He stepped into the damp mist

Michael could hear his own breathing as he slipped toward the beach. An unexpected tension hummed in his muscles. He was anticipating trouble.

A slight motion stopped him dead in his tracks. He couldn't see clearly in the thickness of the night, but someone—or some*thing*—was inching toward him. When he was within fifteen yards of the creature, he saw that it was a person in a black wetsuit.

With a few powerful strides, Michael threw himself on top of the stranger. The body struggling beneath him was lean but gently curved. When his palm and fingers curved around a full, firm breast, he heard a gasp, a curse, then a breathless voice.

"Take your hands off me or I'll bite your face off."

ABOUT THE AUTHOR

As a child, Caroline Burnes and her brothers played on the white-sand beaches of the underdeveloped town of Gulf Shores. Pirates, smugglers, sea monsters and adventures were always close at hand—as well as the terrible undertow, which dragged bad children far into the ocean. Mirage Island is fictitious, but there are several barrier islands off the Alabama/Mississippi coastline which have long histories and beautiful beaches. Caroline has no doubt that the coast has seen plenty of real smugglers and pirates, not to mention more than a few romantic lovers.

Books by Caroline Burnes

Cutting Edge
Caroline Burnes

Harlequin Books

TORONTO • NEW YORK • LONDON
AMSTERDAM • PARIS • SYDNEY • HAMBURG
STOCKHOLM • ATHENS • TOKYO • MILAN
MADRID • WARSAW • BUDAPEST • AUCKLAND

Most writers would never publish without the help and support of friends and family. I've been fortunate to have that support from a number of sources, among them Tahti Carter, editor; Jean Todd Freeman and Gordon Weaver, both teachers. This book is dedicated to them; they offered encouragement when I might have quit.

ISBN 0-373-22267-X

CUTTING EDGE

Copyright © 1994 by Carolyn Haines

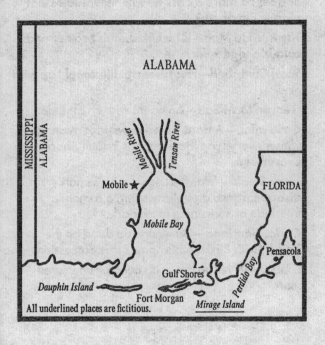

ALABAMA

MISSISSIPPI
ALABAMA

Mobile River

Tensaw River

Mobile ★

FLORIDA

Mobile Bay

Pensacola

Gulf Shores

Perdido Bay

Dauphin Island

Fort Morgan

Mirage Island

All underlined places are fictitious.

CAST OF CHARACTERS

Elizabeth Campbell—Her love for her missing brother put her—and the man she loved—at risk.

Michael Raybin—Is he the man he appears to be, or does he share a dark tie with the troubles that plague Elizabeth?

The Burned Man—Is he Elizabeth's brother or a cold-blooded killer?

Sean Campbell—Has his secret life caught up with him?

George McMillan—An agent with an attitude.

Guy Fallon—A hard-nosed newspaperman who knows everything that happens in Gulf Shores. Everything.

Larry Steele—Was the used-car salesman's disappearance a publicity stunt, a romantic interlude or something much darker?

Carlos Santiago—He wound up dead on the beach, with Elizabeth's name in his possession.

Diablo—Revenge drove his hunt for an injured man.

Chapter One

Michael Raybin planted his feet in the sand and leaned forward into the wind. Cold spray from the Gulf of Mexico whipped across the beach and gusted into his face. He liked the violence of the storm, the sound of the wind howling all around him. The weather matched his mood.

Not fifty yards from where he stood on the north side of Mirage Island, waves crashed over the top of the bridge and lashed the old timbers with an unreasoning fury. Winds of fifty-five miles an hour blasted across the small island, blocking out all visible signs of the mainland. Tropical Storm Marie wasn't a full-blown hurricane, but she was the most recent in a long list of seasonal storms to strike at the gulf coast. Michael was getting his first up-close and personal taste of the storm's power.

Tightening the fastenings of his slicker, he stood for a moment longer, surveying the bridge—the only bridge—that led from the island to the Alabama mainland. He was certain the storm would destroy the decrepit structure. It was a wonder the old timbers held even on a calm day. But the bridge had some give left in it, and it was still holding.

For one intense second Michael felt as assaulted as the bridge. Not by the storm, but by the choices that had been forced upon him. He could only hope that he had a little of the stamina, strength and agility of the old wooden bridge. Perhaps, with some luck, they would both survive.

Tucking his head against the fierce wind, Michael struggled toward the north side of the island. He checked the mooring on the small skiff tied to the island's only dock. The tie lines moaned and complained in the high wind, but the boat was secure. If the bridge went, or the storm got much worse, he'd need the skiff to get over to the mainland, a distance of no more than two miles. The boat was his emergency escape vehicle.

The blowing rain had managed to seep into the collar of his slicker, and even though the days had been unseasonably hot for November, he still felt chilled. The big Victorian house—the only dwelling on the island—had a wonderful fireplace. It was time for a nice fire and a glass of brandy. He could stand by the magnificent windows and watch the storm batter the barrier island.

Michael set his path around the west side of the one-mile spit of sand that was called Mirage Island. He'd borrowed the use of the island from a friend while he sorted through the decisions that would change his life.

Battling the powerful wind, he went to check the toolshed. The door was securely latched and the building seemed to be holding steady against the storm.

The house and outbuildings had survived several hurricanes. He doubted that a tropical storm, no matter how directly it hit, would do much damage. He could only hope that the same was true of all the condos and cheap high-rise construction on the mainland beach. Unlike the house and the bridge, the newer construction didn't have the ability to give with the wind.

He rounded the western side of the island and stood for a moment looking directly out into the gulf. The stormy night sky met the black sea, creating one of the darkest nights he could remember, pitch black except for the faint pale glimmer of the sandy beach. The thick storm clouds shut off everything, as if the rest of the world had disappeared.

Rain trickled down his collar, chilling him to the bone. As he turned to go inside, something on the beach caught his attention. The sand was crystal white, a paradise during the sunny days. He'd walked the beach for the past three weeks. There wasn't a rock or tree trunk or anything to break the monotony of the surf line. Tonight, though, either his eyes were playing tricks on him or there was a dark shape on the sand. He rubbed the rain out of his face with the heel of his hand and walked forward.

The form lay just out of the surf. Several large waves crashed over it, rolling it slightly in an effort to drag it back out to sea. Michael ran, knowing that the tides would pull whatever it was into the water if he didn't hurry.

The wind pushed him backward with a steady fury, blowing rain into his eyes. He blinked. The sprawled form resembled a human. A man. He blinked again, unable to believe his eyes.

Another large wave crashed over the prone figure and then retreated into the gulf. As Michael fought the wind and watched in horror, the body yielded to the demand of the sea. The next wave covered the still form, then retreated, pulling and rolling it into the water.

Michael's feet hit the surf line, and he pounded the firmer sand. The tides were very dangerous, but if he didn't get in the water, the body would be gone. With the next wave, the body started to float.

In a desperate lunge, Michael grabbed the man's sleeve. The tide was sucking and pulling at his own feet, threatening to drag him under. He held firm to the body and struggled back to the shore.

He was fairly certain the man was dead. The limp form felt cold and heavy in Michael's arms. There was no sign of life.

Nonetheless, Michael dragged him to the shore and flipped him over. He drew in a sudden breath. The stranger's face was badly burned. One side was severely damaged, and the other... Well, he wouldn't be able to tell until he had better lighting. There was a cut, but it didn't appear as if the bone structure had been ruined.

Expertly, he felt for a pulse. To his surprise he found a weak, hesitant beat. He cleared the man's breathing passage and started mouth-to-mouth resuscitation. It was hard to tell how long the man had been in the water, but his respiratory system needed a little assistance.

Michael pushed everything else from his mind as he struggled to keep the man breathing.

When a few choking gasps proved the stranger wasn't going to die on the beach, Michael managed to heft him onto his shoulder and head toward the old house. While the storm raged, there was no transportation off the island. No telephone. No medical help available.

Struggling under the weight of the stranger, Michael made it up the steps and in the front door. He carried his burden to the den and deposited the man on the floor.

The electricity was out, so he lit the kerosene lantern he'd readied when reports of the storm had first gone out on the television. In the soft glow of the lamp, he sighed. The injuries were severe. Probably not life-threatening, but certainly disfiguring. The castaway was badly burned, and there was some damage to the right eye. Michael couldn't be certain how much until the stranger regained consciousness. All in all, the man needed a hospital.

In a perfunctory check, Michael loosened the man's clothing and looked for some identification. The only thing he found was an unusual gold coin in the man's jeans' pocket. One side was stamped with what looked like a god of the sea. On the other side was a mariner's quote or toast. He flipped the coin onto the kitchen counter, then went to the bathroom and returned with all the medical supplies he'd brought to the tiny island. After he built a fire, he began the long, slow process of cleaning the stranger's wounds. He had only the basics—novocaine, needle and thread. He was glad the man was unconscious. Otherwise he would have been in excruciating pain. The work Michael did now, while neat, would only be the beginning of the repairs the injured man needed if he was ever to look normal again.

ELIZABETH CAMPBELL PACED the confines of the *Island Beacon* newsroom. The storm was nothing compared to the hurricanes she'd toughed out. After thirty-two years, most of them spent living directly on the Alabama coast, she wasn't intimidated by a tropical storm. But where in the hell was Sean? She looked down at her two nieces coloring quietly at her desk in the newspaper office. They weren't talking—a sure sign they were distressed. What could Sean and Sandra be thinking to stay out in such a storm when everyone in the family was waiting for them? As soon as her brother docked, she was going to deliver him a lecture that would make his dark hair stand on end.

"Aunt Libby, when will Mama and Daddy get home?"

Elizabeth turned to Molly, the six-year-old. Her throat contracted at the look on the child's face. "They've probably docked to ride out the storm, sweetheart. They'll be home as soon as they can." Even as she spoke, Elizabeth felt her own doubts grow.

Sean Campbell was one of the ablest—and most cautious—skippers she'd ever known. The *Sea Escape* was rigged with the latest in radio technology. Sean should have called in. He would have called in.

She turned her attention to Molly and Catherine, the four-year-old. They were beautiful girls with dark curls and brown eyes, just like their father, and like her. The Campbell genes ran strong and true. In fact, Elizabeth was often mistaken for the mother of her nieces. They bore her elfin features, olive skin and dimples. With the same naturally curly hair, it was an easy mistake for a stranger to make. Sandra's blond, green-eyed beauty hadn't made a dent in the Campbell tradition.

"How about a McDonald's treat and home to bed? Your mom and dad can pick you up at my place," Elizabeth suggested. She couldn't keep the kids at the newspaper all night. She'd take them to her cottage and call her friend Abby to come and stay with them while she came back to the newspaper. Back to the newsroom where, if anything had happened, she'd be one of the first to know.

She was bundling up her nieces when Guy Fallon, the publisher of the biweekly newspaper, stopped at her desk. "I just called the Gulf Shores Police Department." He paused, looking down at the girls. "There's been another...death. On the beach again. Young boy. He's on the west end. Dead for a while."

The west end of the beach was isolated, with more private homes and less tourists. This would make the third murder in the small, normally lazy town in the past three months. Elizabeth shivered. Her hometown was under attack, but nobody knew from whom.

"I'm going to take the little ones home. I'll be back in a couple of hours," Elizabeth said.

"No point in coming back." Guy lifted his shaggy eyebrows. "Stay home with the children. You'll feel better and so will they."

Elizabeth hesitated. "Well, maybe until they fall a-s-l-e-e-p."

"I can spell that," Molly said, gathering her crayons.

Guy chuckled. "I'm sure Sean and Sandra will call in soon. If we hear anything, I'll call you at home."

"Thanks, Guy." She bundled her nieces in raincoats and hats.

"Watch those streets. With all the rain, they'll be deep in water."

"Right." Elizabeth held open the door and shooed her nieces into the rain. Together the three of them made a dash to her Trooper. On the way, she scooped Catherine into her arms and hurriedly tucked her into the back seat, assisting Molly next. The rain pummeled them as she slid into the driver's seat and pulled the door closed.

"Whew! What a storm," she said, watching her nieces in the rearview mirror. Molly sat staring into the darkness. The power was out along the coast, and the night was completely black. "This old storm must have your mom and dad holed up someplace. Tomorrow the sun will be shining, and they'll be home.''

Molly looked away from the window and stared into her aunt's eyes in the rearview mirror. "Promise?"

Elizabeth swallowed. She wanted to answer in the affirmative, but something stopped her. It was only the dark night and the howling wind, the rain pelting the windshield so hard that the wipers were useless. It was only her own secret fears. Nonetheless she couldn't make a promise like that. "I love you, Molly. And Catherine, too. I'll do everything in my power to take care of you."

Molly shifted her gaze back to the window, staring toward the raging gulf.

THE PENDULUM clock in the den ticked ominously. Michael checked the stranger who slept fitfully on the pallet beside the fire. The man's heartbeat had strengthened. His breathing was shallow but regular. Apparently he was a tough man, a man with a strong will to live. But once he saw himself, once he realized the extent of his disfigurement, what would he want then?

Michael sighed. He'd spent too long dealing with men and women who thought each wrinkle, each tiny sag of flesh, was the end of the world. Now he was confronted by someone who might actually benefit from the skills he'd struggled to learn. But on Mirage Island, there was no way he could begin the extensive repairs to his latest patient. It would take time and expert surgery to rebuild that ravaged face.

Michael paced the room. He thought the sky had lightened slightly. It was six-thirty in the morning. More than time for dawn. The remnants of the storm were blowing past and in a little while he'd have to go out to check the damage. He hoped to row across to the mainland and make arrangements for a helicopter to pick up his patient. That was the only sensible thing.

Before he left the house, Michael checked the stranger once more. He was surprised to see the man's one unbandaged eye was open.

"Where am I?"

"Mirage Island," Michael said quietly. He knelt on the floor.

The man slowly lifted one hand to his bandaged face. "Who are you?"

"I'm a doctor," Michael said carefully. "You were in an accident. Your face and hands were burned." *Incinerated might be a better word,* Michael thought bitterly. He did not relish the idea of having to tell this stranger the extent of his injuries.

"The boat!" The man suddenly tried to sit up. "The boat!"

Michael put a restraining hand on his chest, gently pressing him back to the floor. "Take it easy, mister. There's nothing you can do. The storm is just breaking up."

"How long have I been here? I have to—" The man's questions gave way to a moan. Everything had gone wrong. The boat. The explosion. The water. He remembered the burn of the salt. The desire to live. Above all, the desire to live. "I have to get up." He thrust himself forward only to fall back with another moan.

Michael wished for a sedative, something that would give this injured stranger a few hours of peace before he had to face reality.

"I need to go to the mainland," Michael said. "I'll get a helicopter out here to get you. At the same time, I can report your boat."

"No!" The man clutched his shirt, oblivious to the pain that must have screamed through his burned hands.

Concerned, Michael put his own hands on the stranger's shoulders and eased him back to the floor. "It's okay," he said slowly. "I won't go for a while."

"The boat," the man whispered again. His thoughts had turned inward. A shudder rippled through him. "My God, my God!" He started to moan again.

"What's your name?" Michael asked.

The man didn't answer, and for a moment Michael thought he hadn't heard him. Then the stranger spoke.

"Just let me die."

"Take it easy and try to rest," Michael said softly. "Try to sleep. That's the best thing you can do for your body now. Sleep and heal."

The man turned his face to the side. Michael got up. "I'm going out to see about the skiff," he said. "We'll talk later, when you feel stronger."

He put on his slicker and went out, glad to get away from the stranger, glad to escape, for a moment, the tragedy that had washed up on the shore of the island. It was a bitter thought that the stranger's problems at least put his own personal dilemma in perspective. Michael knew his reputation as a plastic surgeon was one of the best in the nation. He was the doctor of the stars—or, at least, all of the stars who could afford him. He made more money than he knew how to spend, and he was treated like a god. Compared to the stranger on his floor, he didn't have a problem in the world.

Except that he was tired of playing God. Tired of a lifestyle where wealthy patients expected miracles to stop the natural process of aging. Tired of the vanity and the egos and the money and the hype. Tired of himself.

He sighed as he walked along the beach, seeing but not registering the debris that had washed up on the once pristine sand. In the distance he could see that part of the bridge was missing. The pilings looked straight, but part of the wooden roadbed was gone, a gap maybe one-fourth the size of a football field.

He sighed again. So he would have to use the skiff, after all. He walked on to make sure it was still securely tied. When he got to the dock he saw the little boat rising and falling on the high waves. It was there, thank goodness. And in a few hours, when the water calmed a bit, Michael would row over to Gulf Shores and get some help for the stranger.

Until then . . . What? He decided to go back to the house to see what he could find out about the man. Michael had a good friend who practiced in Mobile. Steve Van Hugh had been a classmate—a very skilled plastic surgeon—who had moved to the midsize city of Mobile, Alabama, to specialize in burn victims.

Michael prepared soup on the butane stove and waited for the stranger to wake again. The old nautical map on the wall beside the fireplace drew his attention once more. He'd studied the map on a daily basis ever since he'd come to Mirage Island. It was quaint, a relic of sailing from days gone by. But it was also a clear map of Mirage Island and the mainland. It showed every inlet and cove, and the sickle shape of the island. Michael didn't know some of the terms written on the map, but he liked it. It gave him a strange sense of the history of the old house.

The stranger moaned and shifted on the floor. Michael could tell by the man's restless twitching that he was in pain. There were many drugs he could have given, but he had none with him. He was helpless, a sensation that didn't sit well with him at all.

When the stranger opened his eye, Michael was sitting across from him in a comfortable wing chair.

"How about some water?" he asked. "Maybe some juice? You have to eat something."

"I want to die." The stranger turned away.

"I thought at first you were dead," Michael said, "but it would seem that your will to live is a lot stronger than your desire to die."

"You don't understand—" The man stopped. "It would be better for everyone if I were dead. Everyone." He watched Michael's reaction to this.

"Surely there's no problem so insurmountable that you'd prefer death?" Michael spoke calmly, rationally, and was extremely aware of the irony of his words. His partner and best friend, Dr. Thomas Chester, had said those same desperate words to him not a month before. When Tommy had discovered that he was HIV positive, he'd expressed the exact same desire to die.

"You don't know what you're talking about," the stranger said bitterly.

"Oh, but I do. I have patients who feel the same way whenever they have a new blemish." Michael laughed, but it had a hollow ring. "It may not seem possible to you, but a tiny imperfection—to them—is worse than a fatal disease."

"What kind of doctor are you?" the stranger asked, accepting a drink of water from Michael.

"At one point in my career, I had the potential to be one of the best doctors around. And then I became a... Well, let's just say that I spend a lot of time making people look good."

"How badly am I hurt?"

The question caught Michael off guard. He'd never lied to a patient, never candy-coated the truth. "The injuries are serious. You're going to need a lot of plastic surgery."

"But I'll look like I did before?" The man's voice was flat, as if he knew better.

"That depends a lot on what you looked like before the accident," Michael said carefully. "The bone structure seems to be intact. Modern medicine can achieve amazing results..."

"It's pretty bad, then," the man said. He nodded slowly. "I remember the water burning. I thought I'd die from the pain."

"When we get to the mainland, they'll give you something. I don't have anything here."

The stranger shifted his one good eye to look at Michael's face. "What are you doing on Mirage Island?"

"That's the question I want you to answer," Michael said. "What was the name of your boat?"

"The less you know about me, the better. People will be looking for me. People I'd rather avoid."

"What about your family?" Michael asked. "Won't they be worried?"

The stranger started. "Yeah, they will." He spoke with some panic. "I hadn't thought of that. They will. My daughters—" He looked at Michael.

"So, you have something to live for," Michael said. "Daughters."

"They'll be better off if I'm dead." The man spoke with sudden anger. "I killed their mother with my stupidity. She didn't want to go out. I insisted. It's my fault. I killed her!" His voice rose into near hysteria. "Listen. Help me get to the mainland and I'll get some money for you. I have to disappear. I can't face them!"

Michael leaned down to the man and touched his shoulders, firmly but gently pressing him back to the floor. "I have every intention of getting you to the mainland. In a few hours, when the gulf calms, I'm going to get some help for you." He hesitated. "I have a friend in Mobile. He's extremely good with burn victims. He'll be able to help you, and I'm certain he will."

"Man, oh, man," the stranger moaned. "My family." He stopped himself. "I have to get off this island. What have I done? Dear God, what have I done to my children?"

"I'll—"

"Listen to me!" he interrupted. "I have an insurance policy. It would pay a handsome profit to my family if I never showed up anywhere alive. I made some mistakes. Serious business mistakes. That's why I made her go out in the boat with me. I was going to tell her what I'd done. I had a plan to get rid of the boat. For money. But the storm blew up." He choked back a sob.

"The worst thing you can do is allow your emotions to run wild." As he tried to reason with the man, Michael felt a surge of compassion. The man's wife had been on the boat. "Maybe your wife isn't dead. Maybe she made it to shore or the coast guard has picked her up."

"She's dead," the man said quietly. "I saw her. I carried her body for a long time, until I couldn't anymore. She's dead."

"Try to rest." Michael felt completely inadequate.

"If I just disappeared, my daughters could have secure lives. If they find me, they'll suffer. They'll be shamed and humiliated. They will never forgive me for what I've done." His voice faded.

Michael could see the man was in more emotional pain than physical. He felt a genuine pang of sympathy. He had the sneaking suspicion that perhaps the man had been in the middle of sinking his own ship for the insurance money when things had gone awry.

"I know you're feeling desperate now, but—"

"You're right. I'm desperate." The stranger stared at Michael. "I'm more desperate than anyone you've ever met."

Chapter Two

Michael watched the boat speed across the distance. Without binoculars, he couldn't be certain, but he thought it was a coast guard clipper. More than likely, it searched for the man who slept fitfully on his floor.

The wind was brisk, and the sun had cleared away the last wisps of gray clouds. It was a beautiful afternoon. And high time he made the trip to the mainland.

Michael had spent the past few hours debating his options where the stranger was concerned. The man was tormented, spiritually and emotionally. He'd asked Michael not to report the accident. He'd insisted once again that his family would be better off if he was dead.

He'd begged Michael not to force him to go to the hospital.

Now Michael Raybin found himself caught squarely between a rock and a hard place. His ethics required that he report the accident and make sure the stranger got competent medical help. That was what he knew he should do. But what about the stranger's wish to control his own fate? Did Michael have the right to decide this man's future?

It was exactly the same problem he faced with his partner. Tommy's life-style was none of his business. But the fact that he now carried a fatal disease was. Still, did Michael have the right to force his friend to disclose his illness? Tommy was an excellent doctor. Not only did he treat the wealthy clients, but he also donated weekends and summers in free clinics to perform surgery on Third World children who needed medical attention.

Did he, Michael David Raybin, have the right to deprive those children of medical attention that no one else would give them? That would be the end result. Tommy's wealthy clients would flee. His practice would be ruined. And the fact that he was an exceptionally talented doctor would not make a whit of difference. If Tommy's HIV positive status became public knowledge, he'd be ruined in Hollywood.

On the other hand, Tommy's patients had a right to know.

Michael shook his head, trapped in the web of his own reasoning. What should he do? He was no closer to an answer than he had been three weeks before when he'd unpacked his car on the island. Now he had two tough decisions to make.

He went back to the house. He would ask the stranger one more time for his name. The man's family must be frantic by now. The coast guard would soon discover pieces of the boat—if there was enough left to find. And the body of his wife would surely wash ashore somewhere. Michael sighed. He pitied the stranger. In an act of desperation the man had lost his wife and perhaps the support of his family.

The screen door on the wide front porch banged behind Michael as he went into the house. There was an enormous living room with two fireplaces and a central hall that led to the kitchen and another porch. The den was near the kitchen, and he walked back, his footsteps soft on the polished oak floors.

Around him, the house was still. Unnaturally still. A sense of unease crept up Michael's spine, and he went immediately to check on his patient.

He never had time to dodge. The blow struck his head and knocked him to his knees. He fell to his side, unconscious before he hit the floor.

"Sorry, doc," the stranger said, stepping from behind the door. He dropped the lamp he'd used as a weapon. "I asked you nicely to let me go. If I weren't such a desperate man, I wouldn't have to hurt you."

He checked to make sure Michael's pulse was strong. He wanted the doctor alive. Just in case. He had no idea what he would do in the future, but he knew he had to get away before they came looking for him. And they would. Even now, as the gulf waters calmed, they would be out there, in boats and helicopters, hoping to find him alive.

He hurried out the front door and toward the dock where the skiff was tied. In a few minutes he had the boat free and was motoring in a northeasterly direction toward the mainland. His destination was a spit of beach that was protected as a bird sanctuary. He knew the coast well enough to know that was his best chance to land undetected.

ELIZABETH DROPPED the telephone back into the cradle and let out an expletive. Across the newsroom, Guy gave her a sympathetic look, which she quickly hid. He knew without having to ask that there was no word on Elizabeth's brother, Sean, or her sister-in-law, Sandra. There was no sign of the *Sea Escape,* the twenty-two-foot sailboat that was Sean's pride and joy. They had vanished into the stormy waters of the gulf. And now, with the storm over for at least eight hours, there was still no sign of them coming home.

"Call the hospitals in Pensacola," Guy suggested. "If there was an accident, they might be there."

"I tried," Elizabeth said, frustration making her words clipped. "I've tried everything I can think of." She looked at Guy. "What do you think happened?"

Guy shrugged. He didn't have a good feeling, but there was no point in indulging his morbid thoughts. Sean was the best sailor on the coast. He knew how to handle storms, and he knew when to head for port.

"Could be he got blown farther out or down than he intended. That was a powerful storm, Elizabeth."

"I told him not to go out," Elizabeth raged. "I told him that the storm was coming. But no, he wouldn't listen. He and Sandra needed the weekend to themselves. They needed the time on the boat. They'd be careful. They had radios." She sputtered to a stop. "Then why in the hell don't they use them to call someone and let us know they're safe?"

Guy knew Elizabeth didn't expect an answer. It was a good thing, because he didn't have one she'd like. "Have you found out anything about the shooting?" A change of topic seemed the safest course.

"It was another kid. About sixteen. Brian Havard. He was on the beach, just down from his house. Whoever hit him went by in a boat. High-powered rifle. Expert marksman. The kid was playing with his surfboard several hours before the storm hit." Elizabeth couldn't suppress the surge of pity she felt for the boy's parents. "What's happening to this town?" she asked her boss. "A kid is out having some harmless fun, and somebody goes by in a boat and kills him. Why?"

"Good question," Guy said. "If you dig up an answer, I'm sure everyone in town would like to hear it."

"I'm going down to the police station to see if they've picked up any clues," Elizabeth said. She'd been there twice that morning, but if she had to sit still a minute longer, she'd have a conniption.

She drove down the strip of beach toward the police station. Halfway there she slowed and pulled over to the side of the road. The gulf wasn't the normal aqua. Mud tinged the waters, and the beach was littered with debris and a few dead fish, jellyfish and seaweed. The storm had done no severe damage—some downed power lines, missing roofs, flooded streets. And now the sun shone brightly, and the waves had begun to fall in an orderly pattern.

An idea struck. She hit the gas and ignored the speed limit as she headed east toward Perdido Pass. When she saw the sign for the boat rental, she knew immediately that she wasn't going to wait for any more reports. If Sean and Sandra were stranded somewhere along the coast, she'd find them herself.

The powerboat she rented had plenty of gas and a new motor. She still had several hours of daylight. She asked the rental man to call Guy and tell him she was going out in the gulf. She didn't want to make the call herself—didn't need the lecture or the loss of time in arguing. She pressed a ten-dollar bill into the rental agent's hand and waved as she headed into the gulf.

She pointed the boat east, pushing the throttle forward until she was skimming the water some hundred yards from shore. She sped past the tall condos that were now the Gulf Shores skyline. Several miles ahead would be Pensacola, Florida, but there was one strip of coast that developers had missed. Her fingers pulled back on the throttle, and she slowed to search the coastline. She saw the skiff, dragged out of the water almost to the sand dunes. Pulling out the binoculars she always kept in her car, she focused on the beach. There was no sign of a person, but one set of tracks led up the sand, disappearing over the dune.

Sweeping the coast with her glasses, she swung her body in a slow arc. The distant outline of Mirage Island came into view.

The sight of the island brought a surge of memories. Elizabeth and Sean had had many adventures on the beautiful little island. Much of the fun had been the fact that it was forbidden terrain. For the children who'd grown up on Gulf Shores, Mirage Island had always been synonymous with adventure. She and Sean and the local teenagers had picnicked and partied there, trespassing and loving every second of it.

She turned the wheel of the powerboat toward the island. There was a chance Sean might have sought refuge from the storm there. As far as Elizabeth knew, the island was inhabited only infrequently. It was owned by a Los Angeles physician who vacationed there sporadically.

As she eyed the old road that cut from the mainland to the island, she wasn't surprised to see the missing portion of the wooden bridge. The old structure had withstood far more storms than she'd ever anticipated. As Elizabeth evaluated the damage, she saw that it wasn't as bad as it could have been. The pilings were still solid. Just some of the planking would have to be replaced. Her hopes rose. Sean and Sandra might have been stranded on the island. The storm had knocked out electricity all over southern Alabama. Some phone lines were down. The bridge was out. There were good reasons they might not have called home.

As she pulled into the small dock, she noticed the empty mooring where the skiff was normally kept. It had to be the same skiff she'd seen beached. Had Sean finally motored to shore and started walking? Maybe he was home already. But there had been one set of footprints, not two. Her pulse accelerated as she thought of Sandra. Was her sister-in-law injured in some way?

She tied up the powerboat and rushed toward the house. As a teenager, she'd trespassed in the old house, too. She and Sean had always been careful not to damage anything. But the house had been irresistible, especially with the legends of bootleggers and modern-day pirates and buried treasures.

Elizabeth hurried up the wide steps to the front porch and knocked at the door.

"Sandra?" She called her sister-in-law's name loudly. "Sandra, are you in there?"

She thought she heard a low moan, and she froze.

"Sandra!"

When there was no response, she pushed the door open. Her heart almost stopped when she saw the tall, broad-shouldered silhouette of a man staggering toward her. She caught a glimpse of thick hair and a strong-featured face, handsome in its planes and angles. Thick eyebrows hid the expression of his eyes, and his mouth was set in an angry line.

It was only when he stumbled against the wall that she realized he was injured. She pushed the door wide and stepped inside, lending him a steadying hand.

"Are you okay?"

"I think so," he said. His fingers probed the side of his skull, and in his thick dark hair Elizabeth saw blood.

She steered him toward the back of the house, into the kitchen and onto a chair. As she tried to assess the damage to his head, she took in his tanned face, his blue eyes and his strong, lean hands, which were presently holding his head. Her first impression had been correct. He was a handsome man with the features of a loner.

"What happened?" she asked.

Michael hesitated. The woman who stood before him was like something out of a fantasy. Her long, dark, curly hair was wind-whipped, partially hiding a gently pointed chin and slightly slanted eyes.

"Who are you?" he asked, still dazed by the blow to his head and her presence.

She shook her head. "Did someone hurt you?"

Michael was certain the injured stranger had taken his fate into his own hands. Maybe it would be better to let it go at that. "The storm. Something hit me."

Elizabeth didn't believe him for one second. Nothing in the house looked storm tossed, and the angle of the blow to his head indicated it had been delivered by someone else. But unless that someone was Sean or Sandra, it really wasn't any of her business.

Without asking, she got some ice from the refrigerator, wrapped it in a dish towel and put it gently on the knot on his head. He closed his eyes, and she gave him a moment to let the cold dull the pain.

"My name is Elizabeth Campbell," she said. She was staring directly at him when he opened his eyes. "My brother Sean and his wife are missing. They were out on their sailboat." Something flickered in his gaze. "Have you seen anyone?"

Michael saw the concern and the worry in Elizabeth's brown eyes, and he turned away. He would not play God with this man's fate. "The bridge is out. I haven't seen anyone."

Elizabeth knew by the way he refused to look at her that he was lying. Or hedging the truth. It was possible that he hadn't "seen" whoever waylaid him. But someone had struck him and taken the skiff. Why was he holding back the truth?

"I love my brother very much. His daughters are worried sick. Not to mention Sandra's family." She paused. "Sean is an excellent sailor. Sandra, too."

For a moment Michael was tempted to tell her about the injured stranger. Then he remembered the man's desperation. "If I see anything, I'll let you know." Michael removed the ice pack and stood. The woman was suspicious of his story. He knew it. He'd never been adept at telling lies. Not even the little white ones his patients wanted to hear. But he'd made a decision to allow Sean Campbell—or whoever the man he'd rescued was—to chart his own fate. And he was going to stick by it. Hell, he had enough on his hands with Tommy. He wasn't about to try to make some errant sailor show up and tend to his family responsibilities. Maybe the guy knew best. Maybe it would be better for all if he was presumed dead.

Elizabeth withdrew a business card from the pocket of her jeans. "My home and office numbers. If you hear or see anything, anything at all, please call me. We're frantic to find Sean and Sandra."

Guilt almost made Michael look away from her intense brown eyes, but he forced his gaze to remain steady as he accepted the card. "You're a reporter?"

"Yes," she said, not smiling. "And you're..."

"Michael Raybin," he answered smoothly. "I borrowed this getaway from a friend of mine."

"How nice for you. We get a lot of wealthy transients here," Elizabeth continued. "Gulf Shores has become a big resort area. Too bad so many of the environmentally delicate areas are being developed. But money talks."

Michael heard the thin edge of contempt in her voice, and he smiled. "I'm not planning on building."

"I hope you enjoy your stay on the island," Elizabeth said. Heat flushed her face, and she wondered about her rudeness. He'd done nothing to bring about her wrath—except that he wasn't telling the truth. Why was a man like Michael Raybin lying about being attacked?

"Would you mind giving me a lift to the mainland?" Michael asked. He knew without looking that his skiff was gone. "I need to call some repairmen about the bridge."

"Sure," Elizabeth answered. "I can drop you off near where your skiff was beached." She smiled. "Maybe you had a houseguest who wasn't happy."

Michael stared at her. She was smart, and bold. There was no point denying that his boat had been taken, but he wouldn't tell her any more. He decided to play as boldly as she had. "Okay, so someone knocked me out and stole my boat. Does that make me a suspect in your brother's disappearance?"

"No, but it makes me wonder why you'd lie. Not many people are interested in protecting someone who physically assaulted them and then stole their property and left them stranded on an island."

Michael shrugged. "People sometimes get desperate."

Elizabeth's clear gaze pinned him. "It sounds like you know more about this person than you're letting on."

"It sounds to me, Ms. Campbell, like you might be better at fiction writing than newspaper reporting. We'd better get moving if you're going to have time to search for your brother."

Elizabeth picked up the makeshift ice pack she'd made. With a flick of her wrist, she tossed the pack into the sink. As she started to drop the cloth on the counter, her eye was caught by a gold coin. She inhaled sharply.

Michael's back was to her as he straightened his clothes, but he heard her intake of breath. He turned to find her staring at him. "Something wrong?" he asked.

Elizabeth knew better than to expect a straight answer from him, so she didn't try. "No." She forced a smile. The gold coin looked exactly like a good luck piece she'd given Sean for Christmas nearly ten years ago. He never went anywhere without it. One side showed a picture of Neptune, his trident raised. On the other side was a saying, "May the wind always blow ye home." The coin wasn't an original, but it was somewhat rare.

She picked up the coin, trying to act casually. "This is an interesting piece. Where did you get it?"

He watched her, knowing that the coin held some significance for her. "I found it," he answered. "Are we ready to go?"

He was lying, she knew it. But there was nothing she could do to make him tell the truth. "You know, smugglers once did business in this house. They said the man who built it, Tommy Sagio, was murdered by his own boss. They ran rum during Prohibition. The rum was supposedly smuggled into the States from here. Sagio came down here, built this lovely old Victorian and moved the liquor from the island to the heartland. It's an interesting bit of local color."

Michael watched Elizabeth with caution. She was a very smart woman, and one who probably never told stories without a moral. Her eyes were glittering, and he couldn't help but admire the color in her cheeks. "What happened to Sagio?"

"A shipment turned up missing. Sagio was blamed, and during a dinner party he was shot in the head and his body thrown into the gulf. Two days later he washed up on the beach."

"I wasn't aware of the local history," Michael said at last. "I'm certain I'll think about your chilling little tale tonight when I get ready for bed."

"The locals all say that Mirage Island is jinxed. The violent death of Tommy Sagio still haunts it. Even as kids, we liked to come over here and play, but never at night."

"I'll be sure to lock my doors and windows."

"Judging by the knot on your head, I'd say you were already a bit late with that safety precaution." Elizabeth turned on her heel and motioned him to follow her toward her boat. "We'd better get moving," she said over her shoulder.

He was unsteady on his feet, so she guided him over to the dock and onto the boat. She pointed it in the direction of the small skiff she'd seen. Michael sat in the passenger seat, turning backward and eyeing the bridge as they left it behind.

"It doesn't seem to be as badly damaged as I thought at first," he yelled over the noise of the motor.

"It isn't. I'm amazed that old bridge has made it through as many storms as it has. If the planking is the only weak point, it'll survive another fifty years." Elizabeth's long, dark curls blew about her face. She pushed them aside with one hand while she steered with the other.

"When was the house built?" Michael asked. "I've been working on it for a while now, and I'd say it was the 1920s."

"Good guess. As I said earlier, it was built by Tommy Sagio during Prohibition. Gulf Shores wasn't even a village then. It was an easy point from which to smuggle booze and God knows what else."

"Architecturally the house is magnificent. Much of it is made of teak."

"Too bad it belongs to an absentee landlord," Elizabeth said.

"Why should that bother you?" Michael was truly interested in her answer. There was something there.

Elizabeth sighed. She was really being a bear for no good reason. Michael was only borrowing the house. He didn't own it. "At one time, there was a group of citizens who tried to buy the house to use Mirage Island as a wildlife preserve.

As you can tell by looking at the beachfront, development has been rampant and without a lot of restraint.''

"It's a pity," Michael agreed. "This is a lovely area. It's a shame to see it begin to look like every other strip of beach in America.''

Elizabeth stared at him through her blowing curls. Along with handsome, fit, a liar and obviously wealthy, she was going to have to consider Michael Raybin a man with a brain. And a conscience?

She was getting closer to the area where she'd seen the skiff. She wanted to point it out to Michael so he'd know where to find it when he started back to the island.

She scanned down the beach. There was no sign of the boat. A couple of beach scavengers were walking along the surf line looking for any interesting shells that might have washed up in the storm. All traces of the skiff were gone.

Elizabeth continued down the beach for half a mile, unwilling to believe the small boat had disappeared. At last she turned back to the west. "That boat was there," she yelled above the noise of the motor.

Michael searched the beach, too, but he didn't expect to find the skiff. If his stranger had chosen to hide his path, then Michael knew he'd do a good job of it. After all, the man had made it perfectly clear that he was desperate.

They skimmed the water in silence until they neared a sailboat rental along the beach.

"I can get help there," Michael said.

"There isn't a dock," Elizabeth pointed out.

"I can wade in from here," he assured her. "I've interrupted your search long enough." He watched her eyes rove restlessly over the beach, searching, hunting for her brother. He felt a pang of sympathy and a twist of guilt.

"Elizabeth, is there any reason your brother might want to disappear?''

"No." She turned to face him. It took a few seconds for the impact of his question to hit. "What are you saying? Are you implying that Sean might *want* to leave his daughters?

That he might have some reason to hide?'' Her voice rose with each question.

Michael knew he'd stepped over the edge, but if the man he'd rescued was her brother, then he did have some reasons for what he was doing. If Elizabeth knew that, she might realize that it might be better to stop hunting for him.

"I don't know your brother. I'm just saying that sometimes we never know the people we love."

The truth of his statement was as sharp and deadly as a knife. Elizabeth felt the breath leave her lungs just as if she'd received a sharp jab. She didn't need to be reminded that a loved one could practice deceit. She'd learned that lesson first-hand from her ex-husband.

"Some people are like that," she conceded, "but not Sean. If you're implying that maybe he wanted to disappear, then you're wrong. He loved his daughters, his wife and his family. He was a happy man. And you seem to forget that his wife was with him. I don't think Sandra would be one to disappear into thin air, either."

"Sorry," Michael mumbled. Her brown eyes were so expressive. He saw her frustration, and her fear. "I really was trying to help," he said gently. "Your brother, wherever he is, is a lucky man to have someone who loves him as much as you do."

Of all the things in the world, Elizabeth didn't expect to feel her eyes fill with tears. "I'll find them," she said. "I won't give up until I do."

Chapter Three

Elizabeth's footsteps echoed off the white tile of the floor and walls. She slowly approached the white-shrouded table where blond hair spilled from beneath a sheet. Her eyes felt as if hot grit had been embedded in them, but she checked back the tears as she nodded her head. The attendant dropped the sheet over Sandra Campbell.

"I'm sorry, Ms. Campbell," the officer standing at her elbow said. "We were fairly certain it was Sandra Campbell, but we had to get a family member to identify the body."

"I know," Elizabeth said. She wanted to get out of the morgue and into the sunlight. Along with the body of her sister-in-law, the coast guard had also found sections of the *Sea Escape* washed up along the sandy shore. The boat had been customized by Sean. It could be mistaken for no other.

Experts were checking the scraps for evidence—at Elizabeth's adamant insistence. She could not believe the boat had disintegrated in the storm. Something else had happened. Only no one wanted to believe it. The police, along with the coast guard and the federal authorities, were more concerned with the murder of Brian Havard than with the disappearance of two adult sailors. The prevailing attitude was that if Sean and Sandra had been silly enough to try to ride out a tropical storm, then they'd brought on their own bad luck.

Elizabeth had checked the pieces of the *Sea Escape*. She wasn't any kind of expert, but she didn't believe waves had destroyed the boat. Not even big waves. She'd lived on the water all of her life, and as a reporter had investigated a lot of drownings. Something wasn't right here.

She walked into the sunlight, wondering what to do next. She thought of her mother and Molly and Catherine. They were waiting for the news. Waiting and hoping against all odds that Elizabeth would walk back in the door and tell them that it was all a mistake.

Elizabeth felt the burn of her tears again. Sandra had been almost as close as a sister. How could she deal with never talking with her again? What would her children do?

Without the stares of the police officers to strengthen her backbone, Elizabeth gave in to her tears. She broke and ran, sobbing all the way to her Trooper. Once inside, she closed the door and leaned on the steering wheel and cried. Where was Sean? There had been no sign of him, but the search boats were still out.

Sandra's body had drifted ashore near Pensacola. The search had moved from Gulf Shores in an eastward direction. No one had to tell her that there was little hope left, except in her heart, that her brother was alive.

She'd almost told the authorities about the skiff and footprints she'd seen along the beach, but something had held her back. Now with Sandra's death, she knew what it was. If Sean was alive, the fact that he'd made it to the mainland and not reported the accident made him look guilty of something. Just what, she wasn't sure. Something was terribly cockeyed about the whole business.

Sandra did have a large life insurance policy, a million dollars. Elizabeth had helped Sean and Sandra select the insurance for each other. The children were the beneficiaries, with Elizabeth as administrator of both policies.

She turned the Trooper toward her mother's beachfront home. Aleshia Campbell would be devastated. But someone had to call Sandra's family. They were in Michigan, preparing for the trip down to help in the search for their daughter. As Elizabeth thought about the Kellers, she felt her tears prickle again.

Aleshia Campbell received the news of Sandra's death with the strength she'd shown all of her life. Elizabeth took her nieces outside to play in the yard while the necessary phone calls were made. They'd agreed to delay telling the girls until there was news about their father.

Putting on a brave front, Mrs. Campbell signaled her grandchildren into the house. "By the way, Guy called," she told Elizabeth as she helped the girls out of their jackets. "He said he wanted you at the newspaper. You'd think that he would understand..." She stopped as she saw Molly looking at her.

"It's Guy's way to keep me busy, Mom. He knows that if he gives me something to do, I'll feel better." She kissed her mother's cheek and for a moment let her hand linger on her shoulder. "He's only trying to help."

"I know. It's just that..." Her voice broke and she turned away.

Elizabeth widened her eyes at Molly's solemn stare. "Grandma said she'd help you two bake cookies. Great idea, huh?" When she'd garnered a smile from her niece, she turned to her mother and whispered, "And that's my way to keep you busy. With Catherine helping, you'll be cleaning up cookie dough for days."

Her mother's smile was teary but genuine. "Elizabeth, there have been times in your life when I'd—"

"I know Sean and I were a trial to raise, Mom, but you loved every second of it." She pulled her jacket on. "See you in a while. Call the office if you need anything."

She hurried out the door, afraid that her mother would see the tears in her eyes if she didn't leave. Going to the office was the perfect solution. Guy was curmudgeon enough not to allow her to cry. He'd humiliate her if she showed any weakness. And she wanted that. He'd make her be strong and help her to keep hoping that Sean would show up—alive.

When she pushed open the glass door at the newspaper office, the brass bell jingled. The paper still sold a few office supplies, and Betty Brown, a society writer and typesetter in a pinch, often took up the slack as salesclerk, too. Betty had a knack for making even the most traditional wedding sound new and fresh, and she loved it.

But Betty's desk was vacant. Guy stuck his head out of his cubbyhole of an office and grunted at her. "Thought you'd want to know they found a case of Uzis down west beach. Not too far from where the kid was shot."

"Uzis, as in the Israeli automatic weapon?" Elizabeth thought she'd misunderstood him.

"Exactly. A whole case washed up on the beach wrapped watertight."

Elizabeth pondered the situation for a moment before she spoke. "A smuggling shipment?"

"Would seem so, but the feds have been called in and they've threatened the lives of any of the local officers who talk to us."

"Gun smugglers in Gulf Shores?" A terrible thought was forming in Elizabeth's head. If the *Sea Escape* hadn't been destroyed by the storm, it could have been blown up by gun smugglers. Over the past several months, pleasure craft up and down the Gulf Coast had disappeared. It was a phenomenon that had been going on for years, but had intensified over the past summer. Drug enforcement officials, better known as DEA, had assumed it was drug related. But it could be guns.

"Gulf Shores isn't a likely spot. Not exactly a ready market here, but it is pretty isolated," Guy said. He came out of his office, and there was the gleam of excitement in his eyes. "This could easily be an entry point before the guns are shipped to places like Miami or wherever the hell else people are running around cutting each other into bits with automatic weapons."

Elizabeth knew better than to be offended by Guy's seeming lack of compassion. He knew Sandra was dead. And he was sorry for it. But he'd never say that. He wasn't the kind of man who would ever be able to openly show kindness or sympathy. His way of being kind was to avoid talking about personal tragedy—the same treatment he'd expected when his wife had died in an automobile accident. He'd shown up for work after the funeral and even written her obituary himself. When Elizabeth had tried to intervene, he'd gotten furious and asked, "Who could write it better than me? Who knew her any better?" And he'd stalked back to his office and pounded on his old manual typewriter.

And that had been that. He hadn't missed an hour of work since then. If anything, he worked ten hours more a week.

"No one's talking about the Uzis?" she asked.

Guy grinned at her. "That's why I called you. Sometimes a pretty face can open a lot of doors."

Instead of getting angry, Elizabeth laughed. "And how would you know that?" she replied.

"Because I've seen you do it," he answered. "Now go work on those feds. The local guys all know you too well. The feds won't have a prayer. They'll see some beautiful gal with legs a mile long and they'll tell you everything you want to know."

Guy was outrageous, but it was his way of trying to show her he cared. He was not a flirtatious man, and after three years of working beside him for sixty- and seventy-hour weeks, she knew he was only trying to take her mind off her own personal troubles. And there was a germ of truth in what he said.

The local police officers had been very chatty with her when she'd first moved back to Gulf Shores from New York. They hadn't expected an experienced, aggressive news reporter in the guise of a young woman. They'd often told her more than they'd intended, and she'd written a multitude of good articles. Now they were more leery of her. But they'd enjoy the spectacle of watching the federal officers fall into the same trap.

"Guy, have you ever thought that we're a bit on the deceptive side sometimes?" she asked as she slipped a notebook into her jacket pocket and a camera around her neck.

"I don't look at it that way," Guy said, sincere for the moment. "Those men are victims of their own preconceived notions. They look at you, and they think 'beautiful broad.' Forgive me, Elizabeth, but they don't get past the obvious physical attributes. As long as you identify yourself as a reporter, you aren't deceiving them at all. They're doing it themselves, because they don't give you credit for being smart and talented."

Even though she knew she was being treated tenderly because of her troubles, Elizabeth warmed under Guy's praise. He was an excellent reporter himself. Trained at the *Charlotte Observer,* he'd come to Gulf Shores in his fifties to take it easy. What a joke! He'd taken on the small newspaper and turned it into one of the most respected biweeklies in the nation. He'd given Elizabeth her first job, during her senior year of high school, and he'd encouraged her through journalism school and onto the staff of a national women's magazine. And when she'd divorced and come home, sick and defeated, he'd given her another job.

"I love you, Guy," she said, grinning as she walked toward the door. "I know it's outrageous to love your boss, but I do."

"Always angling for a raise," he called after her, but his face glowed with pleasure at her words.

The lighthearted feeling evaporated as Elizabeth made her way to the local police department. The feds would have coordinated through the Gulf Shores P.D. It was the best place to begin looking. She thought about the Uzis, about the brutal murder of Brian Havard, and about Sandra's death. In the middle of it all was Sean, her brother. And on the fringes was one Michael Raybin. The man knew something. And he was hiding it. Why?

She went through a number of scenarios. She didn't really know who Raybin was. He could very easily be the pickup man for the guns. He was clever, composed, very sure of himself. He'd make a good money man. Very cool. But there was something in his eyes that gave him away when he lied. And he *had* lied. Elizabeth was willing to bet her life on it. She was a good reporter because of her gut instincts, and this one was telling her that Michael Raybin was hiding something important.

It could be that he was an innocent man somehow caught up in the web of murders and crimes. Maybe the twinge she'd seen in his eyes was regret, or guilt.

She sighed and parked in front of the Gulf Shores police station. The place was a beehive of activity, and when several of the local officers looked up and saw her Trooper, they hurried in the opposite direction. She knew then that there was no new information on Sean. Nobody wanted to tell her that.

Inside, Chief Carl Williams handed her a cup of coffee, black. They'd shared a cup many times over the past two years.

"I'm sorry, Elizabeth," he said. "The coast guard is doing everything in their power."

"Sean's a good swimmer," Elizabeth said, and she kept her voice from breaking. "I haven't given up hope."

Williams turned away and picked up a file from the counter in the main office.

"What about those guns?" she asked.

"The DEA has called in the Alcohol, Tobacco and Firearms guys. Three ATF agents are working that case now. We've got other problems. You remember that used-car salesman who was always pulling stunts to get on television?"

"Larry Steele?" Elizabeth couldn't suppress a smile. Steele was a character. He'd been in Gulf Shores for about a year, and he'd performed as Houdini, thrown knives at his lowest salesman of the year, attempted Wednesday night bingo at his car dealership. He'd do anything to get publicity. A real live wire, he had kept the Gulf Shores P.D. in a constant uproar.

"He's missing. Took a pleasure boat out just before the storm. Rental. Said he was going to Florida to judge a wet T-shirt contest."

"He's probably holed up in some cozy bungalow with several of the contestants," Elizabeth said. Another idea occurred to her. "Or it could be another one of his bizarre attempts at publicity."

Chief Williams scratched his jaw. "That's the problem. If he's fooling around, I don't want to waste any manpower putting out an effort to find him. But he could be in danger. I've alerted the coast guard, so they're hunting for Sean and Steele."

"At least that'll keep them hunting awhile longer." Elizabeth knew that if Sean didn't turn up soon, the search would have to be down-scaled. There wasn't manpower or money to search indefinitely.

"Well, I thought you'd be interested in the story," Williams said.

"Thanks. Now, where are those ATF guys?"

"Try the Perdido Hilton. They've got federal tax dollars," Williams said, and he smiled. "They're pretty excited about those Uzis, Elizabeth."

"And Brian Havard? Is he tied in?"

"Hard to tell. Our investigation shows that Havard had made some enemies. I don't want to think that teenagers are blowing each other away over high school feuds, but it's happening all over this country. Gulf Shores has been a sleepy little town for a long time." He shrugged his shoulders. "But we have a lot of transients here now. Folks come and go. It isn't the community it used to be. We're bound to import a lot of the violence along with the money."

"I hope you're wrong, Chief," Elizabeth said.

"Not nearly as much as I do." He waved her out, and she headed for the Perdido Hilton.

At the desk she discovered that the federal agents were not in their rooms. She knew the desk clerk well and obtained their names, room numbers and a wealth of information. She slapped her notebook against her hand, wondering how to kill time until the ATF agents returned. She didn't want to go home, and she didn't want to go back to the office.

When she got to her vehicle, she found herself driving to the boat rental at the pass. She was going back to Mirage Island. Raybin was hiding something, and she intended to find out what.

As she headed for the island, the sun was behind her, and she had a clear view of the workmen on the bridge. Michael Raybin didn't waste much time when it came to getting things done. There was also a skiff tied at his dock. And the man himself was standing on the pier, watching her glide toward him.

MICHAEL KNEW trouble when he saw it, and Elizabeth Campbell was trouble. He'd seen the tenacity in her brown eyes the first time he'd met her. She loved her brother, and she wasn't going to let him go without a fight. Michael's conscience shifted uneasily. Was he doing the right thing by keeping quiet?

He held out his hand to take her tie line and then assisted her onto the dock. Her lovely hair was windblown, and color had been whipped into her cheeks. She was extremely beautiful, and she didn't seem to be aware of it at all. Her jeans were well worn and her bright coral jacket gave her olive complexion a beautiful glow. He'd seen movie stars who would have paid thousands for her skin.

"Do you have news?" he asked as he released her hand. Her fingers were freezing.

"They found Sandra's body. Sean is still missing." She stared at him, willing him to tell her the truth.

"Come into the house and have a cup of coffee or some hot tea."

His invitation surprised her. She'd come to confront him, to bludgeon him with the fact of Sandra's death. Instead of looking guilty, he was solicitous and kind. She felt her precarious emotional balance slipping.

"I was hoping you'd found something."

Michael saw beneath her steely facade. She put up a good front, but she was torn to pieces inside. He took her elbow and guided her toward the house. "Let's go inside and we'll talk."

Elizabeth let him lead her to the house. In her mind, she'd imagined a confrontation where she forced him to tell her everything he knew. In reality, she saw compassion in the depths of his blue, blue eyes. Whatever he was doing on Mirage Island, he wasn't there to deliberately screw up her life.

Michael seated her at the big oak table in the kitchen. He put the water on for tea and in a few minutes held two steaming cups. When he handed her one, she wrapped her cold fingers around it and let the steam warm her face. She hadn't realized how cold she'd gotten driving the speedboat.

"Ms. Campbell, I wish there was something I could tell you to make you feel better. But there isn't." Michael had had time to carefully think through what he was going to say. If he told her about the stranger, it would give her little comfort. If the man was her brother, then he was either up to illegal activities or he'd done something he was ashamed of. That information would not ease his family's grief. Besides, if he wanted to go home, he would. No one, not even the determined Elizabeth Campbell, could make him.

"I'm not asking for any sugar-coated hopes," Elizabeth said softly. "I only want the truth. If Sean is dead, I can accept that. But whoever killed him will pay."

"Killed him?" Michael leaned forward in his chair and rested his long arms on the table. "I thought he was out in a sailboat and got caught in the storm."

"It's funny, but I think that's what someone wants us to believe. The autopsy on Sandra—" she suddenly choked up, but fought it back "—will be ready soon."

"You don't think she drowned?"

"Maybe she did, but it might have been with a little help."

Michael searched her face for the traces of hysteria he'd learned to recognize. He was used to dealing with women and men who came to him, terrified of the consequences of a few lines and wrinkles. They told him outrageous stories, and underneath it all was that edge of hysteria that meant trouble for a plastic surgeon. He'd become an expert at sensing that desperation.

And there wasn't a trace of it in Elizabeth Campbell's face.

"Exactly what are you saying?" he asked.

"I think my brother's boat was hijacked. My sister-in-law was killed and the *Sea Escape* was blown to bits."

"And your brother?" Michael asked carefully. "What role does he play in this?"

"Hostage. Possibly dead." Elizabeth swallowed. "If he tried to defend the boat, they might have killed him first. He'd never have let them harm Sandra. Not if there was breath in his body."

"Or?" Michael could sense there was more.

"Maybe he escaped. Maybe he swam for it."

"And you think it's possible he could have survived the storm?" Michael was asking questions, but his mind was already at work. The stranger had been badly burned. His injuries could have come from an explosion on board a ship. That made perfect sense. But why was he running? Why had he said it would be better for his family if they thought he was dead? Unless—

"Sean could have survived," Elizabeth insisted. She was watching Michael's face again. He was hiding something. She could see it surface in his thoughts.

"Who do you think tried to hijack your brother's boat?" Michael asked. This was the piece of the puzzle he didn't have.

"Gun smugglers," Elizabeth answered quickly. "A case of Uzis washed up on the west shore after the storm, and a teenage boy was shot and killed while surfing."

Michael held his breath. He'd thought he was coming to an island paradise, a place where he could push aside the ugly realities of the world and concentrate on his personal problems. But ugly reality had intruded on his sanctuary, and the woman who sat across from him was suffering from it.

"And you think all of these things are related?" he asked.

"I do." Elizabeth reached across the table and touched the back of his hand with her finger. "And so do you," she whispered.

Michael couldn't deny it. But the problem was that when he totaled all the answers he had, it seemed likely that Sean Campbell might have been involved in gun smuggling and in that endeavor had managed to get his wife killed and his ship destroyed.

That, indeed, would make a man desperate enough to abandon his own daughters and run as far, as hard and as fast as he could.

THE RUSTED SCREEN balked, but it finally gave. A hand covered in dirty bandages lifted down the screen and eased up the window. The house was abandoned—had been for years. And it was isolated. Not many people remembered the old Cowart place. There was no electricity or hot water, but he was tired, exhausted. At least he could sleep for a few hours. Maybe when he awoke, the pain would be easier. Maybe after a little sleep, he would have a plan. As it was, his life had been torn into tatters. There was no going back.

Everything he'd earned and worked to achieve was dust. With his face horribly burned, there was no going forward, either. No, he needed rest and a plan. He was hungry, too, but that would have to wait.

Grunting with pain, he slipped through the open window. The house was musty, filled with the smell of old moldy things long shut away from sun or fresh air. At another time in his life he would have turned up his nose at the idea of taking refuge in such a place. Now, though, it was perfect. No one would think to look for him at this place.

He made his way carefully through the rooms until he found a bedroom where the meager possessions had been abandoned. Pulling an old spread from the bed, he wrapped it around himself and sank down in a corner. In a matter of minutes, he was asleep.

Chapter Four

As the salt spray of the gulf splashed over the bow of the boat and tingled Elizabeth's chilled skin, she thought back over the scene in Michael Raybin's kitchen. He'd frozen as soon as she'd mentioned the Uzis. It was almost as if he had been shocked or horrified by them. A man from California shouldn't be so naive, not in a state where gang warfare was commonplace. Whatever his reason for that reaction, he'd grown suddenly uncomfortable. She'd finished her tea and left. The tiny hint of tenderness and compassion she'd noticed in Michael when she'd first arrived had completely vanished.

Was it possible Michael Raybin had some connection with the guns?

She shook her head. Anything was possible.

She aimed the boat into the channel that led to the rental agency and checked her watch. The autopsy should be forthcoming. And she wanted to check on the ATF agents and go by the office. When she'd worked for *Glitz* magazine in New York, she'd developed a few Los Angeles contacts. Now might be a good time to make a call or two about Raybin.

She guided the boat to a dock and killed the engine. In a few moments she had the boat securely tied and was hurrying toward the rental office and the worried-looking man who watched her through the window.

"Thanks, Johnny. I appreciate the short notice service."
She dropped a twenty-dollar bill on the counter. Since she'd
grown up in Gulf Shores, she knew almost all of the local
businessmen. The town was changing drastically with the
constant construction of condos and hotels, but there were
plenty of her old friends still around. She and Johnny Belmont had gone from grades one through twelve together.
Johnny had taught her how to snorkel off the coast of Mirage Island. Johnny and Sean. They'd been best friends as
boys.

"Any word?" Johnny kept his voice easy, hiding his own
pain and worry. "Has the coast guard found any sign of
Sean?"

"None." Elizabeth smiled. "He'll be home, though. I
know he will."

"About Sandra..." Johnny stumbled to a stop.

"It's going to kill Sean," Elizabeth said, and her voice
sounded brittle. "Not to mention the kids."

Johnny came around the counter and gave her a big hug.
"I'm so sorry, Elizabeth," he said as he walked her to the
Trooper. "If you need anything, call me. We can get some
of the boats and hunt ourselves."

"The coast guard is still searching." Elizabeth forced a
smile for her old friend. "When they quit, I might ask for
your help."

"You've got it," he said. "And don't give up hope.
Sean's the best sailor I've ever known."

Elizabeth got in her Trooper and fastened her seat belt.
When she reached into her jacket pocket for her keys, she
found the twenty-dollar bill. Johnny wasn't the kind of man
who charged his friends during a crisis.

She went back to the Perdido Hilton. Lawson Wells, one
of the agents, answered her phone call and agreed to meet
her in the lobby. He was polite but brusque. He had nothing to say about the Uzis or the murder of Brian Havard.

Elizabeth studied the slender, balding man who kept
pushing his glasses against the bridge of his nose with one

finger. He wasn't the agent to pursue. He was too regimented, too uptight. She thanked him and drove on to the paper.

Guy was absent from his cubbyhole, so Elizabeth started her calls. There was an Associated Press reporter she'd met in New York but who had recently transferred to Hollywood. She called Leslee Rhodes, and in less than sixty seconds had asked about the stranger on Mirage Island.

"*The* Dr. Michael Raybin? The god doctor of the stars?" Leslee asked in her clipped New York accent. "That one?"

Elizabeth had anticipated that it would take Leslee several days to track down any information on her mystery man. But no, Leslee had him pegged. And according to Leslee, he had an extensive surgical practice. She sighed. "That's him. Tall, good-looking, blue eyes." She stopped. The intensity of his blue eyes was easy to call forth in memory. As were his hands, so tan and slender. So strong.

"He has an exclusive clientele, mostly stars, those on the way up and those on the way down," Leslee said. "You're not thinking of plastic surgery, are you?" Her voice rose.

"Not this week." Elizabeth laughed. "Raybin is vacationing here in Gulf Shores. I met him and..."

"Go for it." Leslee's voice had warmed with enthusiasm. "He's single, wealthy, has a thriving practice and it would get you out of that backwater little town and back where there's some action. I'd even talk with my boss. There aren't many jobs available, but he knows everybody in town who has anything to do with journalism. I'm sure he can find something for you. But, of course, if you're with Dr. Raybin, you won't have to worry about a job, or money, or anything else."

"Easy, Leslee," Elizabeth said. "This isn't a romantic thing. My questions about Raybin were strictly professional."

There was a long pause. "What's going on down there, Elizabeth?"

All of the easy banter was gone from Leslee's voice. She smelled the scent of a news story, and all of her senses were alert.

"My brother is missing, Les. He and his wife went out on their sailboat and the boat cracked up. Sandra's body has been recovered. Sean is still missing."

"Oh, Elizabeth! I'm so sorry."

Elizabeth swallowed. "Raybin is on an island off the coast. I may be grasping at straws, but there's something odd about him." She took a deep breath. "As crazy as it sounds, I get the feeling that he might know something about Sean."

"What would a Hollywood plastic surgeon know about your brother?" Leslee asked.

"I know it sounds insane." Elizabeth didn't have any answers. "Just say my intuition tells me—no, it insists!—that Michael Raybin knows more than he's telling."

Leslee's fingers hit the keyboard of a typewriter. "Okay, so give me a list of questions you want answered. I'll find out whatever you need to know."

Elizabeth thought for a second. "Why is he here in Alabama? This is a strange place for someone like him to show up. Alone. If he was with a girlfriend, it wouldn't be so odd. But Gulf Shores in November is a strange choice for someone with his life-style."

"Okay," Leslee said as she typed. "What else?"

"See if you can find out if there are any malpractice suits against him, financial distress of any kind, that sort of thing."

"Okay, next?"

"Just general stuff like that." Elizabeth tried to think of some more specific questions. "Who's tending his practice? When do they expect him back?"

"I'll do my best," Leslee said. "Hang tight, and I'll keep my fingers crossed for your brother."

"Thanks." And Elizabeth meant it.

"I still think you should come out here," Leslee said. "It's not anything like New York. You'd like California."

"I'll give it some thought," Elizabeth promised before she hung up the phone. California was the farthest thing from her mind.

She called Chief Williams, and to her surprise he asked her to return to the police department.

When she walked into the room, she knew something serious had happened. Williams and two men were waiting for her. The chief introduced her to ATF Agent George McMillan and the agent she'd already met, Larson Wells. Williams had a copy of Sandra's autopsy in his hand, and after he helped her into a chair, he gave it to her.

"Fatal blow to the head."

Those were the only words Elizabeth saw. She looked blindly at the page and then up at Williams, oblivious to the other men in the room.

"What does it mean?" she asked.

"Someone struck your sister-in-law on the back of the head," Williams said. "She was dead before she was put in the water. Or before the explosion."

Elizabeth's heart began to pound. Never in all of her thirty years had she even come close to fainting, but she felt the fiery tingle of her scalp and knew she was about to pass out. Williams grabbed her shoulder and held her in the chair while McMillan got her a cola. After a few sips of the cold drink, she started to feel better.

She looked up at the men in the room and saw the questions in their eyes, and the accusation.

"Sean didn't do it," she said.

"There was some evidence of a sophisticated explosive device," Williams said gently. "Whoever killed Sandra meant to do it."

"And they might have killed Sean," Elizabeth filled in for him. "That's what I've been trying to tell you."

Williams exchanged a glance with the two ATF agents. Elizabeth read it as clearly as if he'd spoken aloud. She rose to her feet, unsteady at first but fueled by her anger.

"Sean didn't do this. I don't know how you can consider such a thing! Sean loved Sandra, and he loved that damn boat."

"There were huge insurance policies," Agent Wells said.

"I know that! I helped pick them out. And they go to the children!"

"A parent or guardian would benefit," Wells said coolly. "That's a reality, Ms. Campbell."

"You can take your reality and shove it—" She turned to the police chief. "Carl, I can't believe you think Sean did this terrible thing."

Williams smiled. "I don't, Elizabeth. I've told both of these men that I've known your brother for years. He wasn't the kind of man who would do such a thing. But you have to realize, with the guns and all coming in on the beach, these gentlemen have to investigate every clue. And I promised them you'd cooperate."

Elizabeth was struck mute. When she finally found her voice, it was to ask, "Cooperate? When they're trying to frame my brother for murder?"

"Not frame, Ms. Campbell," the taller agent named McMillan said slowly. "Explore the possibilities. Now that we know the *Sea Escape* was destroyed deliberately, there's a chance it might figure in with the death of that teenager and the guns on the beach."

"I've been saying this all along!" Elizabeth fumed. "They took Sean and Sandra hostage. Don't you see? Sean might be in danger right this minute."

The two agents exchanged knowing glances, and Elizabeth felt her temper flare. They believed Sean was involved in something, not a victim.

"We'd like access to Mr. Campbell's financial records," Agent McMillan said slowly. "We don't mean to offend you, but we have to check this out. If you refuse to give us the records, we'll get a court order."

Elizabeth looked at Carl. He shrugged, unable to help her.

"I'll get the records for you," she said evenly. "Meet me at 124 Beacon Road. That's his real estate office."

Elizabeth grabbed her coat by the collar and walked out of the room. The autopsy report was still in her hand, and she dropped it at the dispatcher's desk without a word.

"You didn't have to be so damn blunt," she heard Williams berating the two agents. But she kept walking. She had a key to Sean's office and she'd open it for the agents. They could search to their heart's content; they'd never find anything criminal in Sean's activities. Her brother wasn't a crook.

At 124 Beacon Road, Elizabeth unlocked the door of the blue Creole cottage-style office and went in. The office was such an extension of Sean and Sandra's life together that she felt the surge of tears. She walked back outside the building. There were too many photographs of Sean, of the *Sea Escape,* of Sandra and the girls. She found the office depressing. She checked her watch, tapping her foot impatiently until she saw the standard dark sedan headed down Beacon Road. It had to be the feds. They all wore the same style of shoes and drove the same kind of car.

Sure enough, Wells and McMillan got out, slamming their doors in unison. They were like robots.

She held open the door and tossed the key to McMillan. "Lock up when you leave," she said. "You can take the key back to the *Island Beacon.* If I'm not there, leave it with Guy Fallon."

"We don't know how long this will take," McMillan said.

"Don't rush on my account. My brother may be dying at this moment, held hostage by gun smugglers, but don't hurry to finish searching his financial records. I mean, what the heck, the victim is always the first to be suspected." She slammed the door with enough force to rattle the glass window. Damn them all. As she stepped away from the building, she spotted a sports car driving slowly down Beacon Road. The car seemed to move faster as soon as she looked up at it. Almost as if the driver had been watching her and had been caught.

She fished her keys out of her jacket pocket and walked on to her Trooper, never looking at the car again. It had to pass her. There wasn't a turnaround on Beacon. She cast a look over her shoulder. The car had slowed again and now suddenly burst forward with a roar.

As it flew past, Elizabeth caught a glimpse of a familiar profile. The elusive Dr. Raybin! A shot of pure adrenaline went through her, overriding her tiredness, depression and anger. She jumped into the Trooper and tore out of the parking lot. If Michael Raybin thought he was going to spy on her—or her brother—he'd better learn to be a lot more subtle. She rounded the curve and picked up the taillights of the red Jaguar. Raybin should also learn not to drive such a conspicuous car. Tailing him was going to be like taking candy from a baby.

Elizabeth followed him along Highway 59, cutting across the fertile farmland of Baldwin County. Pecan orchards, bare of leaves but heavy with pecans, were scattered among the neatly disked fields where corn, potatoes and soybeans would be planted. As intent as she was on not getting too close to Raybin, she still found a moment to notice the land. Baldwin County was an interesting phenomenon. The gulf shoreline was tropical island beautiful with white sand and aqua water. Only a mile inland, the soil was some of the richest in the South. A perfect blend of worlds.

She let several cars slip between her vehicle and Raybin's when he turned on Interstate 10 west toward Mobile. She followed him over the Jubilee Parkway, noting that the storm had barely affected the low-lying areas of the causeway. Tropical Storm Marie had caused little damage—except to her family. And to the bridge to Mirage Island.

Raybin took the Water Street exit and angled down to Mobile's business section. Elizabeth moved in closer now, afraid of losing him in the slower, heavier city traffic. To her surprise, he stopped at a red brick building on St. Francis Street. The office of Dr. Steve Van Hugh, M.D. Raybin parked in front of the building and disappeared inside.

Pulling into the shade of an old oak, Elizabeth waited. In a few minutes Raybin returned to his car with another man. Together they drove to a restaurant on Dauphin Street.

Almost tempted to give up the chase, Elizabeth sighed and parked her car a block over. She walked back to the restaurant and entered through a side door. Her gaze swept the interior until she saw the two men leaning close to each other and deep in conversation at a secluded table. It took only a winning smile to get a table nearby. The hour was late and the restaurant wasn't busy. She was close enough to Raybin that she could hear snatches of his conversation, but a peace lily offered her some protection from discovery.

She ordered West Indies salad and gumbo and settled back to listen.

The snatches of conversation she heard were too vague. Raybin and Dr. Van Hugh were obviously old friends. They talked a lot about the past. Elizabeth ate her gumbo and the delicious crab salad and tried to follow the drift of their talk.

"He was badly burned."

That caught her attention. Raybin was talking.

"I thought he might die."

The other doctor mumbled something.

"He might be dead somewhere. The burns were deep. There was no way to tell what he'd once looked like."

The voices dropped lower and Elizabeth, heart pounding, lost the thread of the conversation. Sitting alone at her table, she tried to think clearly. There was no reason to believe that Michael Raybin was talking about Sean. No reason at all. He could have been talking about a patient in California, or an interesting case from medical school. But somehow she knew he wasn't. He was talking about the man who'd knocked him on the head and stolen his boat. The man who'd washed up on Mirage Island in a storm. Her brother. Sean Campbell. Alive and badly injured.

Slipping from her chair, Elizabeth paid her tab and rushed out to her vehicle. She couldn't afford to be caught in the restaurant. Especially not now, when her only hope of finding Sean involved tracking Michael Raybin.

ELIZABETH PUSHED the shopping cart through the aisles of the Delchamp's grocery store. Nothing looked good. A week had passed, Sandra was buried, and there was still no sign of Sean. Even the ATF agents had given up on finding a link to illegal activities in his business.

Michael Raybin had returned to Mirage Island the afternoon after his meeting with Dr. Van Hugh, and he had not gone anywhere since. As far as Elizabeth knew, the only people who'd gone near the island were the workmen repairing the bridge. Their job was almost done.

Catherine, sitting in the cart, made a grab for a jar of peanut butter, and Elizabeth captured it and put it in the cart. If the girls would eat peanut butter, she'd be more than glad to buy it. So far, no one in the Campbell house had been able to find any appetite at all.

"When are we going back to school?" Molly asked, suddenly appearing at Elizabeth's side.

"Tomorrow, girls. You've missed a lot of studying."

"I'd rather stay with you." Molly's gaze was solemn.

"And I'd rather have you there, but you have to go back to school."

"Can't I wait until Daddy comes home?"

"Nope." Elizabeth kept her voice light, even though her heart contracted. "When your father gets home, he'll want to see how much you've learned. He'll be disappointed if his girls aren't learning their lessons."

"I can read," Molly said. "Catherine knows her ABC's."

"Daddy will be very proud." Elizabeth lifted Molly and stood her in the cart with her sister and then spun it around. "We have enough groceries, let's go home."

When the girls and groceries were delivered to Aleshia Campbell's house, Elizabeth drove to the strip of undeveloped beach near the Alabama-Florida line. It was late afternoon, a dreary November day. It had become her habit to take a pair of binoculars and search the water. She knew it was impractical to think that Sean might come swimming up on a big wave, but she couldn't help herself. As long as she looked for him, there was a chance he wasn't dead. She could also scan the horizon and watch the bridge to Mirage Island. She'd already checked to make sure the red Jaguar was parked at the dock where Raybin would have to leave his boat. The car was there, the chalk mark she'd put on the left rear tire undisturbed. If Michael had gone to the mainland, he hadn't used the car.

The memory of his face rose before her. She remembered the way his emotions had played across his features. Tension, concern, wariness...guilt. Why guilt? That was the question that plagued her. What did he know?

The binoculars were almost useless for spying on the island. It was just far enough away that she couldn't see anything important. All telling details were obscured by distance. But Elizabeth already had the knowledge that someone had washed up on Mirage Island the night Sean had disappeared. And that someone had taken a skiff and left. Alive.

Frustrated, she dropped her glasses around her neck and started her car. She had to get back to the office. Guy was putting out a special edition of the paper that focused on the recent violence among teenagers. Brian Havard was dead, and the high school had been vandalized. Elizabeth was depressed by the stories she'd written, but she knew Guy was right. They were timely and important stories. Someone had to call attention to what was happening among the local teens.

When she pulled up at the office, she was surprised to see Chief Williams's car parked in front of the building. He was sitting on the edge of her desk when she went in. Guy, his face puckered in worry, stood to the chief's left, a notebook in his hand.

"We think we've found Larry Steele," Williams said as he slowly stood up.

"Think?" Elizabeth held her breath. After more than a week in the water....

"The body had a billfold with Steele's driver's license, credit cards, et cetera, in the pants' pocket."

"So why do you *think* it's Steele?" Elizabeth stiffened her spine for the answer. She knew it already.

"The body wasn't intact. Sharks." Williams cleared his throat. "There won't be any dental records to check."

"I just hope the poor guy was dead before they got to him," Guy said slowly. "Steele was a bachelor. That's good. Tough for us, though. He was a maniac. He made great copy with his stunts."

"Always first in line with compassion," Williams said sourly. "And folks say lawyers are ambulance chasers. They've never met a newsman like you, Guy."

"Hey, I'm only remarking on the truth. Larry Steele could always be relied on to stir up some trouble when things got too calm around Gulf Shores. I mean it sincerely when I say I'm sorry he's gone."

Elizabeth loosened her grip on the back of her chair very slowly. The two men were bantering to give her time to compose herself. As soon as she'd seen Williams, she'd been afraid of what he was going to say. That they'd found Sean's body. At least now she could breathe again.

"Is the search off?" she asked.

Williams nodded. "It's been over a week. They've called in most of the boats. If Sean is out there, he isn't alive, Elizabeth. You know that as well as I do. It's time you and your family got on with your lives."

"We're moving on with our lives," Elizabeth said stiffly, "but forgive me if I don't give my brother up for dead just yet."

"Why don't I handle the Steele story," Guy interjected, picking up several pasted-up pages of the paper and thrusting them at Elizabeth. "You proofread. Check the spelling. Betty helped me typeset. She always thinks she knows how to spell better than I do."

Elizabeth took the pages, but she didn't look away from Williams. "What about the ATF's suspicions about my brother?"

"They went over all of his records and they couldn't find a thing. They have no evidence."

"So they won't try to do anything?"

"He's listed as a missing person. That's all. But they haven't given up entirely." Carl Williams shifted his weight from foot to foot. "Too many things can't be explained. It's unfortunate, but Sean's disappearance seems to be a part of that."

"I agree," Elizabeth said suddenly. "But as an innocent victim." She turned on her heel and walked away, leaving Guy and Carl to stare after her rigid back.

THE WEIGHTS were strictly makeshift—a car axle and pieces of metal wired at each end. Grimacing with pain, the man wrapped his fingers around the axle and hefted it. He counted thirty repetitions before he stopped, grunting with exhaustion. That was five more than the day before.

In the week that had passed, he'd been a busy man. Stealing food and medicines required great planning, especially since he couldn't afford to be seen by anyone. But he was getting stronger. Each day he felt more capable. And more satisfied that he might be able to create a small measure of success out of the tragedy of his life.

He read the newspaper, though usually a day late, retrieved from local trash bins. The search was all but over. No one except Elizabeth Campbell continued to look.

Eventually she'd tire of it. Even the stubborn Elizabeth would have to give up after a time.

Throughout the long days, when he was confined to the old house, he worked with his weights and thought about the doctor on the island. Michael Raybin was going to be his key to the future. With the good doctor's help, he'd stand a chance of returning to Gulf Shores if he wanted, to the little girls who'd lost their mother. Maybe he had something to strive for, after all.

But first he had to get a car. And he had to practice talking. The side of his mouth had been burned, and the tissue was becoming hard, unyielding. He had to work at enunciating his words properly. The more he could do himself, the less time it would take for surgery. And surgery was the only thing that could give him back a life.

He dropped the weights and wiped his hands on the old sweatpants he'd found in the house. He didn't like the idea of stealing a car, but he had no choice. There were, after all, plenty of families with spare vehicles in Gulf Shores, especially in the wealthier neighborhoods. It would be a piece of cake.

Chapter Five

Glancing at the children in the rearview mirror, Elizabeth quickly surveyed her nieces. Their mother's death had devastated them. And they needed a normal routine. But were they ready to go back to school? The school authorities had been alerted to watch them carefully. She sighed. It was so hard to see them struggling to be brave. As she looked in the mirror again, she couldn't help but notice the dark circles under her own eyes. Since Sean's disappearance she'd had virtually no sleep. Or at least, not any restful sleep. She was tormented by dreams, plagued by anxieties, worried sick about Molly and Catherine. It had gotten so bad she'd considered making an appointment with her doctor.

She pulled up in front of the elementary school and got out to assist Catherine and Molly with their book bags. Even though Catherine was in preschool, she took her "homework" very seriously. If Molly brought books home, Catherine felt she had to do the same.

Both girls were working very hard at acting "grown-up" about returning to school. Elizabeth gave them each a kiss and watched as they went in the front door together.

Her mind was in a million different places when she saw the red Jaguar parked some fifty yards from the school and half hidden behind some crape myrtles. Michael Raybin sat in the driver's seat.

The fury that scorched through Elizabeth made her catch her breath sharply. All good sense left and she slammed the Trooper door, oblivious to the cars that waited behind for her to move. Her long legs covered the ground in impressive strides as she walked straight toward the Jaguar.

Michael was staring at his hands on the steering wheel and failed to notice her approach.

"I don't care that you spy on me or my brother's office, but when you follow his children to school, that's taking it too far."

His head jerked up with a sudden motion that revealed startled blue eyes.

"I wasn't—"

"Spying? I think you were. There are laws that make stalking people, particularly children, a crime."

"Stalking?" Michael sat up straighter in his seat, wishing she would back away from the door so he could open it and stand up. "I wasn't stalking anybody, and certainly not children. That's insane."

"Then what exactly were you doing?" Elizabeth's temper had cooled, and her professionally trained journalistic mind kicked in.

Michael looked up into her brown eyes. He could see her anger and her frustration, but beneath that was deep fear. She was worried about the girls.

"I came to make sure the children were okay. I've been thinking about them. Their father is missing and their mother is dead. It must be hard for them."

"It is, but I don't see where this is your problem." Elizabeth let her tone drop, but her words were deadly.

"Maybe it isn't. They're beautiful girls. They look like you."

"My brother and I looked a lot alike. Strong family genes." She couldn't stop herself from saying it, remembering how he'd spoken with Dr. Van Hugh about the badly injured man.

"I'd wondered..."

"Wondered what?" Elizabeth felt her pulse quicken.

"What your brother looked like." Michael shifted uncomfortably in the seat. This was all going wrong. Ever since Elizabeth had come storming onto the island, she hadn't been far from his mind. He'd come to Mirage Island to resolve his personal problems, and he'd spent at least half his time worrying about a badly burned man and a determined woman he didn't even know.

"Why would you care what my brother looked like?" Elizabeth asked.

Michael started to tell her the truth but stopped himself. He'd decided to let the injured stranger handle his own fate. He had to abide by that decision.

"Professional curiosity," he answered, shrugging. "Looks are my stock-in-trade."

"Why do I get the feeling that just when you're about to tell me something I really want to know, you back off the subject?" Elizabeth knew she'd lost whatever chance she'd had to get him to talk. The cautious, distant look was back in his eyes.

"If I told you why I came to Mirage Island, you might understand."

"I've been curious about that," she conceded. Conversing with Michael Raybin was like walking through a field of land mines. He was reserved and then frank, secretive and then disturbingly honest.

"Why don't we meet for a cup of coffee? I think you'd better move your vehicle." He nodded toward the school where a group of angry mothers had formed a mob that was looking threateningly their way.

"Meet me at the little café on the beach beside the Hangout."

"The Hangout?"

"Where all the teenagers go. At the intersection."

Michael understood her directions and nodded. "See you in a few minutes." He put his car in gear and eased away, careful not to spray gravel at her.

Elizabeth ran back to her car. She didn't bother with apologies. The mothers were too mad and she understood exactly why.

She drove straight to the café, and then walked to the little table where Michael sat, his gaze on the constant motion of the gulf.

"Exactly what are you doing in Gulf Shores?" Elizabeth asked as she sat down. She turned her coffee cup upright and watched Michael's profile. His gaze never left the water.

"Do you want the truth?"

"That would be nice for a change."

The waitress brought the coffeepot and cast a curious glance at Michael. He was a stranger in town and November wasn't exactly the biggest tourist month, especially not after a big storm.

"I came here to decide whether I should—or could—continue playing God." He shifted forward in his chair.

That wasn't the explanation Elizabeth had expected. As she watched his profile, though, she knew he wasn't trying to be humorous.

"Things have happened in my personal life. Tragic things. I came here to be alone. To think. To try and decide what's right and what's wrong." He rested his hands on the table and then immediately removed them.

Elizabeth watched him with fascination—and an unexpected desire to comfort him. She could feel the struggle that was going on inside his brain. He was weighing the core of his life, and trying to do the right thing. She wanted to reach out to him, but she didn't. This was something he had to do alone.

"Have you ever found it difficult to know the difference between right and wrong? Or are journalists born with that deep sense of moral judgment?"

He turned to her with a gaze so intense Elizabeth felt her breath catch in her lungs.

"Yes, I've faced some difficult choices," she answered finally. "Sometimes it's hard to know what to do." She held his gaze.

"Sometimes there isn't an answer." He paused, more aware of her unique sensitivity than he'd ever been before. She did understand, yet she needed a more solid answer. "And sometimes it isn't a person's place to make a decision. The difficult part is in knowing which is which."

"Could you be more specific?" Elizabeth felt the undercurrent in his words. He was walking all around the answer she wanted, and she wished she could simply coax him into telling her.

"Let me give you a hypothetical question," Michael said. He studied the beautiful woman who sat across from him. She was listening with all of her heart. "Say I have a patient who's going to die. He asks me not to tell his family, says that he wants to protect them from his distress. He says he wants to disappear. Now, to whom do I owe an obligation—the patient or his family? They love him and don't want to be cheated of his final months. But if he doesn't disappear, they'll have to watch him die. What should I do?"

Elizabeth didn't realize she was holding her breath until she felt her lungs begin to burn. "I don't know, Dr. Raybin. To whom do you have an obligation?"

Michael could see a pulse pounding fiercely at her temple. She understood that he was drawing a parallel. Without thinking, he reached across the table and picked up her hand.

Elizabeth felt his fingers close around hers. She was aware of his touch like no other she'd ever known, but her mind hurtled through the possible meanings of what he'd just said. She had to focus on Sean, on what Michael was saying beneath his words.

"My obligation is to my patient," he said softly. "My oath dictates that. No matter how much I hurt for the family and what they suffer."

"Was my brother a patient of yours?" Elizabeth asked. Her fingers curled around his, holding him.

"Given the hypothetical situation I described, I couldn't answer even a simple question," Michael said.

Elizabeth knew it was pointless. He would not say anything more. She could read into his words whatever she chose, and she chose to believe that he knew Sean was alive. For some reason—to spare his family—Sean had wanted to disappear. It didn't make any sense . . . Unless someone was after him! Someone who might be trying to hurt the girls. Or her.

Michael saw the excitement in Elizabeth's eyes. Their brown depths caught fire. He could feel the strength of her emotions in her hand. The skin was so smooth, the fingers tapered and elegant. She had the hands of a musician.

"What are you thinking?" he asked.

"That perhaps I've discovered something about my brother, after all." She withdrew her hand. "I have a lot of things to check out, Dr. Raybin. Thanks for the coffee and the chat."

Michael stood up, a bit concerned. What had he said that would put such a light in her eyes? "Elizabeth?"

She turned to face him. "Yes?"

"Whatever you're thinking, promise me you'll be careful."

Something in his eyes held her. He was genuinely worried. "I promise."

He nodded, breaking the moment, and she left the café.

When she got to work, Elizabeth found a message from Leslee Rhodes. She called the Hollywood reporter and waited anxiously while Leslee finished up a quick story. In a moment she was back on the phone, breathless with her news.

"Listen, I've got that info on Raybin for you," Leslee said. "It was a pretty good tip, too."

"What kind of tip?" Elizabeth felt a deep uneasiness.

"There's something going on at Raybin's clinic. He left over a month ago and the place has been nailed shut tighter than a coffin. His partner is out of pocket, too, and there's some talk of a serious disagreement between the two. From what I can tell, no one is paying the bills, either."

Elizabeth felt the small shock waves resonate throughout her body. She hadn't expected this! Was it possible Raybin was actually in serious financial straits—serious enough that he might be involved in something illegal? Something like gun smuggling? It didn't make a lot of sense, but sometimes people in a bad situation did crazy things.

"Elizabeth? Are you still there?"

She struggled back to the telephone conversation with Leslee. "Thanks, Les."

"Well, I haven't come up with anything specific, but I thought you'd want to know this. Maybe Raybin is thinking about setting up a practice in—no! Not in Alabama. Well, maybe he's just trying to sort through his life and decide what he wants to do. Along with the financial rumors, I also picked up a few hints that he wasn't satisfied with his practice. He was short with a few stars, sending them out of his office. And the good doctor had been well known for his bedside manner in the past." Leslee chuckled. "I'd like for him to tuck me in at night."

Elizabeth found herself laughing at her friend. "You're incorrigible."

"Thank God there's a few of us left," Leslee answered, still chuckling. "So what are you going to do next?"

Elizabeth smiled. "Maybe pay a visit to the good doctor. There's a full moon tonight."

"Elizabeth, remember the time when you climbed that garden wall to spy on that rock star?"

"I wasn't spying on him. He was making a drug deal and I wanted to get the goods."

"That's not spying?"

"Not technically. I was trying to get a story."

"And you almost got shot. Just remember that before you go gallivanting around Alabama in the dead of night. Alabama may be a kinder, gentler area than New York City, but people everywhere are funny about property rights. Some people shoot first and ask questions later."

"I'll keep that in mind. And thanks, Leslee. I'll let you know what I find out." Elizabeth replaced the receiver before Leslee could give her any more lectures.

It was after six before she left the small newspaper office. The day had been grueling. She knew it was her lack of sleep that was making her so tired and depressed, but there wasn't anything she could do about it. Whenever she lay down to rest, she thought about Sean. What if her brother was injured somewhere? What could she do to help him?

Now she had a new worry. What if someone was trying to hurt him? It was more than possible that Sean had witnessed Sandra's murder. If he was alive, then the murderer would certainly be hunting for him.

Elizabeth went to her cottage, ate a sandwich and took a long, hot bath before she dug her wet suit out of the garage. She got the mask and snorkel, not bothering with the diving tanks. She wasn't going diving, but she *was* going exploring—on Mirage Island. It would take some talking to get a boat from Johnny Belmont at night. He was the kind of friend who'd want to go with her, to make sure she was safe. But she couldn't drag Johnny or anyone else into this. And she had to be absolutely quiet. She knew the coastline well enough to travel without a light, and she had every intention of doing that.

By the time she got all of her gear loaded into the Trooper, a thick, dense darkness had fallen. The overcast sky seemed to swallow the light of the stars, as if all of the sharp edges had been blurred. As Elizabeth drove to the boat rental, she tried to find Mirage Island in the gloom where the water met the night. A shroud of fog seemed to hang over the tiny island.

She heaved a sigh of relief when she found Johnny had gone home for the evening. She knew where he kept the spare key to the office, and she found it with only a whisper of guilt. She'd borrow the boat, bring it back and pay for the rental. Johnny would never miss a wink of sleep worrying about her. It was better this way.

Before she could change her mind, she took the keys, found the boat and headed through the pass to the gulf. She drove slowly enough to allow her ears to pick up any sounds of other small boats moving without lights. Once she was on the water, she realized that she might not be the only boat that didn't wish to be seen. If someone was hunting for Sean, they, too, might be trolling the waters as unobtrusively as possible.

She felt her blood chill at the idea, but she kept her hand on the wheel. She moved slowly toward the horizon where she knew Mirage Island would suddenly appear in the fog.

As the small boat cut through the black water, Elizabeth let her mind drift to Michael Raybin. He wasn't what she'd expected of a Hollywood plastic surgeon. There was a genuineness about the man, a feeling that he was struggling with some deep personal problem. He'd said he was at Mirage Island because he was tired of playing God. Coming from a different man, it might have sounded like nothing more than ego or arrogance. Coming from Michael Raybin, it had sounded like the truth.

Elizabeth sighed. She was feeling a grudging admiration for a man who was causing her nothing but troubles. And she was going to feel like the dumbest kind of rube if she found out that all of Michael Raybin's chest beating was centered on a financial crisis.

Her sharp eyes detected the dim outline of the island. She was on the west side, about forty yards from the coast, and she swung the boat eastward, moving along the north shore where the water was calm. She had to get a bearing on the shore before she anchored and swam in. She wanted to be able to find her boat when she came back.

Inching as close to shore as she dared, she decided to anchor just north of Michael's own dock. It wasn't the most covert maneuver, but she'd be able to find her boat and it would minimize the time she had to be in the water. Swimming in the gulf at night didn't bother her—she'd spent plenty of moonlit evenings swimming and partying with her friends. Still, the water was inky-looking.

With a gasp, she slid into it and started making her way to the island. Without the protection of her wet suit, she knew she'd be freezing, but once she started moving her arms and legs, the icy chill of the water receded. She made her way to shore and eased up to the firm sand of the tide line. Her toes were freezing, but she knew she wouldn't die. She had to keep walking.

She passed the bridge and worked her way to the south side of the island where the waves crashed against the sand. Although she couldn't see, she knew the beach was crystal white. In daylight, the black waves would change to a bright aqua.

Her long strides were carrying her down the beach at a good pace when she stepped on a shell. The sharp edge bit deeply into the arch of her foot, and she barely suppressed a curse as she sat down in the sand and pulled the shell from her foot. It was too dark to be able to assess the damage, but she could feel the blood on her fingers.

"Damn!" Now what was she going to do? She hated to put the open cut in the sand, but she was going to have to do it to finish her surveillance and get back to her boat.

"Double damn!" She put her heel in the sand and started to struggle to her feet. Three sudden flashes of light made her change her plans and drop immediately to her elbows. About a hundred yards off the shore of the island, a boat was signaling the shore.

Elizabeth felt her heart squeeze tight as someone on the beach not more than fifty yards from her responded with a flashlight. There were three rapid return flashes.

Once again the boat flashed, this time, two short, a pause, then three long flashes.

The light on shore replied with one long and two short bursts of light.

Elizabeth looked left and right for some protection. She was on the flattest portion of beach, a sitting duck if someone happened to walk her way. They might very easily stumble over her. She had to find a dune to hide behind or possibly even go back into the surf. The one thing she couldn't do was lie sprawled on the sand like some beached sea mammal, waiting to be captured. Ignoring the pain in her foot, she started to ease inland. There were small dunes, little valleys and indentations where she could hide herself without risking the dangers of the gulf-side tides.

AT FIRST, Michael didn't believe what he saw. The flashes of light were offshore, probably, but it really looked as if one of them was coming from his beach.

Who would be on Mirage Island in the middle of the night? Fishermen? But in his weeks at Mirage Island he'd never seen a fishing boat so close to the shore.

Whatever it was, he needed to check it out. The idea that the injured stranger might have come back passed through his mind. He considered it for all of five seconds before trashing it. That man was gone. He'd walked out on his family. It wouldn't be a simple thing to walk back in.

The night was foggy, and the thick, soupy mist made it even more difficult to tell exactly how far out or close in the second series of flashing lights came from. Michael found his jacket, slipped into it and stepped into the damp mist.

He could hear his own breathing, louder than he'd ever remembered it, as he slipped toward the beach. An unexpected tension hummed in his muscles. The business with the stranger and the death of Elizabeth's sister-in-law had struck deeper at his nerves than he'd first realized. He was anticipating trouble. Only the fact that he was the aggressor made him feel a tiny bit better.

Slipping among the gentle dunes, he moved from shallow valley to shallow valley. The concealing dunes worked to his advantage as he made his way to the beach. Every few minutes he climbed to the top of a dune and looked out toward the gulf. The lights had disappeared.

A slight motion stopped him dead in his tracks. In the thickness of the night, he couldn't see clearly, but someone—or something—was inching toward the safety of the dunes. The figure was black. It moved indistinctly, more a crawl than anything else.

Dropping down to his knees, he studied the creature. Was it a beached dolphin? An otter or sea lion sadly off course and injured? He couldn't tell, but he had the uneasy feeling that it was a human.

Michael dropped back behind the dune and made a wide arc so that he could approach the creature from behind. He had no desire to harm it, but if it was sick or injured, he wanted to help. If it was someone sneaking around on Mirage Island, he wanted to catch them before they could do him any harm.

To his right the surf pounded, covering any noise he might have made. He hurried forward, closing the distance rapidly. Surprise was on his side and he intended to use it.

When he was fifteen yards from the creature, Michael saw for certain it was a human being—a person in a black wet suit. Anger sparked. Someone had deliberately come to the island to...spy? Or steal? Or injure him or someone else? He didn't know, but he was going to find out.

With a few powerful strides, Michael raced toward the prone figure. Before the intruder had a chance to even think of a defense, Michael threw himself on top of the stranger. His body weight pressed the figure into the sand.

ELIZABETH FELT the breath go out of her in a painful rush. Two tons of bricks had dropped from the heavens on top of her and were doing their best to crush the life out of her. Her hands and legs were pressed into the sand.

She fought back with every fiber of strength in her body.

MICHAEL HELD the wrestling person with a growing sense of wonder. The wrists he held were slender. The body beneath his own was lean but gently curved. While he held the stranger with one hand, he explored with his other. When his palm and fingers curled around a breast, he heard a sharp intake of breath and a dire curse.

"Take your hand off me or I'll bite your face off."

He recognized Elizabeth's voice instantly. As he tried to shift away from her, she increased her struggles, breaking one fist free and driving it home squarely in his eye.

"Elizabeth!"

She heard the attacker call her name, but she didn't stop long enough to wonder how he knew it. Her injured foot was a distant throb as she pulled her feet under her and used the force of her entire body to buck the man who pinned her down.

"Elizabeth!"

"I'm going to kill you," she promised as she felt the man lessen his pressure a bit.

Large, strong hands grasped her shoulders and pushed her into the sand. The blow stunned Elizabeth for a moment.

"Be still, damn it," the man said, his voice suddenly cold and authoritative.

Elizabeth didn't know why, but she ceased her struggles.

"It's me, Michael," he said, rolling away and to her side. He kept her pinned down with one long, muscular leg. "There's someone else on the island. Are they friends of yours?"

His harsh whisper brought her back to reality with a jolt. She'd been so certain she'd been captured by the people who'd killed Sandra that she'd been fighting for her life.

"Who is it?" she answered, her gentle whisper almost lost in the sound of the surf. The signal light on the beach had blinked again, this time much closer to where Michael and Elizabeth lay.

"They didn't come with you?" Michael calculated the time it would take for the light-wielder to get to them. They had ten minutes at most.

"No," she answered. "I was watching them. They were signaling a boat."

The sensation that terrible danger was approaching touched Michael like a hand from the grave. Whoever was on the island with them, he didn't want to meet them without a weapon. He leaned close to Elizabeth's ear, noticing for the first time that she was wearing a body suit that covered her head.

"Whoever that is will be on top of us in a few minutes. Let's try to get in the dunes and hide."

Elizabeth nodded. When Michael lifted his leg, she rolled against him, onto her side. His hand grazed her hip as they both got to their feet. It was only then that the burst of pain in her foot made Elizabeth gasp.

"What is it?" Michael asked.

"I cut my foot." She took a stumbling step toward him.

Michael's arm swept beneath her knees, and in a moment she was in his arms as he hurried toward whatever safety he could find in the dunes.

Chapter Six

Elizabeth's slender body was snuggled against his own, and Michael didn't bother to analyze the surge of pleasure he felt. He had to keep his mind on important matters—like not getting caught. He had no idea what Elizabeth was doing on the island or who their other "companions" might be. He only knew that they weren't innocent fishermen trying to make a living. The signal lights were either calling a boat in, or warning one away. Either way, whoever was on the island had no business there. He wasn't about to forget that Elizabeth had told him about the gun smugglers.

She felt his arms tighten a fraction around her, sending a message of security and safety. Her body responded to his touch with a willingness that surprised and frightened her. She didn't know this man.

"I think I should go see if I can find out what they're doing," he whispered.

"No!" Elizabeth's hands clutched his arms and held them at her waist.

"We can't hide here, hoping they won't find us," Michael said. They were in a precarious situation. With Elizabeth's injured foot, their mobility was greatly hampered. He had to take the stance of the aggressor.

"Those people may be killers," Elizabeth said. "You don't even have a weapon."

Michael tried to remember if he'd seen a gun in the house. His friend who owned the island was a pediatrician—not exactly the type to be a member of the National Rifle Association. Chances that he owned a gun were slim.

"If I go after them, I'll at least have the element of surprise." Without a weapon, surprise was the only thing he *did* have.

Elizabeth knew she had to stop him. She had to gamble on a part of his character she'd seen earlier—his desire to protect her. "If you get injured, or killed, I'll be a sitting duck. If those are the same men who killed Sandra, they won't hesitate to kill you—or me."

Michael was all too aware that what he was feeling for Elizabeth at that moment wasn't pure protectiveness. They were nestled at the base of a dune, spooned together with his arms fitted into the natural curve of her waist. The wet suit she wore was a strange feeling to his fingers, but beneath the clinging material of the suit, he could feel the shape of her body. For a slender woman, Elizabeth had plenty of curves.

"Let's try to get back to the house. Have they repaired your phone service yet? We can call the coast guard." Elizabeth took his silence for acquiescence.

"No," Michael said. He let go of the idea of chasing after the invaders. His place was with Elizabeth, to ensure her safety. If he tried to leave her, there was no telling what she'd get herself into next. She seemed to have a knack for landing in difficult situations.

"Well, we'll still be safer in the house."

"I agree," Michael said suddenly. He swiftly got to his feet, lifting her in his arms as he stood.

"I can walk," Elizabeth said quickly. When he started striding toward the house, she realized he wasn't going to put her down. "I mean it. I can walk. The cut isn't bad."

"So you think grinding a little sand in it will help it heal?" he asked. He kept his voice low, a whisper aimed at where her ear should be in the wet suit.

Elizabeth subsided. She turned her attention to looking over his shoulder to make certain they weren't being followed. She didn't want Michael to go after the people on the beach, but she certainly wanted to know what they were up to. Why would someone be signaling a boat? A shipment of guns? That was the most logical answer.

As she and Michael moved silently across the dunes, she could feel the warmth of his body through the suit she wore. She'd long ago given up the idea that her feet would ever be warm again. It was probably a blessing that they were blocks of ice or her cut would be throbbing. But where her body rested against Michael's, there was a definite fire building. One of her arms was looped around his neck and her hand rested casually on the long muscles that ran up his spine. He was in good shape. Excellent shape. There wasn't an ounce of fat on him—at least none that she could feel.

"Do you charge for spinal exams?" he asked. Even the casual touch of her fingers excited him.

Elizabeth's hand halted. She hadn't realized she was moving her fingers all over his back, almost giving him a massage. She felt a blush creep up her face just as they stepped onto the porch.

Michael whisked her into the house and carried her straight to the kitchen table. He settled her into a chair and immediately dropped to one knee to examine her foot.

Elizabeth looked at the ceiling while Michael looked at her foot. He turned it first one way, then another. Gentle fingers probed around the wound, sending a lightning jolt of pain through her numbed foot and up into her leg.

"Is it bad?" she asked. He was taking forever to make the examination.

"It's going to have to be cleaned," he said, still looking at it.

"I'll do it when I get home," she said quickly.

"It would be an act of criminal negligence if I let you leave here with a wound in that condition. Besides, you don't have any shoes. Do you?"

When he looked up, the seriousness of his look disappeared in a grin.

"What? What are you smiling at?" she asked, confused by his reaction.

"You look like a seal," he said.

Elizabeth's hand went to her head. Instead of her black curls, she felt a rubber skullcap. The wet suit. With a quick motion she peeled the headpiece off, releasing her black hair. "I was afraid I'd get wet and then freeze to death. I hate these things." She dropped the rubbery material on the table.

Michael was still crouching on one knee. He watched as she shook her curls again. She was a beautiful woman. Her cheekbones were high, her large eyes widely spaced apart, her lips full, sensual. He wondered what they would feel like against his skin.

"I thank you for everything you've done," she said. The intensity of his gaze made her feel strange. There was definitely some chemistry working, and it would be for the best if she nipped it in the bud. She didn't trust Dr. Michael Raybin—not completely. And she didn't want to feel obligated to him in any way. "But I can clean the cut at home. I've become quite proficient at taking care of myself."

"You might be able to clean it, but I doubt you can stitch it."

Elizabeth swallowed. "Stitches? Surely it isn't that serious. It was just a shell."

"A sharp shell. It went in about half an inch, leaving a gash about two inches long. I'd say seven to nine stitches."

Elizabeth looked down at her foot. "I've never had a stitch," she confessed. "We don't have time for all of this. What about those people out there with the lights?"

"What can we do? I'll be more than willing to sneak out there and see what they're up to, but that will mean leaving you alone, without a weapon."

"But we can't just pretend they aren't there." Elizabeth felt a surge of frustration. "They might be my lead to Sean! We can't let them get away."

"We can go into town and notify the coast guard. Other than that, there's little else we can do. Unless you can think of a safe way to capture them when we don't even have a slingshot."

Elizabeth racked her brain. They were weaponless. She was injured and a liability. They had no idea who or how many they were confronting. Michael was right. They had no real choice. The only path open to them was to notify the authorities.

"Do you think they'll be back?" she asked, and she could hear the defeat in her own tone.

"I don't know, Elizabeth." Michael lifted her injured foot. "I don't know what's going on around here, but I do know that this wound has to be taken care of or you stand a chance of getting a serious infection. Let me clean it and stitch it, and then we'll decide our next step."

"Our next step?" Against her better judgment and good sense, she felt an unexpected lift.

"Somehow I feel involved. Those people are on the island I'm supposed to be responsible for. If something is going on, my friend's property may be in jeopardy."

"I see." Elizabeth dropped her gaze from his and looked at her hands in her lap.

"And there's another reason."

Michael's quiet admission made her look up. She was surprised by the look of determination in his eyes. "What other reason?"

"I owe you."

"I hardly think so," she said. She felt a twinge of irritation. Of all the reasons he could have stated, a sense of obligation wasn't realistic—or flattering. "If you owe me anything, I'd say it's a hard time for trespassing on your property."

Michael's serious features were transformed by a smile. "That's true," he agreed. "I didn't have any idea who you were or what you were doing." He paused. "And I still don't. Why were you crawling around on Mirage Island?"

"I came to spy on you." Elizabeth decided that frankness was the best ticket. "Since the first time I met you, I've felt that you knew more than you'd ever said about Sean. Then when I saw you watching the girls, I knew my intuition was right. You do know something, and it's eating at you. You wanted to make sure Catherine and Molly were okay. You needed to do that because you feel guilty about something."

Michael eased her foot to the floor. He rocked back on his heels. "I'll make a deal with you, Elizabeth. Let me clean and stitch that foot—without a big fuss—and I'll tell you what I know."

"You promise?"

She sounded almost like a child. For a strong, determined, savvy woman, she sometimes let the other side of her nature peek out. And Michael discovered that he wanted to protect that childlike streak in her.

"I promise."

"Then that implies that you do know more than you've told."

Michael lifted his eyebrows. "I would say so, Miss Reporter. Now, part of the treatment is that you can't grill me while I work. I like to concentrate on what I'm doing."

Elizabeth lifted her foot and put it in his hand. "In that case, doctor, you can begin. I have total trust in your skills."

He laughed. "Are you always so...difficult?"

"And I thought I was being cooperative."

"I'll just bet you did." He eased her foot to the floor and stood. "Let me get my bag. I have a few things here, but it's not exactly a hospital."

The dread that Elizabeth had been trying to ignore surfaced. "Is this going to hurt a lot? Maybe this isn't really necessary since the bleeding has stopped?"

"It's necessary," Michael insisted. "I'll have to see what I have to deaden the area."

"Deaden. As in 'shot'?"

"I'm afraid I don't have an anesthetist waiting in the wings." He chuckled. "Does the bold Elizabeth Campbell have a fear of needles?"

Elizabeth made a face. "Nobody in their right mind likes a needle."

"Would you prefer a stick to bite on and a slug of whiskey to deaden the pain?"

Elizabeth laughed against her will. "Maybe a small glass of brandy before you begin."

"That," Michael said, rising, "I can manage."

He returned with a glass of amber liquid and a black medical bag that looked ancient. He carried a thick terrycloth robe over his arm. He dropped the robe on a chair and handed her the brandy. "When I was a little boy, our neighborhood doctor used to come to the house if I got sick. He actually made house calls after his rounds at the hospital. That's when I decided I wanted to be a doctor."

Elizabeth sipped the brandy, relishing the warmth that spread through her. Michael had taken a seat opposite. He was watching her with a mysterious look on his face.

"Are you waiting for me to do something?" she finally asked.

"I thought you might want to change out of that wet suit. The robe is thick and warm."

The wet suit was clammy and uncomfortable. Elizabeth eyed the terry cloth with desire.

"Thanks," she said. "Where's the bathroom?"

"Second door on the left," Michael said. "Shall I—"

"I can walk," Elizabeth assured him. She used her heel on the injured foot and hobbled to the bathroom. It was such a relief to strip the suit off. The robe was as warm and comfortable as it looked. And there was a clean, male scent about it. Soap. Cologne. Michael.

She hurried out of the bathroom and away from her thoughts. He was still sitting at the kitchen table, waiting for her. While she'd been gone, he'd unpacked several items from his bag.

"I'll deaden it before I clean it," he said. "It'll make it easier all around." He patted the kitchen table for her to take a seat.

"Good idea." She tried not to grit her teeth as she sat on the edge of the table and lifted her foot into his hand.

"Tell me about your work," Michael said as he inserted a needle into her arch.

There was a moment of fiery protest, and then a blessed numbness.

"I work for Guy Fallon, a terrific editor." Elizabeth found it was easier to relax than she'd ever thought. She could feel Michael working around the wound, and she preferred not to know the details of what he was doing. To keep her mind occupied, she rambled, giving him a day-to-day description of life at the busy little newspaper.

Michael could feel Elizabeth slowly relaxing as he cleaned the wound and carefully stitched the sides of the cut together. The novocaine he'd used would be wearing off soon, and her foot was going to throb. He didn't have any strong numbing agents. If he'd had any, he would have used them on the poor man he'd dragged in from the sea.

He'd promised to tell Elizabeth the truth. It had been a spur of the moment decision and one that he hadn't clearly thought through. But he knew he was doing the right thing. She wasn't going to give up until she knew all the facts. Maybe it was her right to know. Maybe... Hell, he didn't know who had what right. He only knew that Elizabeth wasn't going to forget about Sean and get on with her own life until she knew everything.

Michael had given the stranger the best he could, more than a week's lead. Now a new set of needs had to be met. Elizabeth's. He had to think of the right way to tell her. A way she'd understand his motives and reasoning. It was very important to him that she understand.

He put the last stitch in. It was a passable job, under the circumstances. "You need to keep that foot dry and elevated," he said, standing up and propping it in the chair he'd vacated.

"Thanks, Michael," she said. She'd finished the brandy and was feeling even more relaxed.

He took her glass, refilled it and poured one for himself. On his way back to the kitchen, he stoked the dying coals in the fireplace. Before he'd gone out for his adventure in the sand, he'd had a nice fire going. When the flames were leaping again, he returned to the kitchen, scooped Elizabeth up in his arms and carried her to the sofa in front of the fire.

With gentle firmness he pushed her back to a reclining position and added several pillows under her injured foot. "Keep it elevated," he warned her.

Elizabeth readjusted the folds of the robe over her long legs. Michael's touch did strange things to her, and she searched for a safe subject to talk about. "I was thinking we were lucky they got the electricity back on for you. They'll have the phone lines repaired by tomorrow."

"I'm hardly a priority," Michael said. He was watching the play of the firelight on her face. She was a creature of fire. It danced in her eyes and hair and heightened the shadows and angles of her beautiful face.

"I've been wondering how I'm going to get my boat and get back home," she said.

"You're not. At least not tonight."

"How did I know you were going to say that?"

"Maybe you're psychic."

"Maybe I recognize a stubborn, hardheaded, bossy man when I see one."

"Could it be because you share those same qualities, in the feminine version?"

She chuckled, easing into the soft pillows of the sofa. "Touché, doctor. Now that you've won that round, how about telling me the truth." Her pose was casual, but her eyes were alert, watchful. "What about that gold coin on your kitchen counter?"

"I told you I'd tell you the truth, Elizabeth, but you have to listen to everything I say without interrupting me."

She felt a flutter of apprehension. There was a darkness in his eyes again, a hint of secrets and lies. She felt her growing trust in him falter. "Okay," she agreed finally.

"There was a man on this island the night of the storm, just as you guessed, and the coin belongs to him. He was a stranger, and he did strike me and take the boat. You already know that much. But he was badly injured. Terribly burned."

Elizabeth had guessed as much, but the words still made her hurt. Poor Sean! Where had he gone?

"How badly hurt?" she asked.

"I thought he would die, but he had a lot of will to live. If he is still alive, he's horribly disfigured."

Elizabeth swallowed the grief she felt welling in her throat. Now wasn't the time to cry. Michael had more to tell her.

"He needed extensive surgery, and I offered to help him find it. I even went and talked with my old friend, Dr. Steve Van Hugh, in Mobile."

Elizabeth nodded, but she didn't interrupt.

"I don't know if I can make you understand why I did what I did," Michael said. Elizabeth's soft brown eyes followed every word he said. She was listening, really listening. Now was the test.

"I came here to Mirage Island because my partner, Dr. Thomas Chester, has tested positive for HIV. Tommy refused to tell his patients. He said if I wanted to ruin him, I could tell. I had to decide what was right and wrong. And I came here because I didn't want the responsibility of that decision. Tommy is a good man, a fine doctor. He helps hundreds of poor, sick people, and if it becomes common knowledge that he's HIV positive, it will ruin him."

Elizabeth reached across the sofa and touched Michael's arm. "I'm sorry," she said. "That's a terrible decision to make. You've been forced to do what your partner should do."

"If you can understand that, then maybe you can understand that when this stranger said his family would be better off if he were dead, I decided that it was his decision to make. Not mine. Not his sister's. Not anyone's but his."

"And so you didn't tell anyone about him." Elizabeth spoke softly. It was exactly what she'd expected to hear— and dreaded. Sean was alive and injured, and he was on the run.

"My decision has tormented me, especially after I met you and realized the anguish you were going through trying to figure out what had happened to him. Those two little girls . . . Well, I know they're suffering."

"They are," Elizabeth agreed. "But I doubt that any of us are suffering as much as Sean. He must be terrified to abandon his children. Especially if he knew that Sandra was dead."

"He knew," Michael answered.

"Do you have any idea where he went?"

"I don't. I was going to help him. I told him about my friend in Mobile, but he left abruptly, as you know. He gave no clue as to where he intended to hide. But he has to get some type of medical care."

Elizabeth was staring into the fire. Now that she knew Sean was alive, what could she do? She didn't want to go to the authorities with the information. If Sean was hiding out, she didn't want to draw attention to him. She was going to have to find him herself and help him.

"Can you understand why I didn't tell you?" Michael saw the faraway look in her eyes. He wanted to pull her into his arms and hold her. She was lost in the folds of his robe, a slender woman with a mass of dark curls.

"Yes, I understand, and I believe you. That's not a decision I'd relish making. I'm only glad you changed your mind and decided to tell me the whole story."

"What are you going to do?" He was afraid of this answer, because he knew Elizabeth was going to do something. Even if it was wrong.

"I'm going to find him," she said simply. "He's hiding from someone and he's hurt. I'm going to find him and get him some help. Then I'll find whoever did this to him and Sandra."

The cold determination in her voice made Michael move closer to her. "These people could be killers, Elizabeth. You aren't equipped to get involved in this."

She looked at him, her brown eyes hard with determination. "No, I'm not. But I have to. My brother would risk his life for me, Michael. He has two daughters who miss him more than I can tell you. Our mother's heart is broken. Sean will be coming home. Whatever surgery he needs, we'll see that he gets it, and somehow he'll begin to rebuild his life."

Michael reached out and touched her cheek. He was overwhelmed by a rush of feeling for her. She was brave and determined, yet so very vulnerable. And terribly foolhardy.

Before he could stop himself, he put both hands on her face. He gently stroked several curls away from her cheek.

Michael's hands were warm, secure. He cupped her face, and for a moment Elizabeth wanted to close her eyes and let him hold her. But she watched as he bent toward her, knowing that he intended to kiss her.

Somewhere in the long night, she'd accepted the fact that she wanted his kiss. The niggle of doubt that had made her keep her distance was gone. Now she knew the truth of his involvement with Sean, and she didn't hold it against him. She lifted her lips to his.

The kiss was gentle at first, a soft brush of lips as they took each other's measure. Michael's lips tasted of the potent brandy, and he smelled of the same soap and cologne that was on his robe. It was a smell Elizabeth associated with the sea and the ocean breeze. His arms slid around her and eased her gently toward him until she was half reclining in his lap.

Her arms circled his neck, and she liked the way his body felt against hers.

"I think I've wanted to kiss you from the first minute I saw you," he said. "I knew you were a storm brewing, but I don't think I realized how much turmoil you'd create."

"Is that California flattery, doctor?" she asked with a grin.

"Maybe I should just silence that sassy mouth with another kiss," he suggested softly.

"Do all doctors talk so much?"

He chuckled before he brought his lips down on hers, and this time there was no hesitancy. The passion that sparked between them caught fire, moving from their lips to the rest of their bodies.

TIRED AND ANXIOUS, the man rubbed his good eye with a bandaged hand and lowered the field glasses. So, Elizabeth had stayed the night on the island. He could see the boat she'd rented rocking gently offshore. Had she been captured? He felt a surge of anxiety. She had no conception of the risk she was taking. To herself, or to him. What had she discovered? Had the doctor told her? As his mind jumped from question to question, his anxiety mounted. One false move and he could die. And Elizabeth could trigger his destruction.

"Damn!" He slammed his hand into the steering wheel of the old car and then winced from the pain. Daylight was flooding the horizon from the east, and he cranked the motor. He couldn't stand watch any longer. It was too dangerous. He couldn't afford to be seen.

With a final curse, he drove away.

Chapter Seven

Elizabeth snuggled beneath the cotton sheet and bed-spread, seeking the warmth of Michael's body. His side of the bed was empty, and she opened her eyes. Dawn light filtered in through the wooden blinds that covered the multitude of windows. It was very early.

Propping up on her elbows, Elizabeth thought back over the events of the night before. Making love with Michael had been one of the most joyous experiences of her life. There was no regretting that. But where did they go from here? That question didn't have an answer. She didn't even know how much longer he intended to stay in Alabama. She only knew that her feelings for him ran deep.

"Morning," he said as he came into the room bearing two steaming mugs of coffee. "Black?"

"How did you know?"

"Must be those old movies where all the journalists took whiskey straight, coffee black and cigarettes unfiltered."

"Oops, I forgot my hat with the press card in the band." She returned his smile and reached for the coffee. "Do you treat all of your patients so well?"

"Only the ones I tackle on the beach at midnight." He sat down on the edge of the bed. "Is there anyone who's going to be worried about you?"

"Like my mother?" Elizabeth felt a twinge of anxiety. Aleshia Campbell would be distraught if she couldn't find

Elizabeth. Not to mention Guy Fallon. "Or maybe my boss?"

"Like them," Michael said. He picked up her free hand and brought it to his lips. "I thought I'd go over to the mainland, return your boat and make a few calls on your behalf. You can rest here. With any luck they'll get the phone repaired sometime today."

"I can't tell you how appealing that is." She was touched that he'd want to do those things for her. That he'd want her to stay.

"Elizabeth, I want you to consider staying on the island for a few days. We need time to talk, to learn more about each other. I feel sort of like I took a step and found myself falling off a cliff." His grin made him look like a young boy.

Her heart was beginning to trip. Was it possible that he felt as strongly as she did? They hardly knew each other. But there was no denying the night had been magical. She'd never felt so completely a part of another person, never so intimately connected. But there was an ugly reality waiting for her that didn't allow for nights of love and passion.

"I have to find my brother, Michael. Sean is out there somewhere, injured and afraid. Last night I was able to put that aside for a few hours. This morning, I have to take up my responsibility."

Michael kissed her hand again, turning it over so that his lips caressed her palm. "I'm not asking you to give up your search for your brother. In fact, I'll help you. It's just that last night was special. I don't want to lose that in the turmoil of finding Sean."

"I don't, either." She lifted the hand he still held and placed her palm against his cheek. Stubble tickled her sensitive skin in a delightful way. Desire began a slow burn. She'd never known such an unstoppable need for a man.

"If I run those errands, you promise you won't run away?" Michael's voice was rough. "I hate to leave, but I want to report the people who were on the island, and I want to make sure that no one is concerned about you."

"You're going to call my mother?" Elizabeth had a flash of amusement. Aleshia Campbell was always trying to matchmake for her daughter. She constantly talked of the need for companionship, for love, for grandchildren! What would she do if a man called and said her only daughter was spending several days on an island with him?

"I can see that wicked little mind at work," Michael said. "You forget, I'm a doctor. I can tell her your foot is cut and that I'm taking care of you."

"My mother didn't just fall off a turnip truck." She laughed at Michael's expression. "An old farm saying, which means she wasn't born yesterday."

"Then you'll have to explain the details when you go home," Michael said, grinning. "Now, what's the number?" He took a piece of paper and a pen from his pocket. "Shoot."

She gave him her mother's number and the one at the paper. "Tell Guy I'll check in as soon as the phones are repaired."

Michael heard the anxiety in her voice. "If you're needed at work, I'll ferry you back to the mainland this afternoon," he said.

"I'm always needed at work, but I might *really* be needed." She laughed. "Guy always has ten more stories than anyone has time to write. But if he really and truly needs me, he'll tell you."

Michael took her almost empty coffee mug. "I'll be back in a minute," he said.

Elizabeth stretched in the big bed. How long had it been since she'd treated herself to a day of leisure? Too long. Maybe if she tried really hard she could put aside all of her worries for ten hours.

But even as she snuggled beneath the sheet, she thought of Sean. Where was he? Was he in pain?

Michael entered with a tray. "It's not much in the way of breakfast, but I haven't been to the store." On the tray, he carried another mug of coffee and toast. "Maybe it will tide you over until I get back."

Elizabeth sat up and took the tray. "If this is your bedside manner, I can see why you're a successful surgeon." She took in his lean body dressed in worn jeans and a soft blue shirt. "Nice package," she said with an impish grin.

"I'd never allow any of my other patients to speak to me that way," he said. "Not a good doctor-patient relationship."

"I should hope not!" She was still laughing as she picked up a piece of toast. "Share with me?"

"No, thanks. I had some before you woke. I want to get to the mainland. Where's your boat?"

"About thirty yards off your dock. Will you grab the bag with my clothes in it? I don't think I can run around here the rest of the day in your bathrobe or my bikini."

"I wouldn't complain a bit." Michael hooked the bottoms of her swimsuit with one swift grab. He lifted it from the floor. "I like this bikini."

"I didn't exactly pack for a social visit," Elizabeth said.

"If you need anything in Gulf Shores, I can pick it up."

Elizabeth shook her head. "I can only stay for today. I shouldn't even do this."

"Well, put your mind at rest. While I'm near a phone I can call the plastic surgeons' association. It may be possible that your brother has sought treatment from a member. If that's true, I may be able to locate him without too much trouble. His injuries will make him relatively easy to identify."

Elizabeth leaned forward excitedly. "That would be wonderful, Michael. What are the chances?"

"Maybe fifty-fifty. Not all plastic surgeons are members. And Sean may not have gone to a plastic surgeon."

The odds weren't great, but it was better than nothing. And while Michael was gone, Elizabeth had a plan to put into action, too. She could hobble out to the beach to see if there were any signs of the mysterious visitors from the night before. If she waited too long, the wind and surf would eradicate all traces.

"What schemes are you plotting?"

Michael's question made her smile. "Maybe I'll just surprise you when you get back."

"Lady, you're the biggest surprise I've ever had." He leaned down to kiss her, and Elizabeth had an urge to push aside the breakfast tray, abandon all her cares and drag him back into bed with her.

"Rest that foot while I'm gone," he said, pulling away from her.

Reluctantly, Elizabeth let him go. "Be careful," she replied.

He left the room, a strong, tall man with a decisive stride. When she heard his footsteps recede in the hallway and then the sound of the front door closing, she looked out the shuttered windows. The pink light of dawn had given way to a bright, clear morning. At least it wasn't going to rain.

She lounged in the bed, finishing her coffee and toast before she got up. Her foot's first contact with the floor was a painful reminder of her stitches. It wasn't going to be as easy to explore the beach as she'd thought.

And what was she going to wear? The wet suit was the warmest thing she had. And the most difficult. A pair of sweats had been draped over a chair, and she opted for them and a sweatshirt she found beneath them. They hung loosely on her slender body, but they were warm.

She felt like a criminal poking in Michael's closet, but she found a pair of old tennis shoes and some socks. She looked like a hurly-burly man and even worse when she hobbled into the hallway and found a battered but warm coat. Another person could have fit with her in the clothes she was wearing, but she was ready to explore a deserted island.

What if it wasn't deserted?

Well, she'd have to be careful when she approached the gulf side. Hobbling down the hallway, she left by the front door. The wind was brisk, but she was warm enough in all

of Michael's clothes. Without giving herself time to recon-
sider, she started slowly through the sand, taking the most
direct route possible.

When she was close enough to hear the intimate whisper
of the gulf, she found a large dune and slowly climbed it.
She had a vantage point over the flat beach. The flat, deserted beach. A flock of five squalling sea gulls cried as they
circled the surf. As far as Elizabeth could see, they were the
only living creatures.

But there was something in the sand. A groove of some
kind, as if something heavy had been dragged along the pure
white beach.

Using her good foot for traction, Elizabeth pushed herself over the dune and struggled through the powdery sand
toward the beach. The gulls moved toward her, looking for
a handout. Her attention focused on the sand. The groove
ran straight from the water up the surf line and into the
beach. It ended abruptly, and as the waves pounded the
shore, the mark was slowly being eaten away. In another few
hours, when the tide rose, there would be no sign of it.

Elizabeth examined the mark, sure that it indicated a boat
had been dragged on shore. But why? She looked around at
the empty beach. There was nothing there. Nothing. Not
even footprints. The wind had filled in all traces except for
the very deep groove. Why would someone land on Mirage
Island? Unless something had been unloaded and maybe
stashed behind some of the dunes.

Her foot was already throbbing from the exertion, but she
knew she had to look further.

The line where the sand met the water was clear as far as
Elizabeth could see. If something had been unloaded, it had
been hauled into the interior. Elizabeth used her hand to
shade the bright sun out of her eyes and sighed. As small as
the island was, it would take a lot of time to search the
dunes. The hills of sand rose in an irregular pattern. She'd
have to walk around almost every dune to be sure she didn't
miss anything. With her foot on fire, she didn't relish the

idea of that activity. Only her determination to find any clue that might lead to Sean made her move forward.

Michael's tennis shoes, even padded with socks, were far too large. They slipped back and forth on her feet, making her travels even more unpleasant.

Elizabeth lost count of the dunes she circled, her foot aching more with each step. The sun climbed higher in the sky, and beneath the layers of clothes she could feel a light layer of sweat touch her skin. "I won't quit," she said aloud. "I won't quit." And she thought of her brother. He'd taught her a lot about not being a quitter. She had to be strong for him.

It was almost noon, judging by the sun, when she saw the piece of crate. She'd circled up and down the dunes, moving inland and then back out. The rough wood of the crate indicated that it had been exposed to all types of weather. Holding the board, she climbed to the top of the dune. She wasn't far from the water at all. It was likely that something had been stored here and then moved again. But how? Why? If guns were being brought in, it would be so much simpler to move them from the importing ship to a smaller ship from the mainland. It didn't make sense to unload them on the beach of Mirage Island and then reload them again. Unless the bigger boat had come in on a high tide . . . or the pickup boat was late.

There were possibilities. She studied the board in the bright sun, an unremarkable piece of wood. There was an indentation where it had been creased, probably by a metal band. No stamps or markings, though. It was jagged on one end where it had been broken. All in all, it wasn't exactly the most impressive lead she'd ever uncovered.

Sinking down to rest in the warm sand, Elizabeth let her fingers run over the board. Its surface told no stories, gave away no secrets. She'd hunted long and hard for virtually no payoff. Now it was time to get back to the house. Michael would be back soon. If he found her gone, he'd be worried.

Ignoring the pain in her foot, she started her trek to the house. It seemed a much longer walk back than it had been on the way out, and the sun was so bright the pure white sand was almost blinding. Her thoughts roamed over the midnight scene she'd witnessed before Michael had found her. No matter how she turned the incident over, there wasn't any clear way to read the turn of events. She didn't know enough. She hoped Michael had been more successful on his errands in town.

Once inside the house, Elizabeth decided a hot bath would revive her spirits. She ran the tub full, delighted to find the old claw-footed relic in the bathroom. The porcelain had been replaced and the faucets had been changed so that they came out of the center of the big tub. It took Elizabeth only a second to understand why—two people could bathe and lean back in the tub at either end, a wonderful blend of antiquity and modern ingenuity. She couldn't help a shudder of pleasure as she thought about spending a bit of time soaking in the tub with Michael.

But for the moment she wanted to soak her weary muscles and be out before Michael returned. Now that they'd been separated for several hours, she felt shy at the idea of seeing him again. They had both taken a big risk. When he came home she wanted to be dry and dressed.

The hot water was soothing, and with her bad foot propped on the rim of the tub, she could immerse her entire body up to her chin. Her dark curls were piled on top of her head and held with an old rubber band she'd found circling one of the doorknobs. She hadn't realized how tired and sore she was until she sank into the water.

Eyes closed, she was drifting pleasantly when she heard the front door open and close. Panic was her first reaction. Since her divorce four years before, she'd lived alone. The idea that someone had entered the house while she was in the bath was extremely unnerving. Even if it was Michael's house and Michael's bath.

Holding herself very still in the water so she could hear, Elizabeth listened. The footsteps came slowly down the hall. But there was something not right about them. She remembered Michael's tread as he'd left that morning. This was different. Stealthier. And it wasn't distinct. Whoever was in the house was moving about furtively, in short bursts.

The warm water was suddenly a trap and her injured foot a terrible liability. Elizabeth eased up out of the water and stood, balancing on one foot as she reached out for a towel. Making as little noise as possible, she stepped out of the tub. In a moment she was dry. The only piece of clothing she'd brought into the bathroom was the robe. Slipping into the warmth of the terry cloth, she caught a scent of Michael's clean, soapy smell. It helped stabilize her. She had to think clearly. She had to move with extreme caution.

In her exploration of the island she'd seen no trace of a boat on the horizon. But she'd explored only the south shore. She hadn't even given a glance to the north shore—or the mainland. A boat could have been lurking around that section of the island all morning. She cursed herself silently for not at least sweeping the island in all directions with her binoculars. Now she was a sitting duck. A stupid sitting duck.

The footsteps moved down the hall and into the den. Pressing her ear against the solid oak door of the bathroom, she tried to listen. There was a thumb bolt on the door, and she eased it in place. Whoever the privacy freak was who'd installed such a lock in a bathroom, she thanked him. The intruder might find the locked door, but if she was very quiet, he might never consider that someone was hiding behind it.

There was the sound of furniture being broken in the den, a terrible rending of wood. Elizabeth thought of the antiques and felt a pang of anger and regret. What if she was cowering in the bathroom while vandals were destroying the house? She'd feel like an utter fool if she didn't step out and stop them. Stop them with what? As soon as she got back on the mainland, she'd buy a gun. A big one. This was the last—the very last—time she was going to be forced to cower while someone wrecked things around her.

"Where would it be?"

The voice that asked the question was male. Elizabeth held her breath.

There was a mumbled reply, a gruff, guttural voice. She couldn't tell anything except the sex—male.

So there were two of them, and they were hunting for something specific.

"He'll be back soon. We'd better hurry."

The gutteral voice responded again.

The first man laughed. "I don't think that would be a good idea. When the boss checked this guy out he found out he's some kind of celebrity doctor. Killin' him would cause a big stink. Besides, the doc don't know anything, and he hasn't shown any curiosity. But if he does, I'll certainly take your advice to heart. What's one less plastic surgeon?"

The indistinguishable voice said something else, and the first man laughed. "Yes, there'll be tears in Hollywood. Real ones instead of crocodile tears if the good doctor don't return. But then, we don't live in Hollywood, so what do we care?"

Elizabeth's heart was pounding so hard she was certain the door would shake. She had to see the men. They were talking about killing Michael as if they did such things every day. And they probably did. Were they the men who'd killed Sandra and tried to kill Sean? An intense, cold fury gripped her. Without thinking, she slipped the thumb bolt back. Her hand was on the door, ready to turn the knob.

"It ain't in here. Let's try the bedroom."

Footsteps sounded along the hall, and Elizabeth froze. Her fingers pushed the lock into the slot just as the knob twisted and the door creaked from the weight of a shoulder thrown against it.

"It's locked." The guttural voice spoke against the door, and Elizabeth could finally understand what the man said.

He had a peculiar accent, one she couldn't place—and she'd heard a million of them in New York City. It was a blend of cultures, with a slight speech impediment of some kind.

"Locked?" There was interest in the other man's voice. "Want me to break it down?"

Instinctively Elizabeth backed away from the door. She almost cried out in pain as she stepped fully on her injured foot. She caught herself, stifling her cry into the folds of the bathrobe. There was no place to hide in the room. The cupboard wasn't big enough to climb into. The built-in laundry hamper was spacious, but she wasn't certain she could get into it without making a lot of noise.

The entire bathroom seemed to shake as someone hurled himself against the door.

"Solid, eh?" the guttural voice said. "Hit it again."

The second man grunted. "I'll break it..." His voice drifted away into sounds, but Elizabeth knew what he was going to do.

He hit the door hard again, and this time it held. But the hinges would not hold forever.

The first man laughed. "You aren't quite the bull you thought you were." There was a squawk. "Hey! Take it easy! I was only kidding. The door's solid. Hit it again. It'll come down this time."

"Damn right!"

Elizabeth tensed. She backed to the far corner of the room so that when the door flew open it wouldn't strike her. Maybe she could brain old Igor with something when he crashed in. She lifted the top off the toilet tank. It would make a very solid weapon. Holding it high above her head, she waited.

"Hey! Somebody's coming!"

Feet scuffled outside the door.

"It's the telephone repairman!"

More scuffling sounds came from the hall, and Elizabeth lowered the heavy lid, her arms trembling. She almost dropped it when the doorbell rang, and her heart kicked

back into high gear. Would the intruders hurt the repairman? She ought to try to warn him.

There was an outside window in the bathroom, and she
might be able to open it and get out. If she could be certain
she could get to the repairman before the intruders did, she
might save him and herself.

She had climbed onto the toilet seat and was trying to
raise the window when she heard the front door open.

"Good afternoon, sir. What can I do for you?"

Elizabeth paused as she listened to the intruder assume the
role of homeowner.

"Phone's out. I need to check in the house. The lines here
seem okay but there's still a problem."

"Come right in. Would you care for some coffee, or perhaps a beer?"

Elizabeth couldn't believe her ears. The guy was acting
like he owned the place. His speech was decidedly strange
compared to what she had heard before, and he was acting
like the perfect homeowner.

"Coffee would be nice," the repairman said. "If you've
got some made. The wind's a bit brisk on the water."

"I'll heat a cup in the microwave," the intruder offered.

The footsteps continued down the hall to the kitchen and
the bedroom where the telephones were located.

"That was a terrible storm," the intruder said. "I thought
we were going to blow away here. I've been renting the
house from Dr. Goodman for the fall season. He warned me
that nasty storms could blow in, but I figured the hurricane
season was over by November. Just goes to show that the
weather can stir up the best and worst of surprises."

"Exactly. We've been working double shifts to repair the
line damage. Looks like this is the last of it, though."

Elizabeth took a seat. It was going to be a long wait, and
she didn't dare try to warn the repairman now. She could
possibly get them both killed. There was no telling where old
Igor was hiding.

It seemed like forever, but it was only about five minutes before she heard the repairman leaving. She fought down the panic and the urge to rush out of the bathroom and beg for assistance. To do such a foolish thing would only invite tragedy. She realized how afraid she was as she heard the front door close. The heavy footsteps of Igor came from one of the bedrooms.

"If you're going to break down the door, do it. We've got to get out of here. That repairman can identify us."

"You. Not me."

"Good point," the man said. "Me. So that makes me even more anxious to get out of here."

There was a rumble of indecipherable talk.

"It's him! Out the back!"

Footsteps pounded down the hall and to the kitchen. Elizabeth felt her hopes rise. Just as the intruders' footsteps disappeared, the front door opened.

"Elizabeth?"

Michael's voice was the best thing she'd heard in a long, long time.

She threw the thumb bolt and opened the door. She forgot about being shy or uneasy at his return. Favoring her injured foot, she ran as fast as she could down the hall and into his arms at the front door.

"I don't know what I've done to deserve this, but I like it," Michael said as he caught her against his chest. But when he saw her face, all humor disappeared from his voice. "What is it?"

"Two men. They were in the house, hunting for something. I hid in the bathroom."

Michael's grip tightened. "I never should have left you. Are you okay?"

"Fine. I'm fine." And she realized she was. Her heart was pounding, but the solid feel of Michael's arms around her made everything better. "They're gone now. They're gone."

And the words were an incantation of relief. "What did you find in town?"

Michael's arms tightened around her as he helped her back to the kitchen and den. "I think you'd better sit down for this."

Chapter Eight

Michael took a seat beside Elizabeth on the sofa. He gathered her cold hands in his. "Just let me make sure they're gone."

Elizabeth's fingers involuntarily held his. "Let them go. They're mean, Michael. They were talking about killing you like it was no more than swatting a mosquito."

"Killing me?" There was real puzzlement in his voice. "Why me? I don't have anything to do with any of this."

"Wrong place at the wrong time." She rubbed her palms along his arms. "You helped Sean, and they mean to kill him. Whatever he saw, it must be incriminating."

Michael stood. "I'll be back."

"They're dangerous," Elizabeth protested.

"I bought a gun in town. That's what took me so long." He patted his waistband in the back. The gun was completely hidden by the jacket.

"Do you know how to use one?" The question popped out before she could stop herself. She didn't question Michael's talent or ability—but he was a doctor, not a sharpshooter.

"I know." His smile was amused. "I wasn't always a healer," he said. "I've seen all of Gibson's movies, and my body is a lethal weapon."

"This is no time for jokes."

He grinned. "I'll be back."

He disappeared like a shadow slipping out of the room. There wasn't a footstep or the sound of a door closing. He could move very quietly when he chose.

Michael headed instinctively for the north side of the island. He hadn't gone far when he heard the roar of a motor. A powerful launch sped toward the mainland from a short distance offshore. It had been hidden by a small curve in the island's coastline. The tiny spit of land had blocked the boat from Michael's view when he'd arrived.

"Damn," he whispered. He could see two men in the launch, one big, gruesomely big, and the other an average size. But he couldn't see clearly enough to identify them. The boat was white with blue markings. Nothing unusual there, but it wouldn't hurt to check the docks around Perdido Pass. Of course, it could be moored at some private home. Michael had been doing some thinking, and he'd come to the conclusion that whoever ran the smuggling operation was living somewhere near Gulf Shores.

He turned back to the house and Elizabeth. Thank goodness he'd gotten back in time!

He picked up the groceries he'd left in his boat and hauled them up to the house. The gun was tucked snugly in his jeans, a reminder that nothing involving Elizabeth was simple or easy—or safe. And the next few minutes were not going to be an exception.

He went back to the den reluctantly. He knew Elizabeth well enough now to know that she'd be fighting to get back to the mainland in the next few minutes. He felt his right pocket. The note from Guy Fallon was still there.

Elizabeth was sitting on the sofa, but just barely. Her eager face showed a moment of pure relief when she saw Michael in the doorway.

"I was getting worried. I wondered if I should look for you."

"They were leaving. I didn't get a good look at either of the men, but one was a bruiser."

"I nicknamed him Igor. He didn't sound very bright, but he was strong."

"Elizabeth..." Michael hesitated. He drew the note out of his pocket. "There's been another murder. On the west end again. A young man. A Latino, with no identification. He was shot with a high-powered weapon. The same type that killed Brian Havard." As he spoke, he watched the color drain from Elizabeth's face. "Guy said to tell you that the federal agents think both murders are connected, and they suspect Sean."

"Great! That's just excellent!" Elizabeth wanted to say a lot more, all of it profane. "My brother is the prime suspect."

"They've put out an all points bulletin with Sean's description. He's been formally charged with the murder of his wife, Brian Havard, and this unidentified Latino."

"This is impossible! I'd like to kill those...creeps!"

But Michael saw the sheen of unshed tears in her eyes. What she really wanted to do was cry. He went to the sofa and gathered her into his arms.

"I have to get back to the mainland. I have to—" She struggled against his soothing grip.

"Guy said for you to take a few days off."

"Guy isn't in charge of running my life!" She knew she was snapping, but she was helpless to do anything else.

"Here." He gave her the note.

Very slowly, she unfolded the yellow news copy. Guy used only a manual typewriter and yellow copy paper that had to be ancient. She recognized the typeface of his old Royal, and the way the *i* rose slightly above all the other letters.

Elizabeth
    Stay away from the newspaper. I'm writing an editorial that will shake those lazy feds out of their black leather shoes. Sean is missing, so he's easy to blame. It's best for you and the paper if you aren't here tomorrow when this edition hits the street. Your mother

agrees. She's fine. Stay away or you're fired.

Guy.

The last sentence was underlined three times with the heavy number one lead pencil Guy preferred. His pencils didn't have erasers because he claimed he never made a mistake. Elizabeth smiled, a vague, watery smile.

"If Guy fired me he wouldn't have anyone to bully."

"That's exactly what he said. He also said you'd see through the threat and call his bluff. That's when he told me to try and reason with you."

"My mother—"

"Call her, Elizabeth. The phones are working. Tell her you're okay and not to worry. She already knows about the charges. I called her when I got to the mainland and told her about your foot. She said for you to stay here and stay out of it."

"My mother said that?" Elizabeth felt a wave of confusion. "She said for me to stay here? With you?"

"I told her I was a doctor."

Elizabeth rolled her eyes. "What a line. Only someone of my mother's generation would fall for that."

Relieved to see even a glimpse of her puckish humor, Michael picked up her injured foot. "And it's time for the examination, to prove that I am a medical man. Good grief, what have you done to this foot?"

Elizabeth wanted to snatch her foot back, but she didn't. It was aching and throbbing, no doubt a result of her very active day stomping around the sand dunes.

"It looks like you've been running a marathon."

"I went to the beach." She gave him a three-sentence summary of her adventure and the dismal results.

"That's how you rest an injured foot?"

The tone in Michael's voice made her look up. He was chastising her like a bad child. "My brother—"

"And a lot of good you're going to do him if you have to be hospitalized with an infection. Let me tell you how infected wounds like this have to be drained. Permanent damage could make this foot susceptible to arthritis, calcification, gout, poor circulation." Elizabeth's face was so serious, her eyes so wide-eyed, that he stopped. "I think you get the idea."

The truth of the matter was her foot hurt like mad. She hadn't really thought about it until she was waiting for him to return. The combination of waiting, anxiety and pain had made her want to get up and go after him.

"Just give it a day or two, Elizabeth. It'll heal faster if you give it a chance, and you'll be back to normal."

"That isn't such an unreasonable request." She put her hand on his. "I know you're trying to help me and I appreciate it. Did you find out anything else on the mainland?"

"I put an ad in the *American Plastic Surgeon's Journal.* I called Dr. Van Hugh, but he's been out of the country at a medical convention. I called around the area. No one from New Orleans to St. Petersburg has treated such a patient." He shrugged. "Dead end, up to this point. But the word is out and maybe someone will call."

"Thank you, Michael." She leaned forward and kissed his cheek gently. "Thank you for helping me. Thank you for being you."

"I'll do everything I can, Elizabeth, but I want something from you in return."

"What?" She didn't have any reservations. He would never ask for something she couldn't freely give.

"I want your word that you won't let this hunt for your brother consume your life." He held up a hand to stop her protest. "Let's hunt him with everything we have. And remember, the authorities will be hunting him, too. They just don't know the extent of his injuries yet. But when they do, they'll be hot after him."

"And what about the murderers? They want him, too." She spoke with more bitterness than she intended. "Sean doesn't stand a dog's chance."

"We'll do everything we can to get to him first. But keep in mind that the accident was severe. Sean has been terribly injured. He may not be the man you called brother."

"You aren't talking about physical injuries, are you?" The horrible thought that he might be mentally different had not entered her mind. Not really. "You think he might have a permanent injury to his personality or his brain, don't you?"

"The psychological trauma he's been through is enough to rock anyone. Not to mention the physical abuse and pain. It's enough to break a strong man, Elizabeth. And once a person breaks..."

"All the king's horses and all the king's men." She swallowed. "Thanks for telling me this. I have to be prepared for every possibility."

"When I found out he abandoned his daughters, I started to think he might be... damaged."

"I guess maybe the thought was at the back of my mind. I just didn't want to recognize it. But if that's the case, then he needs us more than ever. He needs help."

"And we'll help him. If we can. But you have to hang on to your life, to your dreams. In the middle of all of this, you can't lose sight of you. And us. Promise me that."

Elizabeth's smile was wan. "How can I concentrate on the wonderful things we have together when my brother may be dying? It's so selfish."

"Because you deserve to be happy, no matter what happens to Sean. You have to be strong and whole for his daughters, and for your mother. Your happiness takes nothing away from him. Remember that."

"I'll try," she said. One tear slipped down her cheek. She brushed it away quickly. "I'm not crying because you've upset me. I'm crying because you're so wonderful."

Michael laughed and pulled her tighter against him. "I think you're having a weak spell. Too much excitement, only some toast for breakfast, and it's midafternoon. I bought all of your favorite things at the grocery store."

"How do you know what I like?" she mumbled against his chest.

Michael kissed her ear. "Your mother told me. Why don't you give her a call while I make some very late lunch?"

"I should," Elizabeth agreed.

"I'll discreetly leave you to make excuses to your mother. Remember, she thinks I'm only interested in your foot."

"I'll bet." But Elizabeth found she was smiling. Michael had a way of lifting her spirits.

When she dialed her mother, she expected the worst, but Aleshia Campbell was a surprise. She was calm—and firm. She insisted that Elizabeth remain on the island and recuperate. There was nothing she could do at home and no reason to return to Gulf Shores. No one in his right mind would believe the charges that had been made against Sean. It would only help in the long run, because friends were so outraged they were all hunting for Sean. The best thing Elizabeth could do was to give her foot time to heal. Elizabeth finally agreed to heed her mother's advice.

Michael had brought her bag with her jeans and a warm flannel shirt, and she pulled those on before heading for the kitchen. The smell of chicken soup wafted to her and made her mouth water. She *was* hungry. Walking gingerly, she made her way to the kitchen and found Michael busily preparing turkey sandwiches. A bottle of chilled wine was on the counter, so she picked up a corkscrew and opened it.

"I didn't realize how hungry I was until I smelled that soup." She put a glass of wine at his elbow and stood on tiptoe to kiss his neck.

"Eat hearty. I have plans for you later." He arched an eyebrow. "Have I shown you my la-bor-a-tory?"

"I thought I was supposed to be recuperating?"

"Oh, everything I have in mind can be done with your foot on a pillow."

"DR. VAN HUGH, please. This is an emergency."

"May I say who's calling?" The receptionist was bored

and wary. She was well trained at her job of guarding the doctor.

"Listen, lady, I need to speak with Van Hugh. I'm not in the mood to play games."

There was a pause. "Are you a patient?"

"Are you deaf? Get the doctor on the phone." He could hear his own rapid breathing and knew he sounded hostile. Well, why shouldn't he? He was standing in some stranger's kitchen making long distance calls, hoping that they wouldn't return before he could steal some food and escape. He didn't want to have to hurt anybody. But he would. If he had to. If he was forced into it. It had come down to that. His hands and face were hurting. The pain had become a constant undercurrent buried beneath everything else he did and thought. He knew he wasn't thinking clearly. But he just didn't give a damn.

The doctor on the island had mentioned this Van Hugh. He'd said he was a good plastic surgeon, especially with burns. Now it was time to get some help. Before they caught up with him. Before anyone could find him and drag him back to Gulf Shores.

"The doctor is away." The woman's voice was angry, but she kept her words coldly impersonal.

"When will he be back?"

"I'll take a message for him, if you'd like to leave one."

"It's a simple question. When will the doctor be back?" He felt his temper flash. If she didn't give him the answer, he'd go to the office and choke it out of her.

"This evening." An edge of concern had crept into the receptionist's voice. "Why don't you leave your name and Dr. Van Hugh will call you?"

"I'll bet."

"Dr. Van Hugh is always concerned about his patients." There was a reasoning tone in her voice, placating. "He'll want to know who called. Can I tell him what you're calling about?"

"Just tell him I'll be in touch."

He replaced the phone, checked outside in all directions and began to go through the shelves and refrigerator, loading up two grocery sacks. He'd never thought of himself as a common thief, but he didn't have a choice. The world had turned against him, and now he was on his own.

ELIZABETH STRETCHED her foot, testing the stitches in her arch. After twenty-four hours of keeping it elevated—and no matter what else they'd done, Michael had taken care of her foot—it felt much better. The swelling had gone down, and the soreness was rapidly diminishing. She looked over at the man who dozed beside her and pushed a strand of hair off his forehead. If only she could stay with him on the island and pretend that none of the terrible things that had happened were real.

But she'd kept reality at bay for long enough. It was time to go back to Gulf Shores and begin to pick up the pieces. Her respite had done her a world of good.

"What's on your agenda today?" Michael asked.

"Back to the mainland. Back to the paper. Back to the search for my brother."

"I was hoping we'd get a call from a doctor somewhere around the area." He drew her close and kissed her cheek. "I'm sorry, Elizabeth."

"That would have been too easy," she said, allowing her body to luxuriate against the feel of his. It was going to be so hard to leave him. It seemed that with two magical nights and days, Michael had given her a completeness that she'd never even known she needed. Why had he come into her life at a time when she couldn't give him the attention she wanted to?

"That was a mighty big sigh," he whispered.

"I have to go back, and I don't want to."

"I know." He kissed her again, letting his lips move lightly down her neck. "I know."

"So let's get it over with."

Michael didn't attempt to stop her, but he did insist on something to eat before they left the island. He carried the weight of the conversation throughout the meal, talking of the things he'd seen on the island. Casually mentioning his dissatisfaction with his practice and his life. Elizabeth watched him, trying hard to etch every gesture and look into memory.

The last dish was washed, and she could not think of another thing to do to legitimately delay. As they walked together to the boat, she lifted her binoculars to her eyes.

"The workmen have almost repaired the bridge. Maybe by this afternoon you can drive back over here."

"I'll need your help."

Elizabeth looked at him. "How?"

"I can't get the boat and the car over here, and I don't think I want to ever be trapped on this island with just a car. This storm has taught me a lot of respect for old man weather."

Elizabeth kissed his cheek. "Those of us who've lived on the gulf all our lives know how erratic the weather can be. A terrible and devastating beauty."

"Magnificent even in a storm," Michael said, a note of teasing in his voice. "Could it be that it reminds me of someone?"

Elizabeth was quiet on the short ride over. She felt as if she were leaving paradise to step back into a world that was hellish in contrast. Michael took her to the boat yard where she'd left her Trooper, and where a curious Johnny Belmont waited but politely asked no questions.

"I'll call you this evening," Michael said as he leaned inside her Trooper window. He had insisted on walking her to her vehicle.

"Are you going back to Mirage?"

"No, I think I'm going into Mobile. Steven hasn't returned my call, and I know he's checked in with his office."

"He's in Europe," Elizabeth reminded him.

"Ah, yes, Europe! Somewhere I recall reading that they even have telephones there!"

Elizabeth laughed. "Your sarcasm is wasted on me."

"Too bad. But Steve should have called me nonetheless. It won't hurt for me to stop by. Maybe he was in transit and just arrived back. He might have some good ideas on tracking down Sean."

"You know, you're pretty smart—for a medicine man."

"Smart enough to know that you're going to have the last word." He leaned in a little farther and kissed her cheek. "Be careful."

Elizabeth was at the office in less than twenty minutes. There were several strange cars parked in the lot, and she checked out the tags. All Alabama license plates. One was a rental. A dark sedan. Why was it that the feds were so conspicuously inconspicuous?

Even expecting to see one of the ATF agents, Elizabeth wasn't prepared to discover Agent McMillan sitting in her chair. There were three foam coffee cups in a line on her desk. He'd been waiting awhile.

"Mr. Fallon said you'd be back today." McMillan stood. "We have some questions for you. Please come with me."

"You may ask Elizabeth to answer some questions, but unless you intend to arrest her and charge her, don't you ever speak to her in that tone again." Guy was bristling with fury. "This fella's been in my hair for two days. He thought you'd skipped the country and gone to the Bahamas. I told him you'd be back today."

Elizabeth noted the lines of tension around McMillan's eyes. The man was as tight as a piano wire. "What's going on?" she asked, her voice much calmer than she felt.

"Where have you been, Ms. Campbell?"

"I'm not certain that falls under federal business." She deliberately walked around her desk and sat down in the chair he'd just vacated. Without looking at the agent, she flipped through the pink message notes that had been left in a neat stack. She was sure the agent had made it his busi-

ness to look at all of them, too. There was one from her
mother, one from Chief Williams, one from an elderly
woman she'd done a story on the week before, one from the
health department regarding a series of vaccinations that
would be held next month. Nothing to excite the interest of
the federal government. She dropped them back on her
desk. "Why do you want to know where I've been? Since
you've accused my brother of three murders and who knows
what else, maybe I'm guilty by blood, is that it?"

"The man we found dead on the beach. Carlos Santiago.
Do you know him?"

Elizabeth furrowed her brow. "Now let me see. I don't
remember him from high school. No. Maybe college. No, I
don't think there were any Carlos Santiagos in my classes.
How about the local yacht club membership roles? I'm not
a member, actually, but I do go there for some social events.
No, maybe not. Oh, yes. Carlos Santiago. Wasn't he a
member of a hard rock band?"

"Cut the wise remarks, Ms. Campbell. This is a serious
matter."

"I might take it a little more seriously if I knew what it
was about. As far as I can tell, you guys are a joke. You ac-
cuse my brother of three murders because you can't find
another convenient suspect. And you expect me to take
anything you do seriously?"

McMillan put both hands on the desk and leaned forward. His eyes were cold. "We found your name written on
a piece of paper in Carlos Santiago's pocket. The man had
been shot in the chest nine times with an automatic weapon.
Does that sound like fun and games to you, Ms. Campbell?"

Elizabeth felt all of her bravado abandon her, but her
anger at the agents kept her back straight and her eyes
snapping. "So by your twisted logic, that makes me a suspect? Perhaps I was an intended victim, Agent McMillan.
Have you ever considered that?"

"It may surprise you to know we have. That's why we've been trying to find you. To offer protection. If there is a chance that Santiago was looking for you, then what he planned wasn't going to be a picnic. We want to put a man with you day and night. If you'll cooperate, it will make it a lot easier."

"Absolutely not!"

Guy swung around to look at Elizabeth, disbelief obvious on his face. "What?"

The agent gave her a tight-lipped smile. "I didn't expect you to cooperate. You're a difficult woman. So I've been authorized to warn you. Make this too hard on us and you'll find yourself sitting somewhere in custody. We've launched a full-scale investigation down here, and we won't have some female reporter ruining our plans. Do you understand that?"

"Perfectly." Elizabeth wanted to put her head down on her desk and close her eyes. Not only were they chasing Sean, they were going to try to follow her around twenty-four hours a day. If there was any chance in getting to Sean and helping him, the feds were going to destroy it.

"Now I have some questions I'd like for you to answer." Agent McMillan flipped open a notebook.

"Not in this lifetime," Elizabeth snapped. "Unless you have a warrant for my arrest, I urge you to get out of this office. And don't come back until you have some authority."

McMillan stood straight. "If that's the way you want to play this game, we'll be happy to oblige you."

Guy cleared his throat and stepped forward. The look on his face telegraphed worry. "Maybe you should rethink this, Elizabeth. If someone is looking for you, someone who wants to hurt you, maybe it wouldn't be a bad idea to have a little backup."

"Did you see the paper with my name on it, Guy?" Elizabeth looked at her boss. "Maybe these folks just made that up. Maybe it's a ruse to get my permission to follow me around. If they're really looking for Sean as a murderer, they might be trying to use me. Right, Mr. Agent? You wouldn't be above such a trick, would you?''

Guy's face broke into a big smile. "You are brilliant, Elizabeth. Brilliant. They had me going."

"This is a very serious matter." Agent McMillan looked extremely uncomfortable. "Your life could be at stake."

"And it could be a trick." Elizabeth felt her heart pounding in her chest. It could be, but she didn't think so. Not after the visit from Igor and his boss on Mirage Island. Someone had killed one Carlos Santiago—who had been looking for her. Now, who was who, and who was on which side? It was far too complicated. A very deadly game of allegiances.

Chapter Nine

Michael took a sharp corner and felt a deep appreciation for the Jaguar's handling ability. Actually, the Jaguar belonged to his partner. Michael's old Volvo wasn't up to a cross-country run, so he'd borrowed Tommy's new car. It was a fine automobile but a little too conspicuous for Michael's tastes. As he headed toward Steve Van Hugh's office, he would have felt better in a dark blue sedan. He laughed as he realized he'd watched too many cop movies.

His mind was on Tommy as he negotiated the downtown streets of Mobile. There was a touch of New Orleans in some of the architecture, but none of the sense of a big city. Tommy would like Mobile. Lush, subtropical. The vegetation spoke of a mild, humid climate and a place where a daily siesta would be a nice way of life. For years Tommy had been spending the three summer months practicing medicine in Central America. Guatemala, El Salvador, Nicaragua, Panama. He'd gone down to operate on people who would otherwise never have had the services of such a skilled plastic surgeon. Children were his specialty. Especially those savaged by stupid wars fought by power-hungry adults. Tommy called his patients "the innocents." He loved the children and the tropics.

The old familiar pang of anxiety kicked Michael in the gut. What was he going to do? What was the right thing? Why wouldn't Tommy at least discuss the matter with him?

None of it made any sense. Tommy had made his announcement that he was HIV positive more than four months before. Michael had given him time to decide how he wanted to handle telling the patients, or if he'd wanted to quietly withdraw from the practice, or even shift his focus to nonsurgical treatments of patients who were HIV positive.

But Tommy had done nothing, and he'd refused to discuss the subject at all. He'd gone on, acting as if he'd never heard of HIV.

For a while, Michael had simply given him room to work it out. But there came a point where the patients had to be told. They had a right to know.

Since Tommy refused to take any responsibility himself, it was forced on Michael to protect the people who came to him for medical treatment. He was going to have to tell them, or else dissolve the partnership. And that was something he didn't really want to do. He and Tommy had been partners—and friends—for fourteen years. Michael wasn't the kind of man who abandoned his friends.

As he slipped into the parking space in front of Van Hugh's office, he realized that he'd come to Mirage Island for the solitude, but also because of Steve. Throughout med school he'd developed a lot of respect for Steve's thinking and his integrity. He'd come to Alabama hoping that his old friend might help guide him on this tricky path.

Michael left the car in the shade and went to the office door. To his surprise, it was locked. Even if Steve was out of town, he should have arranged for someone to see his patients. There were always stitches to be removed and bandages to be changed. Some doctors might not be concerned about those small issues, but Van Hugh would be.

The click of high heels on the sidewalk made Michael turn around.

"I just don't know what to do," the middle-aged woman who approached him said. She was petite and walking rapidly, her heels clicking on the walk like a flamenco dancer's. "Dr. Van Hugh has never done anything like this before in his life. It doesn't make a bit of sense. Not a bit. That man would hardly take time to go to the bathroom, and now he's gone and no one can find him. Patients are calling me at home. The hospital is looking for him. His son called from military school in Florida. Everybody wants something, and there's no Dr. Van Hugh to give it to them. And no one knows where he is."

As she chattered on, she dug in her purse until she extracted a large ring of keys and opened the front door. "You are the doctor who Steve, uh, Dr. Van Hugh, sent to pick up his patients, aren't you?"

Michael followed her inside the office before he answered. "Not exactly. I'm a friend. I'm looking for Steve, too. My name is Michael Raybin. We went to med school together."

"I'm Gladys Runnels." The telephone started ringing and the woman sighed. "It's going to be a nightmare. I'll let it ring a minute. They'll call back. I don't know what to tell them, anyway. I called all the other doctors, and Dr. Van Hugh didn't ask any of them to fill in for him. He was due back yesterday. He has surgery scheduled tomorrow, and those patients are going to want to talk to someone tonight."

There was worry all over the woman's face, and the jangling telephone made her nervous as a cat. Michael felt sympathy for her. "Maybe it's not so bad. Maybe he got tied up at the airport."

"No. He was due in late yesterday. He would have called me." She glanced around the office quickly. "Well, since I can't help the patients, what can I do for you?"

"I referred a patient to Steve. I wanted to see if he'd come in."

She went behind the desk and pulled out a ledger. "Name?"

Michael hesitated. "I don't know. He was very badly injured. Terrible facial burns and wounds. He looked like he'd been in an explosion of some kind."

"Nobody like that has been here. Dr. Van Hugh has been complaining because our cases have been so dull. Liposuction is the thing. Every woman in Mobile wants it. Stomach, cheeks, saddlebags. An hour or two of vacuuming out that old fat and they go home with a new look. Men, too. As you well know, men are every bit as concerned about their looks as women."

"That I do know," Michael said. Gladys Runnels was a card. A receptionist like her could make, or break, a doctor's practice. Most patients loved the chitchat and the friendly treatment.

"If you had to take a guess, where do you think Steve might be?"

"The hospital. But he isn't there. I called already. No one has seen him since Paris. A couple of the other doctors went with him, but they're back at work today. They said he made it home. So where the hell is he?" She looked around the office as if she expected him to pop out from behind a sofa.

"Mind if I look around? Maybe he left a note or something."

Gladys hesitated as her gaze roved up and down Michael. "Okay," she said. "I've never let anyone back in his office without his permission before. I hope this isn't a career mistake."

Michael laughed. "Steve won't care. I promise. I've known his darkest secrets since we were young men."

"You can go back there—but only if you'll tell those secrets. I need a pay raise and I'm not above blackmail."

Michael couldn't help but laugh. If Tommy met her, he'd be trying to hire her. With her Southern drawl and love of mischief, she'd be a hit in Hollywood.

Gladys was setting up for the day's work when Michael opened the door of the first examination room on the right.

The room was antiseptically clean. Not a tool was out of place. The same was true of the eight other rooms he explored. Steve's office was the last door on the left, and he opened it with a bit of reservation. It was one thing to look at the impersonal patient rooms, but a man's office was a different matter. It was snooping.

Michael pushed the door open and stepped in. The desk was cluttered, but not unreasonably so. The thing that caught Michael's attention was the smell. There was an odor in the room. Slightly unpleasant. He went to the trash can and looked in. A greasy hamburger wrapper from a fast-food joint had been thrown into the can along with some uneaten fries and a milk-shake cup. It was the remnants of the food that stank of grease.

While he was at the desk, he scanned the surface. He stopped short at a small black and white picture that was on top of a pile of other things. It was a young man, a teenager, with dark hair and brown eyes. Michael had never seen the person in the photograph, at least, not looking like that, but he knew it was Sean Campbell. The picture had been cut from a yearbook. He could tell by the size and the pose. Dark suit, tie, white shirt. Senior portrait. A man as handsome as his sister was beautiful.

Michael's pulse increased, and he felt a surge of excitement. So, Sean had remembered Van Hugh's name, and he'd finally come to the doctor for help. Since he couldn't go home and get a picture of himself, he'd probably found an old annual and cut out his own picture.

Just as he was about to pick up the photo, Michael stopped. Better to leave it alone. Better not to touch anything at all. There was something not exactly right about what was going on with Van Hugh. Sean must have visited the doctor after hours. That, or Gladys Runnels was lying. She wasn't the kind of woman who would let a mangled man walk past her without noticing. No, Sean had not come during regular office hours.

It was a hopeful sign that he was attempting to reconstruct his face as it had once been. Maybe he was getting closer and closer to wanting to pick up his old life. That would be impossible, but it was a sign of healing that he wanted to try.

Remembering the terrible burns and wounds, Michael couldn't help the jolt of pity that went through him. Sean Campbell had lost a lot more than mere good looks. His wife was dead. His entire life had been destroyed. And now he was charged with heinous crimes. Even if he wanted to step back into his old way of life, he couldn't. The feds were ready to snatch him up and send him to prison.

Elizabeth would be excited to learn that in all probability Sean had been in Mobile in recent hours. But where was Van Hugh? It didn't make sense that he'd disappear. Steve was too conscientious. Too concerned about his patients and his reputation.

Had he gone somewhere with Sean?

That question had an ugly undertone to it, and one that surprised Michael with its power to unsettle him.

He checked the room again, trying to imagine the scene that must have taken place in that office. The only thing Michael got was the bitter aftertaste of nameless dread. Van Hugh was divorced, one son away in school. He had no day-to-day family responsibilities. Not even any pets as Michael remembered their prior lunch conversation.

But he had patients. Plenty of those and all needing attention.

"Someone's been in Steve's office," Michael told Gladys on his way out. "I wouldn't disturb anything in there." He couldn't think of a better way to tell her.

Instantly she looked up at him, her eyes big behind her glasses. "What are you saying?"

"I'm worried about Steve," Michael admitted. "He's probably busy somewhere and will show up for rounds tonight. But . . ."

"What's in his office?" Gladys was relentless.

"Hamburger wrapper."

"That's not Dr. Van Hugh. He won't touch those things. Won't even let me bring them into the office for my lunch."

"I'll check back with you tomorrow. If Steve comes in, have him call me here." Michael wrote down the phone number to the house on the island. "It's urgent."

"Sure you don't want to handle a few of his patients for him?"

"The Alabama medical authorities might object if I simply hung out my shingle."

"They might," Gladys agreed, "if they caught you."

"Keep me posted, Ms. Runnels," Michael said as he left. Once outside, he walked slowly to his car. There should be something else he could do, but damned if he knew what.

ELIZABETH EASED into one of the slanted parking spaces along Magnolia Avenue in Fairhope and entered the picturesque old restaurant. Michael's invitation to meet him there was a pleasant surprise and an excellent way to escape Agent McMillan's not-so-subtle surveillance. Elizabeth had given the feds the slip in a convoluted series of turns down old county farm roads. She'd learned to drive in Baldwin County, and she knew every pig path and two-lane road that led anywhere. She wasn't doing anything she cared about the federal agents knowing, but it was just the general principle that she was being followed—in the hopes that she'd lead them to Sean.

She'd shaken them easily this time, but the next time they'd be prepared for her antics. She shrugged. She'd worry about that when the time came. Right now, she had a lunch with Michael to look forward to.

The red Jaguar wasn't parked on the street, so Elizabeth knew she had arrived first. She entered the restaurant and took a table where she could watch the door. She'd barely sat down before Michael entered. His hair was windblown, and his eyes were glowing. She knew immediately that he had news.

"I think your brother was at Steve's office." He told her about the photo.

"As happy as that makes me, I'm also worried. Every law officer in ten states is looking for him. He doesn't stand a chance, not injured the way he is." She hated the idea of Sean hiding like a rabbit with the dogs and hunters closing in.

"If he's gotten to Steve, he's in good hands," Michael said. "The only problem is that Steve's disappeared."

"Is it possible he might have taken Sean somewhere else? Someplace to do the surgery?"

"A hospital or clinic, maybe. But Steve should have let his office staff know. There's something wrong there." He shook his head.

The waitress arrived and they placed their orders for steaming bowls of gumbo and shrimp po'boys.

"What are you going to do now?" Michael asked her.

She hesitated before she told him about the dead man on the beach. "He had a piece of paper with my name on it," Elizabeth said, watching the worry spring in Michael's eyes. "Naturally the agents think this is more of Sean's handiwork."

"They should give you some protection." Michael looked around the restaurant as he spoke.

"They did. I lost them." Elizabeth grinned. "How can I conduct my personal business if some cop is following me around?"

Michael reached across the table and took her hand. "This time I agree with the authorities. Someone may be trying to hurt you, Elizabeth. You said those two men on the island were talking about killing me. The same applies to you. If they think you know something, they'll kill you without batting an eye."

Elizabeth felt cold fingers trace her spine, and she remembered her grandmother saying that someone had walked on her grave when she had that feeling. It was distinctly unpleasant.

"Maybe you should consider accepting protection," Michael said.

"Maybe. What about you?"

"I'm peripheral. You're Sean's sister. And you're the one who's stirring things up by looking for him and insisting that he's innocent."

"I'm going to begin canvassing all of his old friends when I get back to Gulf Shores. Someone has to be helping him. And..." She felt her voice begin to crack unexpectedly. "It's so strange that he hasn't made any effort to see the girls. Sean loved them and since he's still in the area, I just believe he must be in terrible pain."

"I warned you, Elizabeth. He's been injured. We have no idea how that will affect him."

"But those two girls were his life—" At the expression on Michael's face, Elizabeth stopped. Michael was right. There was no telling what condition Sean was in—mental or physical. "But that doesn't mean he won't ever be the Sean I know," she said aloud. As she spoke, she realized she was trying as hard to convince herself as Michael.

Michael tightened his grip on her hand. She needed support. The waitress served their food, and even with problems heavy on their minds, they both ate.

"What about the dead man on the beach?" Michael asked her. "Why do you think Santiago had your name on him?"

It was a question that she'd given some thought to—and none of it was very reassuring. "The people who killed Sandra must have sent someone to watch me."

"And who do you suppose killed *him?*"

Elizabeth pushed her plate away. She was finished. "I don't know."

"But if you had to take a wild guess . . ."

"If Sean thought someone was trying to get to me or the girls, he'd kill them." That was the possibility she'd dreaded most. That her brother had been forced to take another's life to protect her.

Michael stood and helped her into her jacket. The afternoon was gone and dusk had fallen with a chilling quickness. He dropped money on the table and bundled her out the door to his car.

"I have to go home," she started to protest.

"I'll drive you." Michael had a sudden feeling that they were sitting ducks for someone or something who meant harm to Elizabeth. "Maybe we should think about what Sean might have discovered before the storm. Maybe he'd taken Sandra out on the boat to tell her something. Something he'd seen or learned. What could it be, Elizabeth? What would make someone want to kill him and his wife, and possibly his sister?"

Michael's questions framed the troubling ideas that had eaten at Elizabeth all afternoon. "Sean never talked much about his work. He was opposed to developing the beach any further, and that was a controversial stand for a realtor to take on the 'finest stretch of prime beach property in the nation'." Elizabeth paused. "That didn't make him any friends, but that was an old battle. It has been raging for years, and Sean never mentioned any new developments."

"It's a good place to start. There's enough money in real estate development to warrant murder. Anything else?"

"Just his boat. He loved that boat almost as if she were a member of his family." A note of sadness had invaded Elizabeth's voice. She tried to shake it off, but she couldn't. "Sean was one of those people who are blessed. Sandra shared his interests, and sailing brought them both a lot of satisfaction. Even the girls loved to go out on the *Sea Escape*. All of us."

Michael looked up and down the darkened street. "Let's get out of here. I'll make sure we get your car back, and I'd feel safer if you were with me."

"I appreciate your interest, but I really want to drive my own vehicle home." Elizabeth didn't want to leave her Trooper. She'd been independent for so long that the idea of being without her own car was a tiny bit disturbing.

"Just because you shook the feds doesn't mean someone else didn't follow you."

"And your car, beautiful as it is, won't attract attention?" Elizabeth laughed softly. "Maybe they'll think I'm dating a private investigator from Hawaii."

"I believe Magnum drives a Ferrari," Michael said, laughing himself. He opened her door and helped her in.

"Well, all of the locals claim that Tom Selleck vacations at Ono Island at different times of the year. Maybe someone will think I'm on a date with him in the wrong car." Elizabeth felt herself relaxing as Michael drove. Night was falling and it was far more preferable to sit beside him, watching his profile in the darkening sky. The countryside blurred past her window as she focused on Michael. He was a handsome man. No movie star or television private eye could be any better looking.

Elizabeth's cottage was on the west end of the island, a small house left over from the days when Gulf Shores was a summer place where locals came to spend the long, lazy days. Since she'd purchased it, she'd added several modifications—insulation and central air, primarily. The second best thing about the small cottage—after taking into consideration how close it was to the beach and how the sound of the gulf could be heard—was the fact that it was isolated. Elizabeth had purchased the property from an elderly couple who'd owned ten acres. They sold it all cheap because she promised she wouldn't develop the property. The area around her was still mostly privately owned, and those property owners valued their privacy.

As they drove through the starry night, Elizabeth felt a sudden tingling of anxiety. The front porch light she'd left on was dark. She'd replaced the bulb shortly before the storm, too.

"There's a possibility someone's been at my house," she said, her voice far calmer than she felt.

Michael cast a glance at her as he brought the car to a smooth halt at the beginning of her long driveway. "No lights?"

She nodded. "Maybe there's a power problem, but I don't think so."

"Where is your federal tail when we need it?" Michael asked. He eased the car forward, letting the headlights illuminate the long sweep of steps that led to the house set high on stilts. Not exactly an incredible work of architecture, the house reflected the basic island survival tactics. When storms blew the water inland, the stilts protected the house and furnishings from damage. Elizabeth, a child of the island, loved the cottage because it was such a visible reminder of the past.

"Let me check it out," Michael said. His voice allowed for no disagreement.

"Okay." Elizabeth folded her hands in her lap. "Be careful."

When she saw Michael reach the base of the steps, she eased open her door and slipped into the darkness. There were stairs at the rear, and if anyone lurked in the house, Michael might need some assistance.

The stitches in her foot made her aware of the injury, but as Michael had predicted, the wound was healing rapidly. At the base of the steps she picked up an old baseball bat of Sean's. She'd been teaching the girls how to bat, without much success. The wooden bat had been too heavy for Catherine, and Molly could barely swing it. Now, the weight felt comforting in her hand.

The back steps were narrower and steeper than the front, and halfway up she heard Michael push open the front door. The lock was obviously gone. In a moment, golden light cast shadows around the base of the house. Michael was inside, and the lights were on.

She heard the footsteps through the house as she fumbled with the back-door key. As it turned out, she didn't need it. The doorframe was splintered and smashed. She opened the door as Michael hit the switch in the kitchen. They stared at each other for a split second before Elizabeth's gaze took in the destruction. Every plate, glass, cup and jar was smashed to bits on the floor. Sacks of flour and grits and sugar were slashed open, the contents dumped onto the shards of glass.

"They were very thorough," Michael said.

"The entire house?" Elizabeth felt a lump swelling in her throat.

"Pretty much."

She stepped over the mess on the floor, her feet crunching in broken glass and the grit of sugar. Her mind blanked as she moved into the small living room/den and saw the broken lamps and photographs. The crystal that she'd collected in the thrift shops in New York with such excitement at each find had been smashed against the floor.

The furniture had been slashed and gutted. And when she went into the bedroom she found her clothes had been pulled from the drawers and closets. She picked up a favorite silk blouse and saw that an arm had been pulled away and the back was split. Without a word, she dropped it on the floor.

Michael pulled her against him. "I'm sorry," he whispered.

She felt the tears so close to the surface, but she struggled to hold them back. "It's not the loss of things," she said. "It's just that I feel so...violated. Someone came into my home and touched my private life. They trashed my home."

His arms tightened slightly, and he kissed her head. "I know, Elizabeth. It's horrible. Thanks goodness, though, you weren't here."

Held tightly against his chest, she felt the pressure of her tears begin to subside. The loss of certain items, special mementos, would make her heart ache for a long time. But it was the sense of someone mean and cruel reaching into her life and touching her in such an intimate manner that was the worst.

"I don't know what to do," she said softly.

"Come with me. We'll come back tomorrow, in the daylight, and try to sort through this. But we have to call the police." He saw the telephone beside the mangled bed and reached toward it. He noticed the answering machine on the floor, the red light that signaled a message blinking again and again.

"There's a call," he said.

Elizabeth picked up the machine and hit the message playback button.

The intimate male voice was like a slap. "Elizabeth. Elizabeth?" A long sigh followed. "I'll be back, Elizabeth."

Before Michael could stop her, she erased the message.

But he knew she was protecting her brother. "Was it Sean?"

"I don't know," she answered, and this time she was beyond tears.

Chapter Ten

Elizabeth accepted the cup of hot tea and noticed that her hand had almost stopped shaking. She was bundled on the sofa in front of the fireplace in the house on Mirage Island. Somehow Michael had managed to get her out of her apartment and down to the police station without any awareness on her part.

Even the time at police headquarters had passed in a blur. She answered the questions that Chief Williams asked in a series of I-don't-knows. The image that kept coming to her mind was the smashed photograph of Sean, Sandra and the girls. The photo had been torn in two. The portion where Sean's face had been was missing.

Chief Williams and Michael had conferred, and then Michael had handed her into his car and driven to the island, with orders to keep an eye on her. Williams took the extra step and sent an officer to retrieve her car in Fairhope.

"Elizabeth?" Michael kissed her forehead and snuggled her into his arms. "I want you to think about going out of town for a while. Maybe to New York to visit old friends. Or even California. I'd love to show you the wine country."

"No." She was tired and confused, but she knew she wasn't going anywhere. "Not while Sean is missing." She realized her tone had been cold and emotionless. "I'm sorry, Michael. When all of this is over, I'd love to travel. Maybe for a long time."

"When all of this is over, I'm going to kidnap you and make sure you're safe."

"Michael, do you think we could try to find Dr. Van Hugh again?"

"I called his office while the tea was brewing. There's no answer there or at his home."

"Could we go there?" Elizabeth let the warm steam from the tea touch her face. Her skin felt tight and brittle, and the moist heat was wonderful.

"Tonight?" For some reason Michael felt a twinge of reluctance. As he'd driven across the bridge to the island, he'd felt a sense of safety. With minimal effort, the island could be made into a fortress. The gun he'd bought was on the end table, within arm's reach, under a newspaper. Whoever was after Elizabeth was mean and ruthless. Chief Williams had given him assurances that the federal agents were monitoring the island, and the single bridge made it much easier to protect than any other place. Strangers were obvious. If they left and went into Mobile, they'd lose their isolation.

"I have a feeling that something has happened." Elizabeth wanted to get up and pace, but she forced herself to sip the tea instead. "Sean must be getting desperate by now. And I think he must be with your friend. That's the only thing that makes any sense."

"Perhaps. I honestly can't think of any other reason Steve would be gone for so long. Even if he is helping Sean, he's being terribly irresponsible about his other patients. That poor Gladys Runnels is about to have a heart attack."

"Can we go to his office?"

Michael saw the pleading in Elizabeth's eyes, but he wasn't fooled for a minute. She would go without him if he refused. "Let's wait for Chief Williams to call," he said.

"And then we'll go?"

He nodded slowly. "Against my better judgment, we'll go."

The sharp ring of the telephone made them both start slightly. Michael picked it up while giving Elizabeth a long look.

"We've gone over the place thoroughly," Williams said. "There's nothing there. Not a print, not anything we can use. It was a professional job."

"Did you see anything obvious missing?" Michael asked.

"Nothing like the television or VCR. There was even some good jewelry left behind. I wouldn't think robbery was a motive. The place was tossed, and we don't have a clue as to why."

Michael thought about the message on the answering machine and rubbed his neck. The muscles there had begun to contract and pull. Elizabeth had erased the one solid piece of evidence.

"Will you let us know if you find something?"

"As soon as we have anything. I spoke with Agent McMillan again. His guys are doing the primary investigation, and he assured me that he'd have someone tailing Elizabeth every step of the way. They're guarding the island now, offshore."

"To make this night a little easier for them, we're going into Mobile to visit a friend of mine."

Michael gave the address and watched the thunderclouds build on Elizabeth's brow. He'd barely replaced the receiver before she rounded on him.

"If Sean's there, you might as well have handed him over on a silver platter," she fumed.

"Custody might be the safest place for him," Michael answered calmly.

Elizabeth wanted to argue, but she couldn't. As much as she hated the idea of Sean behind bars, she'd rather see him there than dead. At least if he was captured—and alive— she'd have a chance of proving his innocence.

"Tomorrow, it might be a good idea to start talking to his friends. If Sean's around this area, he must be getting help

from someone.'' Michael paced the room. "I wonder what
the burglar was looking for in your cottage?"

"I know," Elizabeth said quietly. She reached into the
waistband of her slacks and withdrew a crumpled piece of
cardboard.

Michael took it from her hand. It was a torn photograph. He recognized Molly and Catherine and the green-
eyed blonde who must have been Sandra. "Sean's picture?"

"They're still looking for him," Elizabeth said. "And
maybe they aren't certain how badly he's hurt or what he
looks like."

Michael let the air escape softly from his lungs. "Let's
hope he can stay a few jumps ahead of them until we can
find him. I must tell you, Elizabeth, he's an amazing man.
His injuries would have killed a weaker man."

"We have to find him." Elizabeth got up and slipped into
her coat as she spoke. "I'm ready whenever you are."

THE YEW TREES around Steve Van Hugh's office whipped
in the November wind. Storm clouds had blown up suddenly, covering the starry sky with a gray mist that floated
wickedly across the moon. Even riding beside Michael,
Elizabeth felt the nip of winter and a chill of foreboding. It
was on nights like this that she and Sean had often played
games along the beach. They'd crouched behind the sand
dunes and listened to the sea oats whisper in the wind. Sean
had told her of witches and sea monsters. She could almost
hear his voice as she sat in the car and watched the lightless
front of Dr. Van Hugh's office.

Michael eased the Jaguar into the back parking lot, which
was also empty.

"Looks hopeless," he said.

"Let's try." Elizabeth wasn't ready to give up yet.

Michael got out of the car, and she followed. Together
they went to the back door. To Michael's surprise, the knob
twisted under his hand.

He pushed open the door and stared into the black hall-way.

"Steve?" he called. "It's me, Michael Raybin."

The hallway seemed to swallow his voice.

"Maybe we should…" Elizabeth didn't want to leave and she didn't want to go inside the office. There was something about the place that was sinister. She could almost smell trouble.

Michael took the initiative and stepped inside. His palm found the light switch and he flipped it up, illuminating the rows of fluorescent lights down the corridor. The hallway was empty.

"Would Mrs. Runnels have accidentally left the office unlocked?" Elizabeth was surprised by the hollow sound of her voice.

"It's doubtful." Michael hesitated. He was tempted to order Elizabeth to wait in the car, but there were two problems with that. She never did what she was told, and the car might not be any safer than the office. As he tried to think through the safest option for her, a soft whirring noise drew his attention.

His gaze met hers and they both listened. "What is it?" she finally asked.

"I don't know." Not specifically, but he recognized the sound. "Stay here."

His voice, so flat and controlled, told her more than anything else that Michael anticipated trouble. She nodded, easing back against the wall where she could lift the draperies and watch the back parking lot. The agents who'd been tailing them had ducked out of sight. There was no sign of anyone. Not a living soul.

Michael drew his gun. Clutching it at his side, he started down the hallway. The whirring increased slightly. More of a buzz than a whir. The sound of a dentist's drill. Reflexively he clenched his teeth at the thought.

He wanted to call his friend's name, but he knew better. If Steve was in a position to answer, he would have heard from him before now. Hugging the right wall, Michael moved swiftly down the corridor.

The door to Steve's office stood ajar. Very carefully, Michael pushed it open. In the darkened room, the silence seemed to echo. Hitting the light switch, Michael took in the emptiness. He couldn't tell if the desk had been rearranged, but the room was orderly. A sigh of relief escaped. Maybe the office was empty. It wasn't likely, but it was possible that Gladys Runnels had left a door unlocked and maybe a coffeepot or some other kitchen tool running.

He stepped back into the hall and continued on, listening for the whir and letting the noise guide him. The office contained an outpatient surgery, and Michael pushed through the double doors. When he hit the switch, he was momentarily blinded by the flood of lights. In the seconds it took his eyes to adjust, he saw the blood.

It had begun to congeal on the floor, a large puddle once vivid red now edging into a darker stain. The body on the table was covered with a sheet.

Michael knew it was Steve. Still, he forced himself to walk forward and calmly lift the edge of the sheet. His old friend and classmate stared blankly at the ceiling. The scalpel was still lodged in his neck. A surgical light, going bad, hummed in an irregular rhythm.

Michael dropped the sheet and fought the wave of fury that swept over him. Why? Why had this happened to an innocent man? What possible reason could Sean Campbell have for taking the life of Steve Van Hugh?

Fury was quickly followed by guilt. He'd given Sean Steve's name and recommended him as a surgeon. He, Michael Raybin, had visited this fate upon his friend and classmate. He alone was responsible for his friend's death. If he'd done what he should have done—taken the injured stranger to the authorities—none of this would have happened. Elizabeth would not be in danger. A strange man named Carlos Santiago might be alive. And Dr. Steve Van

Hugh would surely be at home going over his notes for the next day's surgery.

"Steve." The whispered name was a request for forgiveness.

"Michael?" Elizabeth's voice came from the doorway.

He turned around, trying to hide the guilt and pain that engulfed him. "It's Steve," he said, seeing the horror and worry on her face. "He's dead."

"My God." She slumped. "How?"

"Murdered." He didn't want to go into the details.

"By whom? Why?"

He could see that she hadn't connected this with her brother. Even with proof, Elizabeth was going to find it very difficult to believe that Sean had changed. Intellectually, she understood how an injury could affect someone. Emotionally, it was going to be very hard for her to reconcile the loving brother she remembered with the man who could cold-bloodedly drive a scalpel into a man's carotid artery.

"You think Sean did this?" She took a step backward out of the room. "Michael, Sean couldn't do something like this. He couldn't." She looked past Michael and saw the blood on the floor. "My God," she repeated. "Not Sean. He couldn't."

Michael didn't say a word. There was nothing he could say or do that would help Elizabeth come to terms with this horrible reality.

"Even if Sean was injured, he couldn't do this. Even if he didn't know who he was or where he belonged, he's not the type of man who could..." She faded. No matter how many protests she made, no one would believe her.

"We should call the police," Michael said softly.

"No!" She snapped her attention back to him. "They'll add this to the list of Sean's sins. Don't you see? He'll become like some mad dog, and they'll shoot him down without even giving him a chance. Sean didn't do this, Michael. He didn't."

"I'm not saying he did, but this all has to end. We have to find Sean and restrain him. If he's innocent, we'll prove it, but—"

"But what?"

"We can't allow him to run free any longer, Elizabeth. If this is his work, there's no telling who he may injure or kill next. He's a desperate man, and I have the feeling that he's getting more and more desperate with each passing day."

Elizabeth felt the sorrow and anger swell to the point that she could no longer contain them. Tears slipped down her cheeks as she drew in a long breath. "You're right," she said. "Call them."

Michael put his arm around her and turned her away from the surgery room. Together they walked down the hall to the main office. Elizabeth held herself straight, but Michael's arm gave her support and comfort.

"I know my brother didn't do this, but they won't believe that. They think he's hiding something or involved in some illegal activity until he's become a man who would kill to protect and save himself."

Michael hesitated with his hand over the phone. Instead of picking it up, he went to her. Enfolding her in his arms, he held her against his chest. "I believe you," he whispered into her hair. "I believe you, and we won't stop looking for him. I swear it. But if the police look, too, we'll find him faster. We can't allow more time to pass, more innocent people to..."

"Die," she supplied for him. "I know. What am I going to tell Molly and Catherine?"

"There's nothing to tell them, yet." Michael held her close. He shut his eyes and simply pressed her against him. There was no way he could absorb her pain or help her, except to let her know that he cared and that he wouldn't abandon her.

When he released her, he picked up the telephone and began to dial.

Dreading each word, Elizabeth walked to the picture window at the front of the office. Oak trees canopied the street, making an interesting play of shadows with the streetlights. In the warmth of the office it was hard to remember that it was November outside. The street was empty and she stared at a lone car that was headed her way. The car moved slowly, cruising along, and she remembered the long-ago days when she and her girlfriends would drive along the beach at Gulf Shores at a slow crawl, laughing and listening to the radio. Gas was expensive and money hard to come by, so they often drove to a place along the beach, turned off the motor, turned on the radio and talked or danced in the sand. Sean had been so much a part of her life. All of her girlfriends had had crushes on him at one time or another. And he'd played the perfect big brother, standing in for Sally Olfield as her date to the senior prom when her steady had let her down. He'd taught Betty Crenshaw how to dance. And he punched out Corey Bradford when he'd started an unkind rumor about Elizabeth, his kid sister.

"Hello, this is Dr. Michael Raybin. I'd like to report—"

The headlights of the car pinned Elizabeth in the window. "Michael!" Elizabeth came out of her reverie to see the car aimed directly for the plate glass. "Michael!" Instinctively, she flung her body toward the desk just as the rapid fire of an automatic weapon cut through the glass and churned along the paneling of the walls only inches above Michael's head.

He dropped the telephone and leapt to cover Elizabeth's prone body.

The burst of fire continued as bullets tore into the desk, walls and floor. Sprawled beneath Michael, Elizabeth was too frightened to move.

"Where are those feds?" Michael demanded, pulling Elizabeth over and under him as he rolled them toward the desk. With a shove, he pushed her under the heavy counter and followed, crowding her against the far wall.

The wail of sirens cut through the night, and outside the office the car peeled rubber and raced out of the parking lot.

"Get up." Michael rose immediately and pulled Elizabeth after him.

"What?" Still dazed from the gunfire, Elizabeth didn't want to move. She wanted to hide in the safe corner of the counter for the rest of her life.

"Get up," Michael said, this time more gently. "We've got to get out of here."

"Why?" She didn't understand what he was talking about. "Dr. Van Hugh . . . the office." She looked around. They couldn't run away now. The police were coming. The sirens were getting closer and closer. They had to tell the police about Dr. Van Hugh.

"Elizabeth, how did those people know we were here?" Michael's voice was intense. "We were supposed to have a federal tail. Where are those guys? Why didn't they do something when the firing started? As far as I can see, they simply sat back in their car and allowed whoever was trying to kill us fire away."

"You think we were set up?"

"I think it's a distinct possibility." Michael took her arm and started dragging her toward the back door.

"What about your friend?"

"There's nothing I can do for him now," Michael said. "Nothing. Now I have to think about you."

"But—" Elizabeth shut off her questions and forced her legs to move forward. She didn't fully believe, or even understand, why Michael was so determined to get away, but she had enough faith in him not to dillydally with questions. Whatever she needed to know she could find out in the car.

"Be quick," he urged her as he opened the back door of the office.

Side by side, they scurried across the black asphalt and into the waiting car. Without turning on the headlights, Michael drove away. Behind them they heard the approach of the sirens, and the first of the red and blue lights cut through the night. From the residences that interspersed the doctors' and lawyers' offices, homeowners emerged onto the sidewalk to see what the fuss was about. Michael continued to drive.

"You think Sean killed Van Hugh, don't you?" Elizabeth asked. She was calmer now. And rational enough to realize that even she had begun to have doubts about her brother's mental state.

"Maybe." Michael's hands gripped the wheel. His guilt still lay heavily on him. "It could be that whoever is after you saw Sean go there. They might have killed Steve and been waiting for Sean to come back."

"They might have mistaken us for him?"

"Possibly, or it could be that they want to kill you, too."

"Because I won't give up looking for Sean?"

"That or because they think your brother told you something."

Elizabeth felt the car hug the road as Michael took a sharp curve and pulled onto the interstate to head back across the parkway to the eastern shore. Mobile Bay glistened with the lights from the raised roadway and the stars. A quarter moon hung over the water.

"So we're back to wondering if Sean was involved in something illegal." She tried to keep her tone neutral, but found it hard to do.

"Elizabeth, he could have gotten dragged into something innocently enough. When he found out what it was, he might have threatened to go to the authorities. Sean may be innocent of everything and still be involved."

"Or he might be guilty."

"That's right." Michael was too tired to try to phrase it more diplomatically. His friend was dead. That was an inescapable fact and one he'd have to live with for the rest of his life. Because Michael had spoken Steve Van Hugh's name, his friend was now dead.

"You feel guilty about what happened to Steve, don't you?" Elizabeth could read the emotions in the firm set of his mouth. "It won't do any good to tell you that you aren't to blame, but you aren't." She sighed. "We both feel responsible for things we have no control over." She reached across the seat and touched his arm. "We're very much alike, Michael."

"You're in a lot of danger, Elizabeth." Michael's voice was carefully controlled. "We made a decision when we left Steve's office."

"A decision not to trust the authorities," Elizabeth said. She'd thought about it, and understood the implications. But then everyone had been in such a hurry to blame Sean for everything. That in itself looked suspicious. Why wouldn't the federal agents at least take the time to consider the possibility that Sean was an innocent victim?

"Now we're guilty of a crime."

"We didn't notify the authorities when we discovered Steve's body, but I'm not certain that makes us guilty of anything."

"If they find our fingerprints there, they might feel differently."

Elizabeth looked out the car window and realized they were headed neither to her house nor to Mirage Island. "I hadn't thought of that."

"We should stop by your brother's real estate office."

"The feds went through everything. If there had been any impropriety, they would have found it."

"Maybe not anything improper. Maybe a deal, something perfectly legitimate and legal that put him on somebody's list to eliminate."

"Beach development," Elizabeth said. "That's a good idea."

"Someone has killed your sister-in-law and my friend. This isn't some haphazard event, some accident. Two innocent people have paid with their lives. Now I intend to find out who's behind this.''

Elizabeth swallowed. She didn't have to say aloud that such curiosity could prove deadly. Michael already knew that, and so did she.

Chapter Eleven

Scooping up the last of the files, Elizabeth stuffed them back into the cabinet. Sean's once neat office was a wreck, and it wasn't all her fault. The federal agents hadn't taken a lot of care in putting the files back in order, and she wasn't going to try to straighten them. Not now.

"Go Beach seems to be the only development company mentioned." Michael rubbed his left cheek. He was tired. The shock of seeing his friend so brutally murdered had worn on him in many ways. The brutal image of Steve Van Hugh, lifeless on his own operating table, assaulted him when he least expected it. Only sheer hardheadedness kept him going now.

"I don't think Sean took the members of Go Beach seriously," Elizabeth said, slapping another file into the cabinet. "He spoke of them a time or two, but my reading was that they were more of a pain than a real danger. He did get pretty mad when they tried to trap all the sand mice and move them."

"What?" Michael looked up. His bloodshot eyes registered confusion.

"There's a small mouse that lives only in the sand dunes along this stretch of beach. It's held up a lot of development, endangered species and all. Some of the locals wanted to sneak around and exterminate the little mice." She shrugged. "You know that mentality. They thought if they could kill all of them, then the beach would be open for development."

"Very farsighted attitude."

"They were looking long and deep into their own pocketbooks." Elizabeth closed the file drawer and locked it. "Sean threatened to call the EPA and the wildlife people. He did, in fact, spend several nights on the beach guarding the mice."

"That's a way to earn enemies."

"Sean didn't care. He thought it was important." Elizabeth sat down on a stool beside Michael. "See what I mean about my brother? He cared about things, even mice. He couldn't have killed your friend or Sandra. Especially not Sandra."

"We've been over this ground before," Michael said wearily.

"Yes, we have," Elizabeth answered stubbornly. "Now what?"

"Sleep."

Elizabeth stood, offering her hand to give Michael a boost. "I want to thank you for helping me. I know you think you've stepped into a hornet's nest. And you have." Their gazes met and she reached out to touch his cheek. "You've done everything you could to help me, and all it's done is complicate your life. Maybe it would be best for you to go back to California."

"And what will you do?" he asked.

"What I have to. Continue to look for Sean. Try to put the pieces of this together. Take care of my two nieces and Guy and the newspaper."

"And what about us?"

Elizabeth sought an answer in his eyes. "I don't know what to say," she confessed. "My feelings for you don't require that you risk your life . . . further."

"And mine for you don't allow me to leave you unprotected."

"You came here to sort through some problems of your own. Ever since you met me you've been caught up in mine."

Michael's smile was slow and tired. "Maybe that's been the best thing for me. It sort of puts my life in perspective. I've got some hard decisions to make, but I'm not the only one in the world."

"What will you do?"

"I'm going to call Tommy tomorrow, or as soon as I've had a chance to get a little rest. We need to talk, and I want to give him another chance to make his own decisions."

"Ultimately, he's going to have to decide many things for himself. It isn't fair to him, or to you, when he puts the onus on you." Elizabeth finally looked away. Involving Michael in her problems wasn't exactly fair, either.

"Let's head back to the island, catch some sleep and decide what to do. We're both too tired to make any serious decisions now."

Nodding, Elizabeth walked to the door. "The ATF agents will be looking for me."

"Tomorrow," Michael said, walking up behind her and pushing her out the door. "Tomorrow."

THE LIGHTS in the old Victorian house seemed to beckon, and Elizabeth roused herself from the comfort of the car seat to get out. The drive over had been brief, but she'd almost fallen asleep. She stumbled slightly and caught herself just as Michael put his hand on her arm.

"We have company," he whispered, nodding toward a dark sedan.

"Great." Elizabeth wanted to scream. Now wasn't the time for the feds to grill her. They could just go back to the mainland and wait.

Michael inspected the car. "It's a rental. They must be waiting inside."

"Lot of nerve they've got," Elizabeth mumbled.

Michael clasped her arm and directed her toward the front. Before he could insert his key in the lock, the door swung open. A tall, slender man with intense eyes looked at him.

"Tommy." Michael was taken completely aback. He looked at Elizabeth and then back at the man in the doorway.

"I should have warned you I was coming," the man said. His voice was apprehensive. "I was afraid if I didn't just get on the plane and do it, I'd back out. I've been afraid a lot lately."

"Elizabeth, this is my partner, Tommy Chester. Tommy, Elizabeth Campbell."

Tommy stepped back from the door and allowed them to enter. "I should have called. I got a spare key to the house and thought I'd just surprise you." His smile was hesitant and touched with sorrow. "I've been thoughtless."

"It's fine," Michael said. He led the way to the kitchen where he made them all a drink. "Elizabeth and I have had a really tough day. It's a long story and one I'll look forward to telling you after some sleep." He went to his partner and put his hand on his shoulder. "I'm glad you're here, Tommy. Very glad."

"We need to talk," Tommy agreed. "I need to talk." He smiled the same sad smile. "Well, until tomorrow." He nodded at Elizabeth and withdrew.

"Looks like you're going to get your problems resolved," Elizabeth said.

"Tommy is a remarkable man."

"And one who's come to terms with his life," Elizabeth agreed. Michael took her hand and led her to the bedroom. "We'll talk about all of this tomorrow. For now..." He grinned at her.

"I thought you wanted to sleep." Elizabeth feigned shock.

"I do. In a while. I think you've managed to resuscitate me. At least for a limited time." They closed the bedroom door behind them.

WHY DID HE RESIST? Why? He didn't have to die. He didn't have to make me angry.

The stranger paced the small apartment on a narrow, dirty street in Mobile.

When headlights cut through the window, he ducked, then crawled forward and peered into the night. The car continued past him without slowing, and he felt a terrible rage. He wanted to pull out the gun he carried and blast away at the vehicle. How dare they frighten him! "Creeps," he muttered, feeling in his waistband for the gun. The cold steel seemed to soothe him. And after all, the car was gone.

He got back on his feet and paced the small room again. He'd stolen a car and made it across the bay. Steve Van Hugh had been his hope. His ticket to freedom. And now the doctor was dead. All because he'd stubbornly refused to help. He was required by oath to help injured people, so it was his own fault that he was dead.

Still, it had greatly messed up the plan.

The man gently unwrapped the dirty bandages on his left hand and looked at the cracked and bleeding skin. He needed ointment and care. As bad as his hands looked, his face was worse. With his burned fingers he felt the bandages that still wrapped his head. After the initial examination, Dr. Van Hugh had rewrapped him, insisting all the while that he could not agree to perform such surgery in secret. And why not? Because he didn't want to help.

"He deserved to die," the man said aloud.

The injured man paced the room rapidly, stopping at the window and looking out into the night. How much longer would it be before they traced him to this abandoned place? They'd gotten very close to him in Gulf Shores. Very close. They'd sent someone to find Elizabeth.

"Elizabeth." He said the name thoughtfully. "They want her."

He turned away from the window and went back to the small collection of pictures on a table. He picked them up with his unbandaged hand and examined them by the streetlight. That was his face. His future. He might never be handsome again. Not like before, but he could begin to look like normal. If he could find a doctor who would help him.

Two thoughts connected, and he jumped into the air and spun around. "Yes!" he cried. "Yes!"

With Van Hugh dead, the office and surgery would be unused. The doctor on Mirage Island could do the repair work—he now had a facility and no excuses. He'd helped once before. He'd do it again.

"Yes!" He put the pictures on the table and hurried to find the car keys he'd hidden. His vision was not good, but he could see well enough to drive. And after surgery, he might have some sight restored to his right eye. The island doctor had told him that much.

It was risky going back to Gulf Shores. They'd be looking for him. Carrying guns. But he had to do it. He had to. And Michael Raybin had to help him. Whether the doctor knew it or not, he didn't have a choice in the matter.

GUY FALLON was sitting in his cubbyhole of an office when Elizabeth hurried in. He stuck out his head, waved a pencil at her. "All hell's broken loose. There're four rolls of film in the darkroom. Can you process them?"

"Sure." Elizabeth picked up a copy of the morning newspaper from Mobile. Doctor Savagely Murdered In Own Office read the headlines. Even though she'd been expecting to see those words, they still startled her. She scanned the picture of the shattered front window and the lead paragraph of the story, which pointed out the bullet-sprayed front of the clinic and Van Hugh's murder. Authorities were undecided if the two incidents were related or not. The Mobile police chief said he didn't believe in coincidence.

"Know anything about that?" Guy asked. He was still watching her.

"Van Hugh was a friend of Michael Raybin. Michael thinks Sean has been brain damaged and may have committed the murder."

Guy's eyebrows shot up. "Is that so?"

"It isn't true." Elizabeth knew she sounded defensive when she saw Guy's expression. "You know Sean could never kill anyone."

Guy changed the subject. "Agent McMillan was in here bright and early this morning. He's pretty ticked off at you. He said you've been playing cat and mouse with his men and he doesn't have the manpower or the desire to waste that kind of time. He implied that you might know something about that doctor's murder."

Elizabeth felt her heartbeat increase. Michael had warned her that the authorities would put two and two together. "I'd better get that film done," she said, walking swiftly into the darkroom and closing the door.

When she came out thirty minutes later, she found McMillan sitting on the edge of her desk. His face was a total blank.

"We went by your house. We should have been called before the local authorities."

"Sorry. I was never keen on protocol." Elizabeth took a seat in her chair.

"Has your brother made any effort to contact you?" McMillan's small eyes watched every move she made.

"None."

"What was your role at Steve Van Hugh's? Witnesses saw a red Jaguar at Van Hugh's office shortly before it was blasted by automatic gunfire. I believe your friend Michael Raybin is driving a red Jaguar."

"He drives one," Elizabeth agreed. "He and Dr. Van Hugh were classmates." That information would be easy enough to dig up, so she wasn't giving anything away.

"We have some forensics experts at that office now." McMillan leaned forward. "I hope we don't find evidence that you were there. Your brother is wanted for murder. If we discover that you're trying to aid or abet him in any way, you can be charged as an accessory to murder. That's a very serious crime."

"My brother didn't kill anyone. Nothing you say or do will change that. If you had one scrap of evidence that would change my mind, I'd be willing to work with you. But all you have is circumstantial bull. That and a scapegoat. Sean is the easy target. Have you ever considered the fact that he might not come home because he doesn't want to be pinned with crimes he didn't commit?"

McMillan sat back. "We're still looking. The gunfire at Van Hugh's clinic came from an Uzi. We'll speak with Dr. Raybin in a little while. Maybe he can help us."

Elizabeth said nothing as McMillan got up and left.

"Your house was trashed?" Guy looked worried. "There wasn't a report with Carl and the P.D. I checked the dockets this morning. And if Carl had known something, he would have mentioned it. Like everyone else, he's worried about you."

"I'm sure the ATF people are controlling the investigation. They'll do what they can to keep the local police out of it. After all, Carl knows the citizens of this area. He might actually try to defend me or Sean."

"We don't have any leads on your brother, but I did have a little luck with Carlos Santiago."

Elizabeth whirled around and met Guy's excited gaze. "Who is he? What was he doing on the beach?"

"Have a seat," Guy said. "It helps to be an old geezer with a lot of friends."

Elizabeth rolled her chair into Guy's tiny office. "What did you find out?"

"Santiago was wanted down in Miami for the murder of two brothers. He shot them in front of a local Latin club with a handful of witnesses. It took the police several months to get any of the witnesses to identify Santiago. It wasn't that they didn't see him clearly, it was that they wanted to stay alive. Santiago was known as a tough guy around his neighborhood, someone who would kill at the drop of a hat."

Even though the man was dead, Elizabeth felt a rush of dread. The man had known her name. "What was he doing here in Gulf Shores?"

"Things apparently got pretty hot for him in Miami. His family helped slip him out of Florida. There were several agencies after him, most notably, Central Intelligence."

"The CIA?" Elizabeth was confused. "Was he undercover?"

"No one knows for sure, and you know how it is with the spooks. You can't believe anything they say. They have layers of cover so deep they don't even know who's who. But I have some friends in Washington, and they're working on it for me. Just know that Santiago wasn't some illegal alien. He was a U.S. citizen, and his family is still very powerful in Panama."

"I assumed he was an illegal." Elizabeth couldn't help feeling afraid. "What's going on, Guy?"

"I wish I knew and not because it would make a blockbuster story. I want you to listen to me for a moment, Lizzy. Think about going away for a week or two."

Guy never called her Lizzy unless he wanted her complete attention. He was worried sick about her and doing his best not to show it. "I can't," she finally answered when he refused to look away.

"You can and you should. Take Aleshia and the girls and go."

"Mom and the girls?" Elizabeth felt the fear pump throughout her system with each beat of her heart. "Do you think they're in danger?"

"I think the people you're up against are completely ruthless. They'd kill your brother, your nieces and you and your mother without blinking an eye."

"I can't leave if there's a chance Sean might need me."

The pencil in Guy's hand snapped in two. One piece flew out of his office and clattered on the floor. "I knew you'd say that," he said, sighing. "Do you think you could talk Aleshia into taking the girls?"

"Maybe she'd go up to stay with Sandra's family. It would do Molly and Catherine good, and I'm certainly not around enough to make a difference these days." Already Elizabeth was making plans. She could get the tickets for that afternoon, pack her mother and the girls off, and then she'd be able to breathe again. "I'll talk with her right away."

"What about that film?" Guy asked as he saw she was about to leave.

"I'll be back to print it."

He nodded. "Tell Aleshia to go. Make her believe it's for the girls."

"I will." Elizabeth bent down and kissed Guy's cheek. "Thanks, Guy."

"I'll keep digging on this Santiago thing. He's involved in everything that's happened around here. And by the way, Larry Steele's business has been put up for sale."

"So quickly?"

"Yeah. It looks like a car dealer from Pensacola is going to snap it up."

"I suppose that's good." Elizabeth gave a wry smile. "I can only hope the new owner is full of the same high jinks. We haven't needed any extra stories, but eventually things will settle down and we're going to miss Larry Steele." She could only pray that her prediction was accurate. It seemed as if her life had always been turmoil and worry. Would it ever return to normal?

"Get back as soon as you can. The high school is having some kind of memorial service for the two teenagers who've been killed. They're going to hold classes on the beach or something like that. I need you to snap a few pictures."

"You've got it," Elizabeth agreed. She didn't have any real idea how to hunt for Sean, so the best thing was to go about her job and hope he would get in touch with her.

Except for getting her family safely on a plane, her only plans included dinner with Michael. When she'd left him this morning he was getting ready for a long talk with his partner and friend. He'd wanted her to stay, and it was hard for her to leave, but she had her own life, and Michael and Tommy needed some time to talk.

It looked as if Michael would be settling his problems, and then there would be no reason for him to remain at Gulf Shores. Elizabeth knew that reality was hard upon her. If he asked her to leave now, she couldn't. *If* he asked her... He'd spoken about "their future." But what they had was a short-term relationship and a heavy attraction. Realistically they were people who lived on two different coasts with two very different life-styles. Once he was gone, would she be anything but a pleasant memory to him?

As she slid behind the wheel of her own vehicle, she pushed thoughts of Michael aside. Romance was something that had no priority in her life now. Michael Raybin might be the man she'd dreamed of meeting, but he'd come at a bad time. She turned into her mother's drive and prepared to do battle. Aleshia Campbell would not want to leave Gulf Shores when her only son was still missing. It would take all of Elizabeth's skill and determination to get her to go.

"Elizabeth!" Her mother's face broke into a relieved smile as she watched her daughter climb out of the Trooper. "The girls have been asking about you."

"I'm sorry." She kissed her mother's cheek and hugged her tight. "I think you deserve a vacation."

"What's wrong?" Aleshia led her daughter into the kitchen and poured them both a cup of coffee.

Giving as little detail as possible, Elizabeth told her mother about Carlos Santiago and his connections in Miami and the CIA. "It's probably some bizarre coincidence, but Guy and I both think it would be best if you took the girls away. Just for a week or so."

"I wish your father were here." Aleshia couldn't help the way her hand trembled as she lowered her coffee cup to the table. "I feel like some evil force has invaded my family. Sandra is dead ..." Her voice broke.

"Sean may be alive, Mom, and that's why I'm staying here. Someone has to stay so he can get in touch with us."

"You take the girls. I'll stay." Aleshia was getting a determined look in her eyes.

"No, that won't work. Someone already knows I'm looking for Sean."

"Are you in danger?" Aleshia stood. "Tell me the truth, Elizabeth. Are you in danger?"

"No, not really." Elizabeth forced a smile as she met her mother's frightened gaze. "Everything will be fine here. It's just that if you're away, I won't have to worry about you. And the girls."

Aleshia paced the kitchen. "I think I'll go get them from school right away."

Elizabeth could see that she'd frightened her mother badly, but there was nothing she could do to change that. There were dangers, and it would be wrong to lie about them. "I'll drive you to pick them up. While you're packing, I need to go back to the office. Guy has a pile of things for me to do. But I'll take you to the airport."

"Where should we go?" Aleshia looked lost as she turned to her daughter. "We're talking about leaving, and we haven't even thought of a place to go."

Elizabeth put her arm around her mother's shoulders. "How about up to Sandra's parents?"

"That's too far." Aleshia was firm. "We'll go to Aunt Ellen's in Montgomery."

Elizabeth started to speak and then stopped. Montgomery was only four hours away by car. It wasn't really far enough, but Aunt Ellen's was an isolated farm. It was probably the best she could do for the moment. If it looked dangerous there, then she'd have to convince her mother to go farther.

The feeling of abandonment was acute—and frightening. Even Michael would soon be leaving. It wasn't a matter of choice, but he'd been away from his practice for a month already.

As Elizabeth waited to drive her mother to the school to collect the girls, she had a terrible feeling that everything she'd ever loved was being forced away from her.

Chapter Twelve

The fire crackled merrily, casting flickering warmth over Elizabeth's right side. Across the table from her, Michael poured them both another glass of wine. A fast-moving cold front had dropped the temperature unexpectedly into the thirties, and the cold had driven many would-be diners away. Elizabeth and Michael had most of the restaurant to themselves. The fire was cozy and the wine light and dry. Still, Elizabeth had difficulty swallowing. A sense of loneliness had settled deep into her bones as she'd packed her mother and nieces in the car for the drive to Montgomery.

"You look sad," Michael commented, as if he could read her thoughts.

"I am." She smiled with an effort. "And you look relieved. Tell me what happened with Tommy today."

They hadn't had a chance to talk. Guy had been a slave driver at the newspaper, and by the time Elizabeth had finished the list of things he'd had for her to do, she'd barely had time to grab a shower and change clothes at her mother's house before their date.

"Tommy's going to move to El Salvador. He's going to tell the clinic there about his condition. He'll act as a consultant, helping to train the doctors there. They're very lucky to have someone with his skills and ability."

The loneliness lifted a bit, and Elizabeth gave a genuine smile of happiness. "He sounds like a great guy."

"He is." Michael's voice held emotion. "We've been friends for a long time. I'd give anything to change this for Tommy. For me. He'll leave a big hole in my practice."

Elizabeth lifted her wineglass and sipped again. There it was, the first acknowledgment of Michael's life in Hollywood. His practice. It would be demanding his time and attention—and very soon.

"What is it?" He reached across the table and took her hand.

"When will you be leaving to go home?"

He hesitated. "I haven't really thought about it."

She recognized the dodge. She was being unfair to put Michael on the spot. He had to go back. It wasn't a matter of choice. He had patients counting on him to return, people who needed his skill as a surgeon.

"I'm almost tempted to go down to Central America with Tommy. He accomplishes important things there. They work on children who'd never have a shot at a normal life. Those doctors make a difference." He sighed. "I have some decisions of my own to make."

"There are underprivileged people here, too. You could do both, Michael."

"That's a very reasonable approach." He lifted her hand to his mouth and kissed her fingers. "And what did you accomplish today?"

She'd vacillated on whether to tell Michael what Guy had learned about Carlos Santiago. Looking into his eyes, she made an instant decision. If she told him, he'd worry and it might influence his decision about going home. She didn't want that.

"My day was uneventful. Mother and the girls went to visit my aunt." She shrugged. "Guy had tons of things for me to do, none of them extremely exciting. Agent McMillan spent twenty minutes being rude to me. And that's about it."

"What are you planning now?"

How was it that Michael always knew she was up to something? She didn't want to involve him. At best, her plan was half-baked. At worst, it could be deadly. As she'd helped her mother pack clothes for her nieces, she'd determined to solve what had happened to Sean and to help her brother come home.

No matter what Agent McMillan or anyone else said, those events were somehow tied in with the activities off-shore from Mirage Island. They were linked to the deaths of two teenagers on the beach. They also involved the murder of Steve Van Hugh and the drive-by shooting of his office. Why? How? Those were the questions she had to answer.

"I don't know what else to do," she said, looking down at the grilled fish on her plate. "I guess that's why I'm quiet. I just don't know what to do next."

"You're a very poor liar." Michael waited, his gaze intent on her.

"I don't have any real plan," she said again, trying for a more convincing tone. "I haven't given up, but . . . I really don't know what to do."

"Will you come back to the island with me?"

"Not tonight." She forced herself to meet his questioning gaze. There was nothing she'd rather do than follow Michael into a world of sensual pleasure and delight. The intimacy they'd developed had become the only safe haven she had, and she also knew that with each hour she spent with him, her heart would suffer more and more when he left.

"Where will you stay? You can't go to your house. It's too isolated." Worry showed in the furrow between his eyes.

"I'll stay at my mother's."

"I don't know." He shook his head. "I don't think so, Elizabeth. At least let me stay with you."

"No." The word was softly spoken, but there was no room in it for quibbling.

"Why not?"

"I need some time alone. The things that have happened with Sean have unsettled my entire life. If that isn't enough, I also have to come to terms with the things I feel for you. When I'm with you, it's too easy simply to feel. I have to understand what those feelings mean."

Michael's eyes grew more intense. "Don't you know?"

The flutter of excitement left Elizabeth breathless. Yes, she knew. She'd fallen in love wit him. But that didn't change their circumstances. "There's so much to think about. So much for both of us to think about."

"Stay with me tonight," Michael said. "Tomorrow I need to go into Mobile and help Gladys Runnels with Steve's office. I can make some calls and see if there's a plastic surgeon around who can step in for the short term and take over his caseload. I may stay at the hospital tomorrow night and help with some of the patients who should be discharged." He took her other hand. Holding both of them, he kissed the fingers. "Tonight, though, let's be together. I need you, Elizabeth."

"Michael . . ." She meant to refuse, but there was no way she could make herself. Would it be so wrong to have one more night with Michael? It wouldn't change the fact that they would soon part. It might tear at her heart more than ever, but that was a small price to pay for the joy of making love with him, of holding him close and sleeping curled against his body until the sounds of the gulf and the gulls awakened them. Mirage Island was the perfect place to let the sun streak through the windows and stir them awake. It would be one last morning of coffee and juice together, of morning light and the brisk smell of the gulf.

"Okay." Her feelings were obvious in her smile. "I'd love to stay with you tonight."

"Let's go." Dropping several bills on the table, he stood and helped her into her coat. They didn't notice anything except their own, intense reaction to each other as they hurried across the parking lot and into Michael's car.

They were both silent on the ride to the island, and Elizabeth knew they were thinking about the inevitable separation. This night would be bittersweet.

As they approached the bridge, Michael slowed. "When Tommy woke up this morning he was whistling as he packed to go back to California. That crazy man flew out here for a talk, just one night, and now he's gone."

Surprised, Elizabeth realized she hadn't thought about his presence on the island. "He's so quiet." She leaned over and kissed Michael's cheek. "I would have liked a chance to get to know him better."

"Maybe you'll get that chance," Michael said enigmatically.

Halfway across the bridge, Michael slowed. "There must be at least a billion more stars here than in L.A."

"Maybe." Elizabeth leaned out the window. The night was cold and clear. It did look as if the sky had been spangled with more stars than usual. "There aren't any lights out here to interfere."

Michael stopped the car completely. He circled her waist with his arms and drew her back inside the car. "I could get used to this sky, to the smell of the water."

Elizabeth was still pondering his allusion when they pulled up to the house. There were questions she wanted to ask, but she didn't. Those could wait until the light of day. If she had misunderstood what Michael implied, she didn't want to ruin the night.

They parked the car in the garage. The house was dark, and together they stumbled, laughing, through the darkness. Michael opened the door and in a few moments had a fire blazing. Curled on the sofa, Elizabeth was torn between the flicker of the flames and the dramatic view of the ocean. It had crossed her mind that staying on the island would also give her access to the beach. She'd have to be careful and make sure Michael was asleep. But Mirage Island would be the perfect lookout point to watch for boats

and signals. Her plan had begun to take on a more solid
shape.

"That's a very intense look," Michael said, handing her
a snifter of brandy.

"It's a beautiful view," she answered. "It's a shame this
house is empty so much of the year."

"Yes, it is." He walked over to the fire. "It does seem like
a waste. I wonder if something couldn't be done about
that." He took a seat on the sofa beside Elizabeth, drawing
her legs over onto his lap. "I have some ideas." He lifted her
left foot to his lips and kissed her instep. "I see your cut has
healed." He kissed her again. "We can take the stitches
out—"

"Tomorrow," she blurted. "Nothing tonight but pleasure. Tomorrow we'll take care of things."

"As delighted as I was to see Tommy, I'm equally delighted to be alone with you." He released her foot and
slipped his hand around her waist. Slowly he moved his
fingers along her torso, pulling her inch by inch onto his lap.
When she was at last settled in his arms, he kissed her.

The desire for his kiss, the way the touch of his fingers
moving over her shoulder and collarbone heated her body,
was instant for Elizabeth. Her response would have been
frightening had it been anyone but him. When his tongue
caressed her lips and mouth, she responded in kind. For a
moment they played and teased before he suddenly deepened the kiss to reveal a raw hunger.

A log in the fireplace snapped and fell, sending a shower
of sparks up the chimney, but neither noticed. Michael's lips
moved down her throat, searching for the pulse point, where
he lingered for a brief moment and then moved on.

With his arm supporting her, Elizabeth let her head fall
back, exposing her throat to his kisses. Her breathing came
in short, shallow breaths as he moved down to her cleav-
age. He shifted slightly, moving his mouth over her nipple,
and at once Elizabeth responded to his warm breath through

the silk of her blouse. Very carefully, he slipped the buttons, and the red silk pooled on the floor.

Her bra followed, and he settled her back into the pillows as he unclasped her skirt and maneuvered it down her legs. His gaze never leaving hers, he stood and removed his shirt and slacks.

The firelight played over his skin, highlighting the muscles of his chest and thighs. A light sprinkling of hair covered his chest, narrowing to a thin line that bisected his torso and dropped lower. Elizabeth reached for him. She wanted to feel his flesh against hers, his hands on her body.

Michael sat down on the sofa beside her. He ran his fingers lightly across her stomach, sending a shiver through her. The black lace of her panties made her skin look even whiter. He slipped his finger beneath the small edge of lace, a daring exploration that made her gasp.

Catching his shoulders with one hand, she pulled him down to her.

"We could go to the bedroom," he offered.

"No, let's stay by the fire." Pressed against him, she felt her nipples harden at the touch of his hair-roughened chest. The teasing was gone. She moved her hands lower, delighting in the texture of the dark curls. As she brought her teeth against his lip, her hands slipped farther down. He groaned in response and deepened the kiss.

With a single motion he swept the lacy panties away and moved to cover her body with his. Elizabeth wrapped her arms and legs around him and gave herself to the rhythm of their lovemaking.

MICHAEL'S BREATHING was soft and regular. He was sound asleep. Taking care not to disturb him, Elizabeth slipped from the bed. Her clothes were still in the den beside the fireplace. She had only a skirt and blouse, and as an afterthought she searched in the darkness for the sweat suit Michael normally kept hanging on the closet door. It was too big for her, but much warmer than her skirt and blouse.

Grabbing the sweats, she tiptoed into the den. By the embers of the dying fire, she dressed. It was twenty minutes after midnight, about the same time she'd seen the light signals on the night she'd cut her foot. She had no intention of confronting anyone, but she had to know if the island was being used as some type of drop point. She had no proof, but she knew that whatever had happened to Sean involved what was going on on the island late at night.

If someone was transferring goods from ship to ship or ship to shore in the dead of night, the chances were good that the cargo was illegal. The only question was, what was it? Drugs? Guns? The idea that it could be exotic animals or even babies made her cringe. There was a thriving business for children from Third World countries who were slipped into the States for illegal adoptions. All of that was big-city crime. But Gulf Shores was learning about big-city crime. Funerals for two teenagers proved that.

Picking up the large flashlight she'd seen earlier on a bookcase, Elizabeth slipped into the night. A blast of cold wind almost drove her back into the house, but she shrugged deeper into Michael's jacket and forced her body away from the shelter of the house.

The bitterness of the night soon made her decide that no sane person would be on the water unless they had to. Of course, the profits from a drug run would compensate for a night of discomfort. She forced herself on with the thought that she'd be back, warm and safe, in bed with Michael in less than an hour. And if the profits were great for criminals, the chance of helping her brother come home was enough payoff for her. Lengthening her stride, she pushed into the wind.

Tears, driven from her eyes by the cold, leaked down her face and she brushed them away. At times the dunes gave her some protection, but when she hit a space where nothing blocked the bitter wind off the Gulf of Mexico, she thought she'd freeze. At the last line of dunes she dropped into the chilling sand and crawled to the top of the dune.

Yellow stars glittered overhead. The dark water crested into white foam where the waves broke, and the surf was a luminous white as it crashed upon the sand and was sucked back into the gulf. As beautiful as the night was, it was disappointingly empty. There was no sign of any ship, not close or in the distance.

"Damn." She whispered the word as she dug deeper into the sand. She'd wait fifteen minutes to see if a boat came into view. It was probably too cold, and the wind had kicked up a chop on the water. There were a million reasons why a responsible sailor wouldn't choose to be out on the water that night.

"Damn," she whispered again, wiping more tears from her eyes. Not all of them were caused by the wind.

With each passing moment she felt colder and more alone. Was it possible that Sean was dead? Everyone wanted to believe he was some kind of heinous murderer. Everyone in law enforcement, that was. She knew better. But was he dead? Elizabeth thought of her brother. She concentrated on a few incidents from their past. As she shifted from event to event, she tried to feel him, to make that emotional link that they'd shared all of their lives. It wasn't anything concrete, and she'd never tried to deliberately employ it. But like many close siblings, she knew intuitively when Sean was injured or ill, and he had a way of always thinking to call her when she was down. Before she'd told anyone of her impending divorce, Sean had called her, wanting to know what was wrong. He'd sense something even over a thousand miles away.

As her mind raced over incidents of gardening and baseball and swimming and picnics and the births of the girls, Elizabeth felt only the darkness and the night around her.

"Sean?" She called to him softly. "Sean?" Her voice broke, and she rested her forehead on her arm. Of course, if he was injured, he wouldn't respond to her. He would be different, thinking of different things. He might not even remember her.

"We'll find you," she promised, "and we'll help you to come back to us. Whatever you've done, we'll help you." She got up and turned back to the house. She was so preoccupied with her own thoughts that she didn't see the crouched figure hiding in the lee of a tall dune.

THE SQUAWK of a gull awakened her, and Elizabeth opened her eyes to the sunlight streaming in through the open windows. Outside, the sky was robin's egg blue, and the raucous gull that had awakened her swooped by the window, crying again. Elizabeth was curled on her side, and she rolled over only to find Michael's side of the bed empty. The panic was sharp and painful. She sat up, sliding her legs to the floor as she looked around the room for something to put on.

"What's the hurry?"

She almost wanted to cry with relief and happiness when she saw Michael standing in the doorway. He wore the sweats she'd carefully replaced and carried a tray with two cups of steaming coffee.

"I tried not to wake you," he said as he came to the bed and set the tray down. "You're absolutely beautiful when you sleep. And when you're awake. And when you're somewhere in between."

Elizabeth brushed her unruly hair from her face. More than likely she looked like a wild woman, but she didn't care. The coffee smelled irresistible, and she took a mug and allowed the warm steam to fill her nose. "Wonderful."

"You should drink it, not inhale it." Michael took his cup and walked around the bed so he could sit beside her and put his arm around her. "It's a beautiful day today, and I slept like a baby. Most of the night." His voice deepened, shifting into a serious tone.

Elizabeth sipped her coffee, waiting. She'd been so certain that Michael was asleep both when she'd left and when she'd returned. He would expect an explanation for her trip to the beach. And he wasn't going to like what she had to say.

"I dreamed last night that you'd disappeared. I searched everywhere for you and I couldn't find you anywhere. The panic was like a vise, squeezing around my chest and lungs. I felt like I was going to explode, and all along I knew I had to find you because your lungs were exploding, too." He stopped and looked out the window.

"It was only a dream." She kissed his cheek, nuzzling against the stubble on his face. He was such a caring man. "I'm here. I'm safe. Don't worry, Michael, I'm perfectly fine."

"I've never experienced anything so real." He turned to face her. "It was the worst nightmare I've ever had. The worst. And I can't seem to make myself believe it was only a dream."

Chapter Thirteen

Michael and Elizabeth lingered over breakfast. Their hands brushed and clung to each other. Despite a lingering chill in the wind, they took their last cups of coffee with them while they went for a walk on the beach.

"This place must be something during the early summer," Michael said. He held Elizabeth's hand in his, and their arms swung lightly between them.

"You'll have to see it for yourself," Elizabeth answered, looking out to the gulf.

"I intend to."

She turned to give him a kiss. A glint of sunlight reflecting from behind several sand dunes caught her eye, and she squinted.

"What is it?"

"I'm not sure. Something metallic, or glass maybe." She shaded her eyes with her hand, but it did no good. The occasional wink of something reflecting the sun was still there but unidentifiable.

"Let's check it out." Michael poured his coffee into the sand and left his cup on the beach. Elizabeth followed suit. They started inland, where the taller dunes blocked their view.

"I thought I'd walked this entire island," Michael said.

"I know I have." Elizabeth's foot had throbbed for two days after her adventure. "There shouldn't be any metal here."

The loose sand pulled at their shoes as they started to the top of a dune. At the crest, they both stopped. A blue sedan was bogged up to its hubs in the sand. It had obviously been driven as far as it would go into the dunes and then left. There was no one near it.

Elizabeth stared at it, but Michael started forward, his pace showing his anxiety.

"It's Tommy's rental car," he said. "What's it doing here?"

His fear was contagious, and Elizabeth followed him, running to keep up with his longer strides.

The car was unlocked, and Michael pulled the door open. The keys dangled in the ignition, but there was no sign of Tommy.

Unable to think of anything that might explain the car, Elizabeth said nothing. A certainty that something awful had happened gnawed at her. She could tell by Michael's face that he felt the same.

"The first thing to do is call the office in Hollywood and see if Tommy is there." Michael spoke calmly, covering his panic with reason.

"Would he go to the office?"

"If he's in town, he's at least checked in. The receptionist will know when he got back. Let's go back to the house." He closed the car door and turned north.

"Check the trunk," Elizabeth suggested. "We need to know if his clothes are in the car." She knew what that implied, but they had to know the truth.

Michael started to comply, then stopped. "Fingerprints. We shouldn't touch anything. Let's check at the house first."

"Maybe something happened and he took a taxi." Elizabeth knew she was clutching at straws, but Tommy's disappearance was bizarre. "I mean, where else could he be?"

Michael shook his head. "I don't want to think about the answer to that. Steve Van Hugh is dead because I knew him. Tommy—"

"That's foolish," Elizabeth snapped. "No one knew Tommy was here. We didn't even know he was going to be here. Van Hugh had an office, a place where he could be found. If he was killed by someone needing a plastic surgeon—and that's a big if—that has nothing to do with your partner. Tommy Chester was just another visitor to Mirage Island, another tourist as far as anybody around here knew. If they knew he was here at all."

"I hope you're right." But Michael's tone said he felt otherwise.

Elizabeth tried to keep her thoughts from circling the black wave of panic that kept threatening to rise up and paralyze her. In a strange twist of fate, everyone that came into contact with her was pulled into a vortex of calamity. And whether she wanted to admit it or not, her brother Sean was involved. He was the gossamer thread that bound them all together. Never seen, but always there.

Once in the house, Michael went to the bedroom Tommy had used. It took him several minutes of searching until he found his partner's suitcase stuffed back into the furthest reaches of the closet. All of his clothes had been crammed into the suitcase. He came out, holding the leather bag.

"Tommy never left Mirage Island," he said softly.

Elizabeth looked at the case and then at Michael. "I think we should call Carl Williams at the Gulf Shores Police Department. He'll help us hunt without making a big issue out of this." She hesitated. "I don't want to ask this, Michael, but I have to. Do you think Tommy might have...done something to himself?"

"Like committed suicide?"

She could hear the angry denial in his voice. "He was sick. Maybe he just didn't want to go through the whole horrible process."

"Some people might think that way, but Tommy wouldn't. He had a lot to give, and he took that very seriously. There were children he wanted to help, and he had hopes that they might discover a cure for AIDS before he died. No, he didn't kill himself. If he's dead, he was murdered."

Watching Michael's face, Elizabeth understood that Michael was as certain of Tommy as she was of her brother Sean. "The police will ask you that," she said softly.

"They have no reason to assume anything about Tommy. Besides, what did he do? Drive his car into the dunes and them walk out into the gulf to drown himself?"

Michael was correct. The authorities would have no way of knowing about Tommy's illness. Besides, a man bent on suicide wouldn't attempt to hide his rental car. "Tommy's illness is his business, and yours. The police won't learn anything from me," she said quickly. "Call your office, just to be sure, and then let's get busy. We can search the island while we're waiting for Williams to get out here. I doubt Tommy's anywhere around, but it's the logical place to start."

As Michael feared, the receptionist at their office had received no word of Tommy's arrival back in L.A. She was quick to tell Michael, though, that patient requests were growing to a staggering heap, and she urged Michael to begin to make his preparations to come home.

Listening to Michael's end of the conversation, Elizabeth got a quick understanding of how lucrative and busy his practice was. His extended vacation had cost him plenty. Each day he was away, he lost thousands of dollars. It was mind-boggling. Once Tommy was located, Michael would have no reason to stay in Alabama.

Michael dodged the receptionist's questions about Tommy, saying only that he was looking for his partner to return to California at any time. When he hung up, his face was ashen and drawn with worry.

"Vicki, the receptionist, said he called in night before last and said he had a reservation on an 11:00 a.m. flight out of Mobile yesterday morning. He should have arrived sometime yesterday afternoon, but he hasn't called in, and there's no answer at his house. Vicki's been trying to call him about a patient."

Elizabeth took the phone and spoke with the police chief. Carl Williams assured her he'd personally make the trip to the island and help them search for the missing doctor. He cautioned her not to become unduly worried, pointing out that most missing persons turned up again within three days.

The advice was standard, Elizabeth knew, but she couldn't help the fact that she was worried about Tommy Chester.

A call to the ticket counter at the airlines confirmed that Tommy had not boarded the plane. Michael's expression grew grimmer and grimmer.

"Maybe we should look around the island," Elizabeth suggested. It would take the police chief at least half an hour to finish with the staff meeting he'd interrupted to take her call.

They walked back to the abandoned car, but Michael made no effort to touch it. It was unspoken between them that he didn't want to disturb any fingerprints that might be on the vehicle. They might not admit it out loud, but they'd both come to believe that the sedan was part of a crime.

The sand was so deep that it was impossible to tell if there had been footprints. They circled the car in vain for several minutes before Michael picked an easterly direction, and Elizabeth followed him toward the most isolated part of the island.

The rolling dunes of sand blazed white in the morning sun, and a gust of wind sent a sand devil spiraling off in front of them. Michael walked into the sun, shading his eyes with his hand as he searched for any sign of his friend and partner.

Elizabeth saw him first and knew by the way he was lying face down in the sand that he was dead. A small sound escaped her, and Michael turned from her to find his friend lying at the base of a dune, his feet and legs partially covered by sand.

"Tommy!" He ran forward.

"Michael!" Elizabeth ran after him, grabbing his shoulder and holding him back. Up close she saw the piece of board protruding from Tommy's back. It was a splinter of a crate, possibly the same splinter she'd found on the beach. It had been used as a spear.

Michael's eyes held rage and pain as he turned to Elizabeth. "I know who did this. We both know! He came back here looking for me. He wanted me to help him." His voice was low, steady and dangerously calm. "Instead he found Tommy, and when he discovered that Tommy was a doctor, then he wanted Tommy to help him. When Tommy wouldn't do it, he killed him."

"You don't know that. It could have been someone who came to rob the house. Or someone from one of those boats that lurk around on the fringes of the island. Maybe Tommy saw something he shouldn't have seen."

"You're going to have to accept the truth, Elizabeth." Michael's voice was was hard, cold. "Steve Van Hugh didn't witness illegal activities before he died, and he wasn't robbed. He came home from Europe and was killed."

"Why are you and everyone else so quick to assume my brother did this?" She took a breath and tried to calm herself. Michael had suffered a terrible shock. It was natural for him to be angry, to lash out. His friend was dead, and it was a vile, irrational crime. She could understand this and forgive him for what he said. What he had to remember was that her brother was missing, and she intended to defend him—until he could be found to defend himself.

"If the man I saved is your brother, you're going to have to realize that he's different. There was an edge to him. He could have had my help then. I offered to make the arrangements with Steve to take care of him. Instead he knocked me out and stole my boat. If that man is your brother, he's already demonstrated that he's capable of going to great lengths to protect himself and gain his freedom."

"He hit you and he stole, that's true enough, but that isn't murder. Especially not the murder of two men who posed no threat to him. He had to have the boat to get away. I believe Sean is capable of that. He didn't have to kill Van Hugh or Tommy. Until he confesses it himself, I won't believe that he did that."

Her argument had some merit, and even more, the look in her eyes held deep pain and a determination to hang on. It took all of the anger out of him. Michael looked down at his partner and felt the swell of unmanageable emotions. There was nothing he could do for Tommy. Nothing. He took Elizabeth's elbow and started back to the house. "I hope Chief Williams is there," he said. "I want fingerprints off that plank. The car. The suitcase. I may have messed up some of them, but certainly not all of them."

Elizabeth grabbed Michael's shoulder. "What if he's still here, on the island?" Her voice rose with excitement.

"He couldn't be. There's not an extra car or boat."

"None that we've found. But we haven't looked very hard. We came in late last night and didn't really take notice of the area around the house. It could have been there all along. We've only used the front door today."

"Damn! You're right!" Michael started toward the house with long steps that soon turned into a jog. Elizabeth raced beside him.

If Sean was on the island, now was the perfect time to get him. She had Michael to help her, and Carl Williams was on the way. Carl knew Sean. Had known him for years. If Sean had to be taken down like some wild animal, Carl and Michael were the men she wanted to do it. They'd do everything in their power not to hurt him. She increased her pace. This might be her last chance to help Sean. If McMillan and his men got involved, they would be capable of killing her brother—and asking questions later.

Glancing down at Elizabeth's face, Michael could almost read her thoughts. He felt a surge of tenderness that he didn't dare express. She was so set on believing her brother was an innocent victim. Her heart was riding high for a terrible blow, but he could do nothing to protect her. All evidence pointed to the fact that Sean Campbell, whatever he'd been before his boat exploded, had become a cold-blooded murderer. When she finally had to face that truth, he wanted to be there for her.

If the change in Sean Campbell was a result of some blow to his head or some other injury, there was a chance that her beloved brother could be reclaimed. Michael wasn't a neurologist or a psychiatrist. He didn't know the odds, didn't want to know. Not now, at least. He only knew that the longer Sean Campbell was on the loose, the more danger everyone in the Gulf Shores area was in. The more danger Elizabeth was in, because she'd taken to heart everything Sean did. His actions would become her guilt. Once she finally had to accept that he was criminally dangerous, she'd believe everything that had happened was her fault. The man had to be stopped.

Michael came out of his musings when Elizabeth ran forward a couple of steps and motioned to the police cruiser on the bridge. Stopping in the side yard, she waved her hand. Michael could make out two men in the car, and he assumed Carl Williams was the driver.

"I don't know who he brought with him," Elizabeth said. She gave Michael a worried look. "I was hoping he'd come alone. If Sean is still on the island, Carl might be able to talk him into surrendering. Another officer might interfere."

Michael didn't offer his opinion, which was that a squad of officers would make him feel better. Because he was unbalanced, Sean Campbell was more dangerous than any sane man. People who were insane often had incredible willpower and strength. Sean had proven that—just to remain alive and on the loose.

Williams climbed out of the car and gave Elizabeth a worried look. "Agent McMillan insisted on coming." He spoke softly to her.

Elizabeth's heart dropped to her shoes. McMillan would just as soon shoot her brother as bring him in alive.

"Good morning, Ms. Campbell. I hear we've got another missing person. A plastic surgeon." McMillan spoke as he got out of the car. He gave Michael a thorough once-over and continued. "Seems strange to me to have one plastic surgeon killed in Mobile and another disappear here in the peaceful little town of Gulf Shores. Not to mention two teenagers murdered. This is a happening place."

"Tommy isn't missing," Michael said quietly. He glared at McMillan. Whatever Sean had done, the ATF had no right to treat Elizabeth as if she were a criminal, too.

"He's turned up?" Williams said, ignoring the tension around him.

"He's dead," Michael answered softly. "We found him out in the dunes. He was speared with a piece of planking from a crate. In the back."

Williams couldn't hide the dismay that crossed his face, and the look he turned on Elizabeth was filled with compassion. "Let's have a look," he said, forestalling any comment McMillan might have wanted to make.

Michael, with McMillan at his side, started back to the dunes. Elizabeth held back, touching Carl's sleeve. "He might be on the island still," she said, watching as Michael and the ATF agent walked on out of earshot.

"Who?" Carl asked.

Elizabeth hesitated. She looked at her old friend. "Michael believes it's Sean. He thinks the accident has damaged his mind and that he's killing these doctors because they won't help repair his face."

"How badly damaged is he?" Williams took the tidbit of news without any emotion. "How do you know he's injured?"

"Carl, if he's on this island, you can reason with him. He knows you. He won't be afraid." Her voice broke. "Sean would never do this. Never."

"Not the Sean we know. But if he's hurt..." Williams let the sentence hang unfinished.

"I don't know what to believe anymore," Elizabeth confessed. "Whoever it is, he has to be stopped."

"I'll do what I can to protect Sean," Carl said. "You know I will. A lot depends on him."

"He'll give himself up to you if he will to anyone." Elizabeth shook her head. "I'm asking you to possibly risk your life. I know what I'm doing, and I can't help myself." Tears trickled down her cheeks. "He's my brother."

Carl's arm went around her. "I'll do what I can. Right now I'm going to radio the station and have someone on the bridge and on the lookout for any boats docking. I'm certain he's gone back to the mainland by now. Just in case, though, if we could trap him on the bridge or get him offshore where we could control his docking, we'd stand a better chance of getting him without anyone getting hurt."

Elizabeth nodded and turned away to wipe her face and allow Carl to do his duty. Once the dispatch was made, they followed the path taken by McMillan and Michael.

STUPIDITY! I'm surrounded by total stupidity.

The man pressed the gas pedal closer to the floor as his car sped along the interstate. This was a new car, sleeker and more powerful than the one he'd stolen to drive to Mirage Island.

He'd come upon a strange, slender man in the house on the island. Instead of the doctor and Elizabeth, he'd found a man called Tommy Chester.

At first the man had been startled by the bandages. Then he'd agreed to look at the injuries. Finally he'd given his idea of what would be necessary to make repairs. "Extensive and prolonged surgery." That was the diagnosis.

The only drawback was that then the doctor had refused to do it. He'd given excuse after excuse, using some of the same lame reasons the other doctor had given. The other dead doctor.

The capper was, though, that he'd tried to pretend he was sick. Him, with his tanned skin and Rolex watch. Sick. That was a joke. Well, he was worse than sick now. He was dead. He'd made a run for it, but he hadn't gotten far.

The man took the downtown exit off the interstate, heading for a section of Mobile where the streets were narrow, dark and filled with litter. There were several children playing on the edges of the road. When night fell, they'd be inside the ramshackle houses. The streets they lived on weren't exactly safe.

He turned a corner and eased the car up onto the weed-choked lawn of one of the houses. It had been a mistake to steal such a new car. But then his taste had always run to fancy cars. He'd have to dump this one soon.

As an afterthought, he left the keys in the ignition as he made sure no one was around to watch him get out of the car. His bandages were a dead giveaway. People would remember a man wrapped in dirty bandages. But it was even worse if he took them off.

A fresh spurt of anger made him clench his teeth. That doctor on Mirage Island had escaped him once more. The next time he'd make sure the doc cooperated. He knew just how to do it. Elizabeth was the key. Elizabeth, or the girls. Why hadn't he thought of that before?

ELIZABETH BLINKED, hoping that she'd wake up to find that the entire morning had been a nightmare. No such luck. Tommy Chester, a man whose only sin was to stay for the night on Mirage Island, was dead.

She looked at Carl Williams's profile as he drove her back to the mainland. Agent McMillan had opted to remain behind with Michael and the body while the crime team went over the premises. At Michael's request, she'd left. He didn't want her to have to hang around and witness every gruesome detail.

"Elizabeth, has Sean made any attempts to get in touch with you or Aleshia?" Carl's question was softly put and he kept his eyes on the road, giving her as much privacy as possible.

"No. Not the first word." She didn't have to lie about that. She'd told Carl everything about the injured man who'd washed up on Mirage Island and how she and Michael had figured it was Sean. Though Carl had every right to be angry with her for withholding evidence, he didn't say anything. If Agent McMillan forced the issue, she supposed she could be charged with some crime. And Michael, too.

"I know this is painful, but the feds have gone through everything of Sean's, personal and businesswise. I can't help but think we're overlooking something. There's a journal—" he shrugged "—but it's all pretty humdrum. Am I overlooking something?"

"Not that I know of." It was another honest reply.

"No hang-up calls? Nothing?"

Carl was fishing, and he was getting too warm. Elizabeth considered her reply. "When my apartment was broken into, someone tore up a picture. They tore out the part with Sean in it. At Dr. Van Hugh's office, there was also a photograph of Sean cut out of a yearbook. Michael saw it. And there was a call on my answering machine. I couldn't tell for certain who it was... And I erased it."

"My, oh, my." Carl sighed. "This doesn't look good."

"I know." She found it easier to admit that to Carl. He'd known Sean. Maybe that was why it was so hard to acknowledge to Michael that he might be right about her brother. Michael had never known the kind, generous older brother who'd often stood in as a father for her after Brett Campbell had died of a stroke.

"I'll let you off at the newspaper."

"Guy will take me to my car," she said. "Thanks." When the car stopped on the gravel drive in front of the building, she hurried out. If Carl said anything kind to her she'd probably cry, and she just didn't have the time or energy to spend on wasted emotion.

"Elizabeth!" Guy leaned out of his cubbyhole, and his face had lit up when he had seen her. "You just missed a visit from an old high school friend of yours."

"Really." Elizabeth wasn't too interested in renewing old acquaintances at the moment.

"She was a nice girl. She said you two were cheerleaders together."

Elizabeth looked up. "I was never a cheerleader." She took the few steps so that she could stand in Guy's cubbyhole.

"Well, that's what she said. She was very emphatic about it, too. Told several stories about the two of you. Said she'd been gone for a long time. Living out of the country down in Central America somewhere. And now that I think back on it, she looked maybe to be a little Latin. Very pretty woman."

Elizabeth sat down unasked. "Guy, I knew everyone in my class at Foley High. What was her name?"

"Connie. Connie Smith." He leaned forward. "Are you okay?"

"There wasn't a Connie Smith in my class."

Doubt and then concern touched Guy's face. "Could she have married? Smith may not be her maiden name." He saw the look of real fear on her face. "What is it?"

"What did she want?" Elizabeth's eyes were round with near panic.

"She wanted to know where your mother and the girls had gone. She knew about Sean." Guy realized his mistake. "She said she'd spoken with you..."

Elizabeth lunged across the desk to the telephone. Her fingers fumbled on the buttons as she tried to punch in the long-distance number to her Aunt Ellen's house. Her first two attempts ended in recordings. On the third try she got the number right.

"What in the world is wrong with you?" Guy asked. He hadn't shifted his body since she'd leapt from her chair.

"That woman wasn't a friend of mine. I think she was pumping you to get information about my mother and the girls. She might be involved with someone who intends to hurt them."

Guy sank back in his chair. "I told her where they were. She seemed like such a nice woman, and a friend of yours. She was so concerned about them, and about you. She even talked about how Sean was such a decent guy." Guy was stricken. "What have I done?"

"If they'll answer the damn telephone, nothing." She counted the twelfth ring. "Come on, Mother, Aunt Ellen, answer the phone." Her fingers closed on the receiver as if choking the telephone would make her mother answer.

On the thirteenth ring, she hung up. "They're out."

"Call the Montgomery sheriff."

Elizabeth hesitated. "Maybe I should drive up there myself."

"That woman was here about thirty minutes ago. She's got too much of a head start on you, even if she doesn't know the area outside Montgomery."

"Aunt Ellen's farm is isolated. If they get there, no one would be around to help mother and the girls."

"Call the Montgomery County Sheriff's Department." Guy reached over as if to take the phone himself. "They can drive out there and get Aleshia and the girls."

"Who could this woman be?" Elizabeth asked. Certainly it was no one connected with Sean. Where could he meet a woman? And if she'd been local, Guy would have known her.

"Agent McMillan had a talk with me, Elizabeth." Guy was clearly worried. "He thinks you're somehow involved in the murders of those two teenage boys. That Santiago guy who was killed on the beach. He had some bad connections." His mouth was a thin line of worry. "This woman, she could be connected somehow with him."

"If that's the case, Mother and the girls may be in terrible danger."

Chapter Fourteen

Each minute seemed to drag on for at least an hour as Elizabeth and Guy went through the Foley High School annual. The woman who had called herself Connie Smith was not included on the pages. Elizabeth wasn't shocked, but Guy was even more distressed.

"She gave me so much detail. Things about the football team and games and road trips. She talked about boys you both had dated. I guess she made the whole thing up."

"Why?" Elizabeth closed the book and held it on her lap. "Who is this woman and why did she do that?"

Agent McMillan, who had for once taken a sideline position, finally spoke up. "We can only assume she was fronting for someone who wants some leverage on you, Elizabeth. The only value your mother or those two little girls might have is blackmail potential."

His words were a cold dagger in Elizabeth's heart, because she knew he was correct. She looked at the telephone again. They were waiting for the Montgomery County Sheriff's Department to call back and tell them that they'd found Aleshia and the girls and had taken them to a safe place. So far, they'd been waiting two hours—and still no word. Elizabeth tried to rationalize the long wait by thinking of all the places they might be. Shopping, visiting friends and relatives, exploring the hill country around the farm. There were a hundred things they might be doing. But the one that captured her mind and imagination was not pleasant. They could be hostages even as she waited to hear from them.

"Mr. Fallon, do you think you could help an artist put together a composite of this woman?" McMillan asked. "We'll get one here."

"I remember her vividly," Guy said.

McMillan nodded and made the call. "Brad Redmond will be here out of the Mobile office. Once we get a likeness of her, we can try to pick her up."

One of the local policemen entered the newspaper office and looked at McMillan. "Chief Williams asked me to stop by here and tell you that there's been no sign of any disturbance at Mrs. Campbell's home. Everything there is just fine. But someone's broken into Larry Steele's home."

"That's the car dealer who drowned during the storm?" McMillan asked.

"Yeah. His house was down on the west end. More isolated and not too far from Mrs. Campbell's cottage. It seems that area has become a target for burglars. And Steele had acquired some expensive possessions. He was the kind of man who liked to show off."

"The house was empty?" McMillan continued.

"It was up for sale. Sign out front. Perfect for vandals or burglars. Just an advertisement that no one was going to be around."

McMillan nodded. "Keep an eye on Mrs. Campbell's house. If anyone makes an effort to get in, we want to be able to nab them then. Might save us a lot of work in the long run."

The police officer nodded, then turned to Elizabeth. "Chief Williams wanted me to ask if there's anything he can do for you."

"No, thanks." There wasn't anything anyone could do. She had to wait. That was the bottom line.

MICHAEL CLOSED the hospital door behind him. His visits with Steve's patients were strictly nonprofessional, a courtesy he performed for his friend and colleague. Something to take his mind off Tommy.

Tommy and Elizabeth.

He could feel the net tightening around her, and he knew she'd never believe she was in danger from her own brother. He started toward the nurses' desk to use the telephone to call her, but stopped. She'd left the island in the company of Carl Williams, a man she knew and trusted. Maybe the police chief could help her see the truth.

He went to the desk to check the room listing of Steve's remaining two patients. He was almost done at the hospital. Then he'd go to the office and meet Gladys Runnels. The receptionist was distraught, and she needed some support while she tidied up some records and tried to think about her future. Steve's son was only seventeen. He had no idea what to do with his father's practice. The police investigators had finally allowed them access to the building, and there were a lot of decisions to be made. Michael felt it his responsibility to help as much as he could. Soon, he'd have to confront some of those same decisions for his own practice.

"Dr. Raybin?" The nurse spoke with some hesitation. He didn't have a name tag and was wearing street clothes instead of the traditional doctor's coat.

"Yes."

"You had a phone call about half an hour ago." The nurse pulled a pink memo slip from a clip and handed it to him.

He scanned the note quickly. It was from Elizabeth, and she asked him to meet her at eight o'clock at her cottage. Concern was his first reaction. Elizabeth had no business out on that lonely stretch of beach, not even if she was waiting for him to meet her.

He thought to call her but knew it would do no good. She was as headstrong as a mule when she'd made up her mind.

He checked his watch and sighed. He'd have to hustle if he was going to get everything done and still have time to meet her—and he wanted to get there a little early, just in case.

THE CAR HE DROVE was a 1987 Camry, not new enough to attract attention and not old enough to give him any trouble. One thing he couldn't afford was car trouble. He checked the gas gauge. He had three-quarters of a tank left. That was enough for the day. There was no way in hell he could stop to buy gas. With each passing day he was looking worse and worse. The bandages were filthy; he needed fresh ones. He should have taken them from the doctor's office while he was there, but he'd had other things on his mind.

He couldn't go back there now. He'd seen the newspaper where the office had been sprayed with gunfire. They were after him. He could almost smell them. The money he'd hidden wouldn't do him a bit of good if they got him. His plan had been infallible—except he hadn't anticipated getting injured. The *Sea Escape* should have blown like a land mine. He knew that boat inside and out. He knew exactly where to put the explosives. But it hadn't worked that way. No, he was living proof of that.

But it should have! Damn them all! His plan was perfect. It should have worked. He'd had everyone fooled. Every blasted one of them. And he'd gotten the money, just like he'd planned.

But they were after him now. They knew he wasn't dead. And he was as good as caught in a trap as long as he looked like some kind of freak.

He eased the car past the newspaper office. The plate-glass windows gave him a good view of the interior, but he couldn't make out who was in the office. There were several men, all standing around a desk. Was Elizabeth there? He couldn't be certain. He'd simply have to wait her out. Eventually she'd be alone. Once he had her, then things would begin to go his way. It was a shame. She was so worried and concerned, so determined to help. And all she was doing was making matters worse. But she did have the help he needed—Michael Raybin's skilled hands. Yes, indeed.

He turned the corner and cruised by Aleshia Campbell's darkened house. He struck the steering wheel with his fist and mumbled a curse. Why wasn't she home? She was always home. She never went anywhere! Before he drew attention to himself, he drove on.

Out of the rearview mirror he saw another car parked among the crape myrtles that sheltered the Campbell house from view. Was it cops, or them? He slowed slightly, but his impaired vision prevented a clear look at the occupants of the car.

The Camry he'd stolen had tinted windows, a small risk if the police decided to stop him. But they hardly ever stopped a car for tinting unless it was speeding or violating the law—or reported as stolen. Which this car would be in a matter of hours. So he had to take care of his business and get back to King Street, where he'd found the perfect hideout. Not clean. Not warm. But totally safe.

That was it. He had to get back to safety—with his prey.

ELIZABETH VAGUELY recognized the ATF agent who slipped into the newspaper office and made a beeline for McMillan. She watched with open interest as McMillan started forward, excitement touching his thin features.

He cleared his throat before he spoke. "Another boat has been reported missing out in the gulf. The *Pleasure Lady,* a twenty-eight-foot powerboat out of Fort Myers. She was headed in to port here, according to the relatives. She's been missing for twenty-four hours."

"Doesn't sound good," Guy offered. "The gulf's been pretty calm. Maybe mechanical problems."

"Maybe," McMillan allowed, but he didn't believe that.

Elizabeth looked down at the stack of work on her desk. She didn't believe it was mechanical problems, either. She believed the people who'd left for a vacation on board the

Pleasure Lady were dead. When she looked up at Mc-Millan, she could tell that he believed the same thing.

"The coast guard has been notified and a search is being organized," McMillan said.

"You're awful helpful all of a sudden," Guy said, eyeing McMillan with some concern. "Why?"

"This may be our chance to catch whoever is doing this." His gaze lingered on Elizabeth. "She may be able to help us."

"How?" Guy asked, immediately wary. "You aren't going to put Elizabeth at any risk."

"She may be able to help us bring her brother in alive." McMillan shrugged. "It may be the only shot he has."

"That's blackmail!" Guy fumed. "You're trying to make her risk herself to save someone who may not even be her brother."

"And he may be. In fact, I strongly believe he is."

"You are a cold-blooded, black-hearted—"

"What do you want me to do?" Elizabeth stood. "I'll do it."

McMillan's grin was humorless. "Good. I'll let you know."

"What do you mean?" Guy was ready to throttle the agent. "You'll let her know now so I can talk some sense into her. She'll do anything for her brother and you know that. You're using her love to threaten her."

"I'm simply giving her a chance to help her brother," McMillan said. He walked to the door, the ATF agent right behind him. "I'll be in touch."

As the glass door closed behind the agent, Guy went to Elizabeth. "You can't put yourself in a dangerous position. Think of your mother, Elizabeth. Think how she'd feel if she loses Sandra, Sean and you."

"If there's anything that I can do, I have to do it." Elizabeth was tired, far too tired to argue further. "It's just something I have to do, Guy. If I don't, I won't be able to live with myself."

"If you do, you may not live, period."

Arguing wouldn't change a thing. "What about a follow-up on those murdered high school kids? Carl told me he was checking the high school to see if he could turn up any link between the two boys. The rumors that the killings were gang related continue to persist."

Guy threw his hands in the air. "Check it out, if that's what you want to do. Do whatever the hell it is that you want, Elizabeth."

She swallowed the pain. She was hurting Guy, and she knew it. But there wasn't any other route she could take. He'd do the same if it were his brother or sister. He understood that, deep inside.

"If Mom calls, will you get word to me? I'm going by the police department and then out to the high school."

"Fine." Guy went to his desk, pointedly turning his back to her.

Elizabeth picked up her coat and purse and left.

IT WAS NEARLY THREE when she returned. The only message on her desk was from Michael, written in Guy's penciled scrawl. "He said he was running late at the hospital. Would you meet him at Mirage Island at eight? Lobster for dinner."

Elizabeth smiled. In a day of hell, the idea of seeing Michael was the only good thing she'd heard. Pleasure gave way to panic as she realized there was no note stating that her mother and the girls had been found. Guy's office was empty, and the only people at the paper were the typesetter and the pressman. She checked with them to be sure, but there were no more messages for her.

The choices were untenable—sit and wait or sit and wait. At least she could finish up a few of the stories Guy needed. The leads at the high school had not panned out. There were definitely toughs and bullies at the school, guys capable of beating each other to a pulp, but she had found no evidence of gangs. At least not the kind that rode in speed-boats, packed Uzis and cut innocent kids on beaches in two.

When the front door opened, she looked up expectantly. Betty, the society editor, gave her a hurried grin and went to the desk that overflowed with papers. "I haven't said anything before, because I didn't know what to say," she said suddenly. "If there's anything I can do, just say the word."

"Thanks." Betty was a no-nonsense person who bull-dozed her way through mountains of work. When she said something, she meant it. "If I knew what to do..."

"That's the hell of it, isn't it?" Betty picked up an article and bent to her work.

Her concentration scattered like leaves in a storm, Elizabeth sat and stared at the phone. It took her several minutes to realize that someone was parked outside the building constantly blowing a car horn.

"What the heck?" She got up and went to the window. She recognized her mother's blue station wagon and burst out the door.

"Mom! Molly! Catherine!" She tried to hug them all through the open car window.

"What's happened?" Aleshia Campbell's eyes were puffy and tired. "I came as quickly as I could. What's happened? Is it Sean? Have you found him?"

"What?" Elizabeth stepped back and dropped to a crouch so she was eye-level with her mother.

"Ellen's Sookie answered the phone. She said you couldn't give any details over the phone. She said you told me to get in the car and drive as fast as possible home and to bring the girls."

Molly leaned over the back seat and reached out for Elizabeth's hair. "Is it Daddy? Is he home?" She put her finger in her mouth.

"I never called." Elizabeth hunted for an explanation. "We've been trying to locate you all morning up at the farm."

"Someone called. Sookie thought it was you." Aleshia was more angry than confused. She blinked back tears. "She said it was urgent for me to come straight home and to bring the girls. Ellen and the girls and I were fishing down at Big Creek, and Sookie was so upset she rode her three-wheeler down to find us. She said you were very upset and said to get home right away. I was certain it was Sean."

"I'm sorry, Mom." Elizabeth signaled her mother to slide over to the passenger seat. She got into the car. "Let's get away from here and go somewhere we can talk."

"Take me home." Aleshia sounded defeated.

As Elizabeth made the turn toward the gracious old clapboard house, she looked at her mother. "Maybe we'd better go to a hotel," she said.

"I'm going home. I've had enough of this." Aleshia looked at her daughter and dared her to refuse.

"For the girls, Mom. Something strange is going on. I didn't call to tell you to come home. I was trying to call to warn you. Someone has been running around town pretending to be an old friend of mine. Guy told the woman where you were. We were trying to find you to warn you."

"To do what? Run and hide somewhere else?"

Casting a glance at the two girls in the back seat, Elizabeth could see they were afraid. How could they be anything else? Every bit of stability they'd ever had had been snatched away from them. And now they couldn't even go to their grandmother's house.

"I'll take you to the Hilton."

"I want to go home." Aleshia's jaw was set.

"I don't care. You're going to the Hilton, and we're stopping by the police station first to tell Carl you're here. Maybe he'll assign someone to watch you."

Worn out with the whole situation, Aleshia leaned back against the seat. "Is there any word?"

Elizabeth saw that her mother's eyes were closed, but she couldn't stop the tear that ran down her left cheek.

"I'm sorry," she whispered, about to cry herself. "I need to talk with you, but not now. When we have some privacy."

"Daddy isn't home, is he?" Molly asked softly. "He isn't ever coming home again."

Elizabeth gripped the steering wheel and drove along the beach toward the hotel near the Florida line.

She'd forgotten that ATF agents were staying there until she saw McMillan at the registration desk. She almost changed her mind about the Hilton, but Molly and Catherine looked so woebegone that she didn't have the heart to load them back into the car to go to another hotel.

McMillan waited until they had a room and a bellhop had taken their baggage before he touched Elizabeth's elbow and asked her for a word.

"Go on, Mother. Take the girls and get them a bath. Carl said he'd have someone down here in a couple of hours, so try to rest. I'll be up in a few minutes."

"Elizabeth, what are you up to?" Aleshia gave her daughter a disapproving look. "I can tell when you're getting ready to do something . . . unreasonable."

"Agent McMillan has a plan, a way to try to locate Sean. That's all."

"If my son were alive, he wouldn't have to be trapped." Aleshia didn't wait for a response. She went to the elevator and didn't turn back.

When they were alone, Elizabeth turned to the agent. "Now what exactly do you want me to do?"

"We found the *Pleasure Lady.*"

"Where?" Elizabeth couldn't help her curiosity, and the sudden hope that the crew was perfectly safe.

"Adrift, off the coast. She was out of fuel, and there was no sign of the couple who owned her. They're towing her in now so we can do a more extensive investigation."

"What do you think happened?"

"They were anchored somewhere, or else cruising along, it doesn't matter much which scenario you prefer. Pirates took over the boat, killed John and Susan Brown and used the boat until they ran it dry. I'm surprised they didn't scuttle it. That's usually what they do. Use it for a run and then punch a hole in the bottom."

"Just what is it you think they're running into this country? Drugs?"

McMillan shook his head. "We got the lab analysis on that piece of wood Tommy Chester was killed with."

"And?" It was part of a crate. The type of wood didn't seem all that significant.

"It's teak."

"For a packing crate?" He had her attention.

"In some Central and South American countries teak is not an expensive wood."

"Which means?" Elizabeth felt like she was dragging information out of him. That was typical of McMillan. He had to be in control.

"That's what has us confused. We're pretty certain it's a gun smuggling operation. But they wouldn't be bringing in guns from any of those countries. It would be the other way around. That's been the problem with this case all along. Nothing fits." He motioned her over to a small love seat against a wall.

"I need to see my mother." Elizabeth didn't like the agent, and she wanted to check on her family.

"You need to hear this, and I'd prefer that you sit."

She allowed him to lead her to the seat. The truth was, if he was going to deliver bad news, she wanted a seat. For the first time she saw a glimmer of compassion in the agent's eyes, and it scared her far more than any of the hardness she'd seen before. Instead of questioning him, she waited.

"Your brother..." He paused. "I'm sorry to have to tell you this, but your brother had invested heavily in a company, an investment firm, actually. It was a bad decision. He'd lost a great deal of money."

The facts registered, but Elizabeth couldn't fathom the reasoning behind McMillan's obvious concern for her. "Was it illegal?"

"No. But it does give him motive. The insurance policy on his wife."

Elizabeth shook her head. "How long have you known about this?"

"I'm telling you now because I want you to know before..."

She finally understood. "Before I put myself at risk. Before you use me as bait to get Sean to turn himself in."

"That's right. I felt you should know. Your belief in your brother is admirable. It's obvious that you love him deeply. You just need to know the truth before you agree to put yourself at risk."

More than anything, McMillan's concern almost made her falter in her belief. All along he'd had reason to believe Sean was committing illegal acts.

"What exactly do you want me to do?"

"Your brother has been injured. We know that. We'd like for you to let him think you can help him."

"Don't you think I've been trying to do that? The fact that you've had agents tailing me hasn't helped a bit. If he'd once been inclined to get in touch with me, he wouldn't now if he thought I was going to lead the law to him."

"We haven't tried very hard to keep up with you," McMillan said pointedly. "You gave some green men the slip once or twice, and then I ordered them to back off. I was hoping you might establish contact."

"Sean hasn't even tried to call me."

"There's more to this." McMillan leaned forward. "We believe Sean tried to contact Dr. Raybin. He obviously needs medical help and he thinks Raybin can give it to him. We need you to convince the doctor to meet with Sean, to agree to help him."

"If you really believe Sean killed Van Hugh and Tommy Chester, you're asking Michael to put his life on the line."

She dug her fingernails into the palms of her hands. "It's one thing for me to risk myself with Sean. Even if he's sick or hurt or deranged, I don't believe he'd hurt me. Michael is another matter completely."

"If you ask him to do it, he will." All traces of compassion were gone from McMillan's face. He was driving a hard bargain.

"I won't ask him. This isn't his problem. He's already suffered enough. Tommy was his friend as well as his partner. Steve Van Hugh was a classmate and a friend. I won't ask him to step up to be the third victim."

"I thought your brother wasn't a killer?" McMillan countered.

"Someone killed those two doctors. Michael won't be the third."

"This may be the only bait that will bring your brother out into the open. His time is running short, Elizabeth. He's stealing necessities. We have a series of stolen cars, minor break-ins. He's taking what he needs to survive, but he can't hide forever. A man with his injuries will be spotted eventually, and when that happens, in his unstable condition, a lot of innocent people could get caught in the cross fire."

"Just what is it you think Sean has done? Aside from murdering two doctors, his wife and blowing up his boat."

"We checked the logs of the *Sea Escape*. The boat made some unusual trips. She was spotted in small harbors, far from where the logs indicated she would be. It was apparent she was rendezvousing with another boat."

"So? Sean had a lot of friends. He and Sandra liked to cruise the coastline and explore different places. I don't think that indicates he was some kind of pirate."

"Some of the boats he became friendly with are ones that later disappeared."

"You think my brother is involved in some kind of smuggling ring? That he set up innocent tourists to become victims of pirates and smugglers?"

"He's ruthless, Elizabeth. You may know only one side of him. The other side is dark and cruel. Know that before you agree to anything."

"I'll think about it." She stood. She was badly shaken, and she didn't want McMillan to know how badly.

"Talk it over with the doctor."

"I'll think about it," she said again before she turned away.

Chapter Fifteen

Michael pressed the gas pedal a half inch closer to the floor. The Jaguar smoothly purred up another thirty miles per hour. It was a responsive car, and it had given Tommy a lot of pleasure. Michael had no idea what to do with it when he returned to California. There were so many dangling ends and unanswered questions.

Darkness had fallen more than an hour earlier, and as he hit the tunnel that dove beneath the Mobile River and came out on the other side where the Jubilee Parkway glittered over Mobile Bay, he inched his speed up even more. If a cop stopped him, it wouldn't be the worst thing that had ever happened to him. In fact, if he could take a few officers of the law along with him, he'd feel much better.

The more he drove, the more certain he became that something was wrong with the note Elizabeth had left him. Why was she going to her cottage? She might want some of her clothes and things. That was reasonable enough. But she'd had all day to go there, get what she wanted and leave. And she'd also had agents and local policemen all too willing to go with her. Why was she waiting until nighttime for such an escapade? It didn't make sense. Unless she was hoping to meet her brother there. And if that was the case, Michael wanted two dozen law officers to be on the scene.

He'd tried to call Elizabeth from Van Hugh's office, but he hadn't been able to track her down at the newspaper or anywhere else he thought to call. Betty, the society editor at the paper, said Elizabeth had gone out to talk to someone. She hadn't come back to the office, and she hadn't called in. As an aside, Betty mentioned that Guy was frantic with worry.

That didn't help Michael's feelings at all.

He took the exit for the beach. It was four-lane and deserted, and he notched the car up to ninety miles an hour. Each second that passed was a second longer than he cared to be away from Elizabeth. He'd wanted—had planned—to make it to her cottage by seven-thirty. That would have given him a good thirty minutes to scout the place out. But he'd been delayed. Gladys Runnels had clung to him and cried, begging him to stay in Mobile and take over the practice. He'd had to forcibly extricate himself and then drive like a bat out of hell to try to make up the lost time.

He pushed the car through the small towns, obeying the speed limits only as long as he felt it was strictly necessary. When the road opened in front of him, he zoomed forward.

It was another clear night, and the air had a slightly balmy feel to it. If Elizabeth was sitting beside him, and if they could remove themselves from the troubles that had visited themselves upon them, he could well imagine himself in paradise. He tried to think about the future, about a time when he could walk with Elizabeth on the beach and not feel as if someone might jump out from behind a dune and try to cut them down with automatic gunfire.

At last he came to the intersection where Highway 59 ran into the gulf. He turned right, going to West Beach and the cottage. It was ten before eight. He'd make it on time, but just barely.

The drive that led back to the cottage was unlighted, and Michael pulled the car far enough away from the main road that it was partially secluded. The beach terrain didn't allow for a lot of vegetation. Only the rolling dunes gave any cover. He stared down the drive, alert for any sound at all.

He had the feeling that he wasn't alone, yet he couldn't say where he thought someone might be lurking.

It was a small sound that stopped him. Something like a stick breaking, or two pieces of metal snicking together. A click, or a snap. He stopped, frozen with one foot ready to step forward.

The scent of some exotic blossom came to him, unidentifiable and completely out of place. It was sweet and fresh, a taste of the paradise he wanted to share with Elizabeth. He was totally unprepared for the rapid gunfire that chattered out of the dunes. Sand danced only inches in front of his feet.

He saw the black shadow of a man leap toward him, striking him at the waist and doubling him over as all of the air was driven from his lungs. He hit the ground with the man atop him, and they rolled, tangled and grunting, into the base of a dune.

"Get down!" The man growled.

Michael needed no encouragement. He flattened himself in the sand as the man crawled off and signaled for Michael to follow him behind the dune.

"Send in the units," the man said into the shoulder of his uniform.

Gunfire burst into the night again, this time followed immediately by the sound of sirens. In a matter of seconds, the driveway filled with at least ten cars. Some carried the traditional red and blue flashing lights of the law. Others had a single revolving red light. They drove madly into the sand, slewing in all directions as they formed a line that effectively sealed the drive. Policemen opened the car doors and crouched in the protection offered by the metal.

"We have you surrounded," Chief Carl Williams called out. "Throw down your weapons and give yourself up."

Michael tore his attention from the scene playing out in front of him and looked at the man who'd tackled him.

"Officer Estis," the man said. "We've had the house under surveillance. Good thing the chief recognized the description of your car or we might have hurt you."

"What's going on?" Michael asked. "Where's Elizabeth?"

"We haven't seen Ms. Campbell," the officer said. "Chief Williams was certain they'd return to the cottage. We've been waiting for them for several nights. Now we have them."

As he spoke, a vicious round of automatic fire covered the area. Michael and Officer Estis ducked instinctively. At the same time there was the sound of a motor revving, and a big truck suddenly burst from behind the dunes. A gunner stood in the back, secured to an upright post. He opened fire and continued to spray the area with bullets as the truck sped across the sand toward the road.

"Radio for a block at the intersection! Do whatever it takes to stop him!"

Michael recognized Williams's voice. There was frantic movement as the officers ran to their vehicles to give pursuit. Officer Estis hesitated, then started after them. "You need to talk to the chief," he said.

"I will," Michael replied. "I damn sure will." Now that the excitement had begun to subside, his worry about Elizabeth had rekindled. Where the hell was she? Maybe Williams had put her someplace very safe. It was the best Michael could hope for.

In the lights of a remaining car he saw a tall silhouette that resembled the Gulf Shores chief of police. He hurried toward the man, relieved to recognize Elizabeth's friend.

"Chief Williams, where's Elizabeth?"

The chief gave him a concerned look. "Isn't she with her mother?"

Michael's reaction was just as confused. So much had happened in the brief time they'd been apart. In a few minutes Williams was on the radio, calling the police dispatcher to call the hotel. As the two men waited impatiently, the dispatcher placed the call. In a moment she returned with the news that Elizabeth had gone to Mirage Island to meet Michael.

"Let's go," Michael said. "I never asked Elizabeth to meet me there. She's been tricked, and so have I."

"I'LL BE CAREFUL," Elizabeth promised as she kissed her mother goodbye. "Officer Jenkins will make sure you and the girls are safe."

"But who'll look out for you?" Aleshia wasn't thrilled with the idea of Elizabeth traveling to the island alone. She'd begged her daughter to call Michael and ask him to pick her up on his way. But Elizabeth had insisted that she didn't want to disturb Michael. He had enough to do.

Elizabeth had spent the early evening talking with her mother. While the girls napped, she laid out the charges as Agent McMillan saw them. She and her mother had agreed that Michael could not put himself in danger, not even to help Sean. What Elizabeth had not told her mother was that McMillan's proposal had given her an idea.

As she came down the elevator and started through the lobby, she tensed. A man waiting at the desk was staring at her. He had to be one of the feds. But on this night she didn't want anyone intruding on her and Michael. It seemed that each time she saw him, it might be the last for a long time. She wanted to savor each second, each hour of bliss. That would be difficult to do if she thought someone was watching every move she made.

She reversed her footsteps and started toward the dining room, as if she'd suddenly decided to eat in the hotel. The man didn't move. He remained in line, waiting to register.

Laughing a little at her own foolishness, Elizabeth turned around once again and went to the parking garage to get the station wagon.

As she eased into the westbound lane, she noticed a pair of headlights coming out of the parking lot behind her. Remembering how she'd jumped to the wrong conclusion about the man in the lobby, she turned her attention back to the oncoming traffic. McMillan had said he'd quit dogging her. He wanted something from her, and he couldn't afford to irritate her. The idea that the car was following her was all in her mind—a justifiable bit of paranoia. McMillan would honor his word and leave her alone. At least for a little while.

In the thick traffic that clustered the highway, she lost the headlights of the car. When she took the turn to the island, she felt a thrill of anticipation. Michael. She'd been waiting all day for a few hours with him.

Halfway over the bridge she saw the car turn in behind her. Panic squeezed, a sensation that made her short of breath and nauseous. The only person who should be on that bridge other than herself was Michael. In the rearview mirror she watched the headlights advance.

"Hold on," she whispered, clutching at the idea that it was Michael coming just behind her. That was who it had to be.

The car behind her was picking up speed, closing the distance at an alarming rate. She gassed the station wagon, realizing for the first time how big and lumbering the car was.

The house on Mirage Island grew steadily larger, and she focused on that, thinking of how she'd get inside if Michael wasn't there to open the door. Mentally she tried the windows, trying to remember if any had been left unlocked. There was a gun tucked in the drawer beside the bed. At least, that's where she'd last seen Michael put it. She prayed it would be there, and that she could get inside. She tried to remember how to slide up the safety on the gun and hold it so that the kick wouldn't throw her off-balance. She concentrated on any tiny thing to keep from screaming with fear. Once she lost control, they'd have her.

Who?

That question stopped her runaway fear. Who exactly was after her? Igor and some foreigner? She'd almost forgotten those two. Another idea came to her. If it was Sean, this might be the chance she'd hoped for. If she could only talk with him, she might be able to bring him around. If he believed that someone still loved him and wanted to help, even if he was unbalanced, he might respond to that, to her voice, to the past they'd shared.

She came off the bridge, checking below her to make sure the skiff was still tied to the dock. The small boat bobbed gently in the soft swells. If worse came to worst, she could always strike out in the skiff. And if that didn't prove feasible, she could swim. The water was calm enough, and if she didn't freeze, she'd stand a better than average chance. She was one of the best swimmers around. Except for Sean. He'd always been able to best her, but that was before he'd been injured.

She made up her mind on a plan. She'd swing behind the garage, make a run for the house, and hide where she could see whoever got out of the car. If it was Sean, she'd talk to him.

And if it was someone else?

If she couldn't get inside, she'd make a dash for the water.

As she swung the wagon around the garage, her heart plunged. A strange vehicle was hidden behind the garage. She'd never seen the car with the dark tinted windows before. The glass was so dark her headlights couldn't even begin to penetrate enough to allow her to see how many people were inside.

She was trapped. Someone on the island was waiting for her, and someone was behind her, coming on fast. She watched the headlights advance.

As she hesitated, she saw the door of the small car open. Someone was getting out. Her headlights picked up the man. Bandages, tattered and coming loose, covered half of his face. He stood by his car door and stared at her.

"Sean." She spoke his name in a whisper, and she felt her throat close with emotion. He looked terrible. He was hurt.

Badly hurt. And he'd been running and hiding from everyone.

She opened her car door and got out, standing still, as he did. Waiting for a moment to allow him time to see her, to remember, if he could. "Sean," she called softly, "it's Elizabeth. I want to help you."

He lifted one hand, as if pleading with her.

The car careened off the bridge, striking one post lightly as it swerved toward the house.

Elizabeth looked from her brother to the car. When she looked back, Sean was leaping back into his car and turning it on. He burst forward with a rush of gravel spraying out behind him. Instinctively, Elizabeth followed suit. As the third car came off the bridge and swung around toward the house, someone on the passenger side opened fire. Bullets chattered along the garage, striking the side of the wagon. Elizabeth stomped on the gas pedal, following her brother onto the bridge as fast as she could. Behind her, the third car swerved, narrowly missing the house. The tail slithered back and forth in the sand, enough to throw the aim of the gunman off for several seconds. It was long enough for her to make it to the bridge.

Sean's headlights were already a hundred yards ahead. She pressed the gas pedal even harder, but the wagon was going as fast as it could. Up ahead, Sean was pulling away.

"Wait," she called after him, knowing he couldn't possibly hear her. Frustration and fear and anger and love all combined to make her feel as if she had to catch him. "Wait. I want to help you." She was so intent on getting to her brother that she ignored the car that pursued her.

As she watched helplessly, Sean crossed the bridge to the main highway. He wove expertly in among the cars and disappeared. He was gone.

Elizabeth thought to use the station wagon to block the bridge. If nothing else, she'd make certain that Sean escaped. But she knew the people behind her would think nothing of cutting her to ribbons. She turned left and headed for the police department. Carl Williams would believe her, and maybe he'd help. In her rearview mirror she saw the other car turn right, after Sean.

Up ahead the scream of a siren warned her. Instead of slowing, she pushed the wagon to the maximum speed. Let the cops chase her! Nothing had ever sounded like a better idea.

"Elizabeth!" Michael recognized her before she could even get out of the car.

"I thought that was her mother's station wagon," Williams said as he opened his door. "Sometimes working in a small town has its advantages."

"It was Sean! It was him! He wanted me to help him and then they ran him off." She let Michael fold his arms around her and hold her. It was the only place she knew she'd ever find such solace.

"Easy," he whispered. "Calm down."

"What happened?" Williams asked. "We were headed for the island. Your mother said—"

"I *did* go there. I had a message at the office to meet Michael there for dinner. But when I got there, it was Sean. He held out his hand . . ." She swallowed. "He was asking for my help. He wasn't going to hurt me."

"What happened?" Michael and Chief Williams asked in unison.

"This other car came and started shooting at us. We both drove away, and Sean escaped. They went after him."

"Pull the wagon off the road," Williams directed Michael. "Elizabeth, get in the patrol car." There was cold fury in his voice.

"Where are we going?" Michael asked. He helped Elizabeth into the back seat as he looked over the roof of the car at the chief.

"We're going for a visit with that moron McMillan. He was supposed to keep an eye on Elizabeth. So far, he hasn't been able to accomplish that at all. I'm beginning to wonder if he's even tried."

Michael had started toward the wagon and stopped. "What are you saying?"

"If he can't do a better job than he's been doing, then he doesn't deserve to be a federal agent. If he *can* do a better job, it sort of makes you wonder who he's working for, doesn't it?"

Michael didn't answer, but moved the wagon far off the highway. He pocketed the keys and returned to the patrol car and slid in beside Elizabeth. It was a different perspective from the back seat.

Williams drove straight to the Hilton. He opened the door for Michael and Elizabeth to get out of the car, but he didn't wait for them. He stalked inside and gruffly asked the desk clerk for McMillan's room.

They caught up with him in the elevator. Elizabeth had never seen him so furious.

"Give him a chance," Michael said.

"Oh, I will, and then I'm going to kick his butt all over that room."

The rest of the elevator ride was silent. At Room 979, Williams knocked softly on the door.

When McMillan answered, the chief booted the door hard, forcing it back on the agent's forehead. Williams kicked it open the rest of the way.

"I want a word with you." Williams's tone was black.

"You'd better have a damn good reason for this." McMillan finally saw the chief's companions. The expression that crossed his face was hard to name.

"Come on in," Williams said, motioning to Michael and Elizabeth to enter the room. He closed the door behind them.

"You were supposed to protect her." Williams nodded to Elizabeth. "So far you've done a pitiful job. If you were on my force, I'd fire you."

McMillan grinned. "I'm crushed."

It was the final insult. Williams drew back his fist and prepared to hammer the agent. Only Michael's hand on his arm stopped him. "Let it go, Carl," Michael whispered.

"Elizabeth is bait!" McMillan walked away from them. At the sofa, he stopped. "She agreed to do it. No one forced her." He looked at Elizabeth. "Tell him. You said you'd do anything to help your brother. Tonight was an opportunity. Unfortunately, things didn't go as we planned."

"Tell that to the owners of the *Pleasure Lady* or the *Hummingbird.* Tell that to the parents of those two teenagers gunned done on the beach. Better yet—" Williams's voice grew dangerously angry "—tell that to your boss, you worthless piece of scum."

McMillan didn't flinch. "My boss is aware of every decision I make. I have his total confidence."

"Well, that tells us what kind of moron he is," Williams responded.

Elizabeth stepped forward. "You knew Sean would be at the island tonight?"

"We knew he was bird-dogging you. We expected he would make some attempt to contact you for help." McMillan paced back across the room to the door. "We anticipated that he would come late at night. We were planning to stop the doctor at the bridge when he tried to go over to the island, and then move in by water to take your brother. It seemed like the best way. No citizens would be endangered."

"No one but Elizabeth!" Michael regretted that he'd stopped the police chief from decking McMillan. "Did it ever occur to you that if Sean felt cornered he might hurt Elizabeth?"

"She was so certain he wouldn't. He's her brother."

"You think he killed his wife!" In his entire life Michael had never wanted to hurt someone as bad as he wanted to hurt Agent McMillan. His blood pumped with the desire to inflict damage on the other man.

"Elizabeth was certain." McMillan's grin faltered slightly. "If she'd had any doubts, we'd never have allowed it."

"My brother and I were nearly killed tonight. Were those your men?" Elizabeth wanted answers. "Sean was ready to respond to me. He was reaching out to me for help. I could have talked him into giving himself up. Were those your men?" she repeated.

"No."

The one word echoed around the room. Williams's hand dropped to rest on his holster. "I should shoot you now," he said, but his voice was deceptively emotionless. "What happened to Elizabeth's protection? Just who were those men, or don't you have any idea?"

"We got a tag number on the car, but we found it abandoned about ten miles down the beach." McMillan paced back to the sofa. "We believe it may have been the smuggling gang we're pursuing."

"Elizabeth was on the island with her brother and a carload of gun smugglers." Michael didn't believe it. "She had both elements of the crime you're trying to solve, and all of them got away."

"As I said, we anticipated that the opposition would move in at a much later time. Campbell must have been on the island for the better part of the evening. He was smart enough to hide out there and wait."

"A lot smarter than you," Michael said. His arm went around Elizabeth. "I'm telling you now. Stay away from her and her family. You've done enough damage to the Campbells and to everyone else here. If I catch you or your men around any members of this family, I'll personally do my best to make them very, very sorry."

"I'm calling your superior, McMillan. You may have his complete confidence, but he's going to have my full report. I'm going to do my best to have you removed."

"Be my guest," McMillan said. He took a seat on the sofa. "The agency operates very differently from your hick police department. You'll find that out." He looked up, his face unperturbed. "In more ways than one."

Chapter Sixteen

Michael held Elizabeth against him. He listened to the soft rhythm of her heart, felt the gentle movement of her chest in and out as she breathed. He wanted nothing more than to hold her, to feel the softness of her hair against his chin, to breathe the clean smell of her.

"It'll be dawn soon." Elizabeth watched the sky lighten to the east.

"I'm sorry to see the night end." He kissed her again. She'd never know how close she'd come to death. Agent McMillan wasn't giving away any information about who the men were who had tried to kill Elizabeth and her brother, but Michael had drawn his own conclusions. The idea that McMillan might have deliberately been working to get Elizabeth and her brother killed gnawed at Michael. It was insane. McMillan was a federal agent, a man handpicked and trained. But the more he thought about it, the more plausible it seemed.

McMillan had never made a sincere attempt to protect Elizabeth. It wasn't realistic that she could outdrive and outmaneuver trained agents who'd been assigned to tail her—if they really wanted to follow her. All along McMillan had been using her as bait to lure Sean out into the open. And then what? Was the ATF man really intending to kill brother and sister?

Possibly, if Sean had something on him. Something like the fact that McMillan was involved in smuggling. Especially if Sean could prove it.

"What is it?" Elizabeth felt the tension in Michael's body.

"Nothing," he whispered, turning his thoughts back to her. When the sun came up, he'd confront McMillan. Without any witnesses. One way or the other, he'd wring the truth out of the agent. For now, he wanted to savor every second of time with the beautiful woman curled against him.

Elizabeth knew Michael was deep in thought, unpleasant thoughts judging by the way the muscles along his back had ridged and knotted. She also knew whatever was troubling him, he wasn't going to tell her. More than likely, it was Tommy Chester and Steve Van Hugh. Two friends who were dead. Michael carried an enormous amount of guilt for their deaths.

Elizabeth understood how heavy a burden that could be; she carried her own guilt. She couldn't shake the image of Sean standing beside his car, his hand outstretched toward her for help. If no one else believed in Sean, she did. And she wouldn't abandon him. Especially not to the likes of McMillan. She didn't want to discuss it with Michael, but she knew the ATF agent had set her up. She suspected that he'd deliberately allowed the gunman to drive to the island with the express purpose of killing her and her brother. The question was why?

What did Sean know that would make McMillan so afraid to let him live? What had her brother discovered? There had to be some evidence that she'd overlooked somewhere. McMillan had allegedly found some evidence that Sean was in debt. She didn't believe that for an instant. But she knew McMillan, with his connections, might be able to fabricate such evidence. If McMillan was a rogue agent, then Sean was indeed in terrible danger.

Michael's soft kiss on her temple stopped her feverish thoughts. She lifted her lips to his, shutting her eyes and closing out all of the torment of the past several weeks. It wasn't daylight yet. She could have a few more hours, a little bit more of heaven, until the sun came up and there was no escaping.

Michael meant only to comfort her. They'd made love during most of the night, and they were sated and tired. His kiss was meant to give her a measure of tenderness, and love. She was so brave and so foolish, so fiercely loyal to her brother. She wasn't even aware of everything she risked, and if she were, it wouldn't stop her. He'd never met a woman with such heart.

His lips traced a path along her cheekbone to her mouth. Her soft lips opened, and she offered herself to him. Comfort quickly turned to hunger. Michael felt a rush of sudden joy as Elizabeth began to respond to him. She gave herself in love as she did everything else, with her complete heart. He had never met a woman like her, and he never intended to let her go.

MICHAEL WALKED along the beach, watching the waves crash against the deserted shore. Elizabeth had expressed her belief that the beach was more beautiful during the winter, when it wasn't filled with bright swimsuits and laughing teenagers. The summer season would have its pleasures, but he had to agree with the woman he loved, the winter was spectacular in its solitary beauty.

A brisk wind was blowing from the west, and the latest weather reports warned of a storm being pushed their way on the gulf stream. One thing he'd learned since coming to the gulf coast of Alabama was the necessity of paying attention to the weather. Accepted wisdom was that Marie had been the last of the dangerous tropical storms for the season, but bad thunderstorms could still blow up on the water. And there were always water spouts, those tornadoes that formed over water and wreaked havoc on unlucky ships or the shore. Yes, the gulf waters were usually warm and gentle, but they could be as savage as any other.

As he walked the beach, he examined the restaurants that offered scenic views of the gulf. He hesitated at the Pink Pony. He'd talked with Elizabeth there. It seemed like a million years ago. From the surf line where he walked he could see activity in the restaurant. Missing Elizabeth, he suddenly decided to go in for something warm to drink. What he really wanted was twenty minutes alone with a particular ATF agent, but McMillan had suddenly been called to "a meeting in Atlanta." No one would say when he'd return.

As Michael pushed into the welcome warmth of the dining room, he was surprised at the number of tables occupied. There were at least three elderly couples and a threesome over by the kitchen, heads bent in some earnest conversation. A mother with two rowdy children tried to feed them while grabbing a bite herself. She needed four more hands and a couple of strong ropes to subdue the little boys. He couldn't help smiling at them.

He took a table and ordered, wondering what Elizabeth was doing. She'd refused to let him go with her to the newspaper. She said she had work to do and that she'd meet him for lunch later. Until then, he had time to kill. He was terrified to let her out of his sight, and afraid to hang around. Elizabeth's independence was important to her. And to his dismay, she'd come up with some angle on her brother she was dying to look into. He could see it in her eyes even though she wouldn't talk about it.

The waitress brought his breakfast, and he turned, sensing that someone watched him. It was the threesome, a big man with a smaller man and woman. It was the woman that drew his eyes. With her dark hair and eyes, she reminded him a little of Elizabeth. They were about the same age. Trying not to draw attention to himself, he studied her and realized that other than coloring, there was nothing really to compare to his Elizabeth. This woman was attractive, but she was a dim light compared to the woman he loved. He smiled, remembering Elizabeth's face as they'd made love the night before. She radiated her feelings. It was extraordinary.

He looked up and caught the big man staring at him again. The little man and the woman were looking, too, and whispering.

Feeling like a fool, Michael looked away. He'd been thinking about Elizabeth with a goofy grin on his face and staring right at the woman. If one of those men were her husband, there might be trouble.

He ate a bite of toast and drank his coffee, turning his gaze out the window to the gulf. In the plate-glass window, he could still see the threesome staring at him. They whispered together, never looking away. Using the glass as a sneaky mirror, he watched them watching him. There was something troubling about them. The smaller man was speaking some strange language, and his expression was ferocious. As Michael took a bite of bacon, it struck him.

Igor! Was it possible the big man was Igor? And the little man had been his partner in breaking into the house on the island? The woman? Was she the one who'd gone to the newspaper and pumped Guy for all the info on Aleshia and the girls? She was pretty, dark, with a Latin flavor. He lifted his napkin and wiped his lips.

As he watched them, he realized they knew exactly who he was. So now what was he to do? He took a bite of egg and spread jam on another slice of toast. The most important thing he could do was pretend he knew nothing at all about them. His heart was pounding, but he moved slowly, as if he had the rest of his life to complete his breakfast. When the waitress came by with the coffeepot, he asked her to refill his cup.

He didn't taste anything he chewed. The hot coffee almost scalded his mouth, but he swallowed it and pretended to be having the most enjoyable breakfast of his life. He noticed that they'd paid their bill, but they, too, asked to have their cups refilled. The little man spoke to the waitress, and Michael heard his voice again. He couldn't place the accent, but Elizabeth had been emphatic about the strangeness of the man who'd broken into the house, the gruffness of his voice. It had to be them, and they were going to wait him out.

Michael surreptitiously pulled ten dollars from his pocket and slid it under the edge of his plate. He got up, strolled to the newspaper box and bought a paper. Holding it up, he scanned the headlines and then put it at his plate as if to imply he intended to read it momentarily.

Still standing, he signaled the waitress and loudly asked for more coffee before he walked into the men's room. He could only pray that there was a window. His breath escaped on a sigh of relief as he spied the window over the hand-towel dispenser. It was big enough for him to wiggle through, which he promptly did. Dropping to the ground, he ran as hard as he could to the point where he'd left his car. Driving like a mad man, he hurried back to a place where he could watch the exit door of the Pink Pony. It wouldn't take long before those three realized they'd been duped and left holding the bag in the restaurant.

That's when the fun would begin, because he fully intended to turn the tables on them and follow them.

The big man came out first. He looked around, then signaled the little man and the woman. They held a conference beneath the pilings that supported the Pink Pony and appeared to be arguing. The woman pointed east, toward the island, while the little man pointed west, toward Elizabeth's cottage. The big man simply waited, looking from one to the other as they spoke.

The woman threw up her hands, and the two men walked off. They got in a brown compact, cut a tight circle and headed west, away from Michael and the woman. Torn between following the men or waiting to see what the woman did, Michael hesitated. He settled on the woman. She would be the easiest to subdue, if he had to. She might talk more readily than the men, if properly motivated. Besides, she had to be fairly articulate—she'd tricked Guy into spilling his guts. Michael wasn't certain the shorter man spoke fluent English, and Igor hadn't spoken a word at all.

As the woman turned to survey the parking lot and the roadway in both directions, Michael slipped down farther in the seat. She might recognize the car, and then again she might not. He waited a few minutes, then looked over the steering wheel. She was walking down the road. Apparently the men had driven off, leaving her without a ride. It was a stroke of pure luck for Michael.

He waited until she was on a stretch of road without a business near. He slowly rolled the car up beside her, then swerved ahead of her and jammed on his brakes. She turned, frightened, and he opened the passenger door.

"Get in," he ordered, pointing the pistol he'd purchased. When she didn't respond immediately, he pulled the hammer back. "I mean it. Get in."

She glanced around, probably hoping to see her friends. She saw no one. Very slowly, she slid into the front seat.

"Close the door," Michael ordered.

She did, not looking at him.

"We're going for a little ride, and you're going to tell me everything you know." Michael eased the hammer back into place. "And if I get wrong answers, you aren't going to like the way you look or feel afterward. Okay?" He felt like a creep. The woman was literally shaking.

"Yes," she answered, her voice unsteady. "Just put the gun away."

Michael thought about taking her to Mirage Island, but he had no faith that the island wasn't being watched. He drove down the beach, trying to calculate which road would take them into the rural heart of Baldwin County. If he wasn't careful, he'd end up in Florida, and he didn't want to cross the state line.

He saw a narrow road that looked promising, and he turned left. The blacktop cut between rolling dunes that were soon topped with pine trees. Away from the beach, the land started to flatten out. White sand gave way to darker, richer soil.

"Where are you taking me?" the woman asked. She cast one quick look at him, her dark eyes wide and afraid.

"Who are you?"

"Carmalita del Reyo."

"Why are you snooping around about Elizabeth, Carmalita?"

"Who is this Elizabeth?" She gave him an innocent look.

"Cut the stupidity and the phony accent. I heard you talking in the restaurant, and I know you speak flawless English. You've been raised in this country."

She remained silent, and Michael mentally cursed himself for speaking so abruptly. If he frightened her too badly, she wouldn't be able to tell him what he needed to know.

He decided to try again. "Why are you asking about Elizabeth? What is it you want to know?"

"I cannot say." She looked straight ahead and seemed determined not to show any more emotion.

Michael took her measure. She seemed less afraid. "You could be in serious trouble. People are dead. Others are missing. That's murder and kidnapping. Those crimes carry a lot of weight. Now tell me what you're up to, and maybe I'll try to help you."

She kept her eyes trained out the window, but she bit her bottom lip.

"This is the last time I'm going to ask. Why were you asking about Elizabeth?"

The tone of his voice was cold, flat and impersonal. She looked again at the pistol that rested in his right hand along his thigh.

It was a moment of drama, and highly unethical, but Michael was desperate. He picked up the gun and made sure the safety was on. Aiming it at her temple, he said, "Talk or die. It's your choice."

"My cousin is Carlos Santiago. I came to avenge his death."

Her eyes snapped with fire and all of her fear seemed to suddenly leave her. "He was shot down on the beach like a dog, and the person who did it will pay. Carlos was good to me. He helped me to go to school. He gave money to my mother for medicine when she was sick." She looked away. "Why should you care?"

"What did you intend to do with those two little Campbell girls if you had gotten them?"

She glanced over at him. "I don't know," she said. "I thought I could make her pay." There was cold anger in her words. "Carlos is dead because of her."

Michael whipped the car suddenly to the left. The unexpected movement slammed the woman into the door. "Your loving cousin had been sent to kill Elizabeth. It just so happened that someone killed him first."

"Diablo," she whispered, saying the name like a curse.

"The Spanish name for devil." Michael's soft tone belied his intense anger. "So who is this Diablo?"

"He is the man." The woman smiled this time, a grimace of fear and disgust. "The bad man. He runs the business and he doesn't like people who mess him up. Be careful, Dr. Raybin. Diablo has contracts he must meet. You're beginning to interfere."

Michael wasn't certain, but there could be no other explanation. "Tell me something, Carmalita. What does Diablo deliver on these contracts? Is it guns?"

She shrugged. "Perhaps. There is always a need for guns. As long as there are men, there will be guns and wars. It would not be a bad business for a man with nerve who wanted to make money."

"Well, it got your cousin three slugs in his chest." That took the wind out of her sails. She sagged against the seat.

"Those two men with you, who are they?"

"They worked with Carlos. They were helping me." All arrogance was gone from her voice. "They are nitwits.

Fools." She threw up her hand. "Bart is like a trained bear, and Rupo is a weasel. They are impossible."

Michael's thoughts had rushed ahead. "I need to speak with Diablo. Could you arrange it?"

Fear sparked in her eyes, though she tried to hide it. "No. I could not do that. He makes his own appointments, and believe me, you do not want to talk to him."

"Oh, but I do. I believe he may have made a terrible mistake with Sean Campbell. Now I believe he's trying to correct that mistake by eliminating Sean and his sister if Elizabeth gets in his way. I'd just like to explain to him that Sean and Elizabeth will be no trouble to him. None at all. If he'll just leave Sean alone and let us get him to a hospital."

She shook her head. "Forget it. The mark has been made on the injured man that your woman has been trying to help. He will die."

"Do you know why?"

Carmalita looked at him. "Because Diablo wishes it. There does not have to be another reason, and I don't want to know it if one does exist."

ELIZABETH COULD BARELY wait for Michael to leave her at the newspaper office. When his car disappeared, she immediately coerced Guy into taking her to her Trooper. With Guy's reluctant approval, she drove to West Beach to talk with the parents of both boys who'd been murdered. There had to be a connection, and she had to find it.

It was painful and difficult, but the mothers of both boys willingly talked with her. They had no explanation for the horror that had happened. They both retraced the steps their sons had taken. It was at Brian Havard's house that Elizabeth found the link. Both boys had been boating the evening before they were killed. It wasn't the fact that they were on the beach, it was that they'd been on the water—and very near Mirage Island.

They'd seen something there!

Driving like a maniac, Elizabeth went back to her brother's real estate office. She'd been through all of his documents, but there were several records from the *Sea Escape* that Chief Williams and the ATF men had examined and returned. Elizabeth had not examined the logs, but she intended to do so. Sean had always kept a journal of observations, small details that struck him about his home and how the coast was gradually changing. The logs had been thoroughly scrutinized by the authorities and might prove one reason McMillan was so interested in making sure that Sean was not taken alive.

As she hurried along the beach, she tried to convince herself that she was being foolish. It was impossible that she'd finally come up with the connection. But all along Sean had been the thread, and now she was beginning to see the pieces of the pattern he'd irrevocably stitched together. Pulling into the lot, she hurried inside the building and locked the door behind her. There was the vague sensation that someone followed her. She racked it up to bad nerves and paranoia. If anybody had justification for feeling any of those things, it was her.

She found the marine manuals on Sean's desk. The notations inside were both cursory and personal, not anything of significance to anyone except the author. Sean was no literary stylist, but he had an eye for detail. As Elizabeth read Sean's brief notations about a curious sea gull or the changing colors of the waters, she fought back tears. At last she found it. On the day that Brian had been gunned down, Sean had been on the *Sea Escape*. He marked his location a half mile south, southwest of Mirage Island. He noted the passage of Larry Steele, several bikini tops tied to the stainless steel railing on the front of his speedboat and flying impudently in the breeze as he headed out to the gulf. Sean also noted two strange ships anchored off the shore of Mirage. There was nothing else, just a brief mention. Two boats anchored off an island in the middle of a crisp November afternoon.

What else had Sean seen to bring this terrible disaster down on his head? And poor Larry Steele. He'd been out hunting nubile young winter beach bunnies and found his own death.

Elizabeth closed the book. Her evidence wasn't solid, but now at least she had some defense for Sean. She couldn't take it to McMillan. All trust in the agent was gone. He'd do whatever he could to make Sean guilty. Right or wrong, Elizabeth believed he was involved in the smuggling.

All of the pieces fell into place. McMillan had been bought off by the smugglers. They were bringing the Uzis into the States at Gulf Shores because it was such a small town. There were no federal agents, no real interference, especially not in the winter when the tourists left and the town shrank to less than ten thousand permanent residents.

There were empty harbors, boats and condos all over the coastline, and discreet smugglers could bring in anything they wanted. That was it! The boats had been meeting off Mirage Island, using the island as a visual block so that no one on the mainland would see the cargo being exchanged. They were transferring it from one boat to another so that known boats could return to harbor. That would arouse the least suspicions. The smugglers were using stolen boats to make the runs, but they weren't docking them. That was far too dangerous. They'd have to transfer the guns and then scuttle the stolen boats. And the guns were probably coming in from Miami. Not some foreign place, but some U.S. city overflowing with crime—and cops.

That's what had happened to Larry Steele. They'd taken his boat, killed him and thrown him overboard for the sharks to enjoy. Then they'd sunk his boat and pretended it was all part of Tropical Storm Marie. And it had almost worked. Because McMillan was in a position to make everyone believe it.

Elizabeth clutched the journal tightly in her fingers. Now what was she going to do with everything she'd learned? Who could she tell? Carl Williams!

Edging sideways, she went to the phone. It was broad daylight outside, and she was acting like someone was trying to kill her. But she felt so vulnerable. Now that she understood about McMillan, she knew she was a sitting duck. She picked up the phone. Instead of a dial tone, there was silence. Rattling the switchhook, she tried again. Nothing.

It wasn't a matter of a line down or the fact that someone had cut the power because of Sean's disappearance. Neither was true. In a small town like Gulf Shores, power and phone outages were big news. She would have heard if there'd been trouble with the lines. And she'd personally paid the utility bills for Sean.

Someone had cut the line to the building. And it could have happened days ago—or moments before.

Elizabeth replaced the phone and froze. Someone was at the back door. They were inserting a key into the lock. Who else but McMillan would have a key to her brother's office?

Chapter Seventeen

The Trooper was angled into the most secluded place in the parking lot of Sean's real estate office when Michael finally caught sight of it. He and Carmalita had been driving around futilely looking for the vehicle and its owner. In a town as small as Gulf Shores, he was becoming frantic with worry. But there she was, digging away at any slim hope of proving Sean's innocence.

Slowing twenty yards from the office, he looked at the woman beside him. "If you try to get out of this car, I won't hesitate to shoot you." He never looked away from Carmalita's frightened gaze. Barely touching the gas, he pulled up to the front of the building and got out. He pointed the gun through the car window at the silent woman to let her know he meant business. Where had he gotten so tough? And could he shoot a woman? The answer was no, but he sounded like he meant it, and maybe that would be enough.

He tapped on the locked door of the real estate office while keeping his gaze on Carmalita.

There was a startled scream from within, and he put his shoulder to the door, slamming into it with the intention of breaking it down.

"Elizabeth!" he called in between battering the door. All thoughts of Carmalita vanished from his mind.

"Michael!" The relief was audible, and he heard the lock turn. In a moment the door swung open and she tumbled out into his arms.

"There's someone at the back door. He has a key. The phone is dead." Elizabeth spoke in staccato rushes. She clung to him, her body shaking.

"Who?" Michael gripped the gun he held at his side.

"I didn't look." She noticed the gun and looked back over her shoulder. "I could only think to escape."

"I'll go around and check the back."

"No!" She grabbed him tightly. "There could be more than one. They could have Uzis. They'd cut you to pieces."

He didn't want to admit it, but she was right. The sound of running footsteps made them both swing around to look.

"Who—" Elizabeth didn't get to finish.

"Hey! Carmalita!" Michael started to run after her. She was flying along the rocky side of the road. He'd never seen a woman run so fast. "Carmalita!" He started to go after her, then realized that he would have to leave Elizabeth alone. For an instant he was undecided, then he admitted to himself that Carmalita had told him everything she was going to tell. He let her go.

He turned his attention back to Elizabeth. Someone had been trying to break into the office while she was alone there. Was it McMillan, her brother, or one of the Miami gun smugglers? "I'll check the back." He didn't give her time to argue.

He eased around the corner of the building. The office was not part of a complex. It occupied a half acre that Sean had landscaped with sea oats, pines and scrub palm. There were only a few places where someone could hide, but he was extra careful. Automatic weapons didn't require a great deal of skilled marksmanship, and from what he'd learned about the people after Elizabeth, they didn't spare the ammunition.

He heard no sounds as he maneuvered around the building. When he made it to the back, he saw more sand, more pines, and no sign of a human being. Whoever had been there had been frightened away. There wasn't any indication that a car had been parked nearby.

After another quick look, he went back to Elizabeth. She was hugging her arms around herself and waiting beside her Trooper.

"Nothing," he said.

"Who was the woman?" She looked down the road where Carmalita had disappeared.

"Long story. Let's get out of here."

"I've found something that may really be helpful, at least in proving Sean's innocence." Elizabeth walked away from the Trooper and got in the passenger seat of Michael's car. She was eager to tell him what she'd found regarding Mirage Island. He didn't believe that Sean was an innocent victim. No one did, except her and her mother. Maybe this would wake everyone up.

Instead of getting in the car, Michael lingered outside her open door, looking down the road again. "Is there a place where we can rent some scuba gear, a telescope? And maybe some specialized equipment?"

"Sure." She felt a flare of excitement. "Why?"

"We're going to do a little surveillance work tonight. At the island. I believe we may be able to figure out what's going on if we can find out for sure what those boats have been doing off Mirage."

"That's exactly the same conclusion I came to!" Elizabeth got out of the car and hugged him.

"We have to be very discreet. We can't let McMillan or any other of the agents know what we intend to do. I don't trust that man, and therefore I don't trust anyone associated with him."

"And we shouldn't, from what I've been able to piece together."

Michael's plan had not been fully formed when he mentioned the scuba gear to Elizabeth. It struck him that she intended to make the dive with him, to be exactly where he was. And the truth of the matter was, the way he had it figured, she was as safe, or safer, with him than anywhere else.

Except that he could easily lead her into the hands of the very men who wanted to kill her.

"This could be pretty dangerous." He glanced at her to see how she would react.

"I know. For both of us."

She wasn't going to let him go alone. It was pointless to even argue. "Let's go rent some equipment. Can we get a boat? I don't want to take the skiff. I want to make it look like we're both on the island, having a late dinner, shutting out the rest of the world."

"Good idea." If only that was their real agenda. Elizabeth wanted nothing more than to have dinner, alone on Mirage, with Michael. Nothing more except to have her brother home, safe and sound. And the two goals seemed diametrically opposed.

"If anyone figures out what we're up to, we could be in big trouble."

"No one will know. The guy who will rent us the boat is a lifelong friend. And it just so happens that Sean and I have our own diving gear. We simply have to get the tanks ready."

"That could be a problem." Michael didn't want any loose ends.

"It could be, except the couple who run the scuba shop went to high school with Sean. They'd do anything I asked, without question. They'll prepare the tanks and deliver them, along with the special things you need, to the boat rental. Johnny will load them on board, and all we have to do is show up, undetected."

"It sounds easy enough." Why did he have such a feeling of foreboding? The more they talked about the plan, the more he felt it was a bad idea. Even though everything was working out perfectly, he realized they were stepping into grave danger.

"Let's go. Sean's tank and mine are at my mother's. We can pull into the garage and load up without anyone seeing a thing." She shut the door to the Jaguar. "But let's take the Trooper. It's a little more practical for what we have in mind tonight."

"Elizabeth . . ." He was ready to cancel the whole thing.

"Yes?" She turned back, her face alight with anticipation. "Is something wrong?"

"Probably not," he said, walking after her. "It's probably just my imagination."

A FIGURE DRESSED in dark clothes flattened itself to the roof of the real estate building as Michael and Elizabeth passed not five feet below him. One dark eye followed their movements to the Trooper.

"Wrong, my good doctor. It isn't just your imagination. But there's nothing wrong in your life now compared to what's going to be wrong later," he whispered to himself as he pressed his body to the roof.

His hands, curled into painful claws by the skin that had been burned and then pulled taut, gripped the edge of the roofline while his toes dug in behind him and held him steady. He'd been almost ready to smash the back door and grab Elizabeth—until he'd heard Michael stop the roar of the Jaguar in front.

He'd watched, furious but unable to do anything, as Carmalita had run barefoot down the road. She was another loose end he was going to enjoy tying into a knot. He wasn't certain how much she knew about his involvement with Diablo, but she was easily neutralized and perfectly expendable. That thought gave him a great sense of control.

If everyone would simply stay out of his way, he'd be able to get what he needed and leave. If people got hurt, it was their own fault. Take Elizabeth, for instance. He had no wish to really hurt her, but she was so uncooperative. Even when she pretended she wanted to help, it was only a game. Like the other night on the island. He'd given that a lot of thought. She'd never really intended to help him. It was a trap, and she'd been the willing bait.

Now, she was going to help. Like it or not, she'd messed up his plan and now she was going to have to fix it.

She was amazingly beautiful. Funny how he'd never noticed that before. Hell, they were all a good-looking family. If he could only get his face fixed, then he'd be handsome again, too. And maybe he could get everything back—and more. And with all of that, he'd have the money he'd stashed. Money that he'd risked his life to have, thank you very much. No one had ever given him a damned thing.

The past was something he couldn't worry about now, though. He had to keep his mind on the problems of the present. Like, who was trying to kill him. He knew all of them. He'd seen them before, working the boats. Trouble was, they knew him, too. It wasn't enough that Diablo had sent Santiago to nail him. Now there was some evidence that Diablo himself was in Gulf Shores. Yes, there'd definitely been the smell of sulfur in the air.

The very thought made him nervous. Diablo wasn't someone to play with. He'd known that from the beginning. All along, Diablo had intended to use his skill with boats and people and then kill him. That was how Diablo worked. And since his plan had backfired, the devil wanted his money—and his revenge.

Pain like a forked bolt of lightning struck behind both eyes. It was hard to think sometimes. His head ached all the time, but there were moments when it was worse. So much worse that he felt as if his skull might pop open.

Oblivious to everything except the sudden, blinding pain that almost paralyzed him, the man clung to the roof. Fragments of conversation drifted up to him. Mirage Island. Scuba gear. Mother's garage.

He heard them but couldn't think about what they meant. All of his concentration was focused on surviving the pain. It was getting worse. He couldn't deny it any longer. He had to get that doctor, and he had to get him soon.

Below him, Elizabeth and Michael got into the Trooper and drove away.

The man's clawed hands curled even tighter. He slid down the back incline of the roof and dropped clumsily to the ground. For the first step or two, he seemed unstable but righted himself and hurried to the back door. From his pocket he withdrew a key and slipped it into the lock. A moment more, and he was inside the office.

He looked around. The pain was much better. He could think again, and if he wanted to stay alive, he had to be able to think. The office contained everything he needed. Water, a bathroom, food. He went to the refrigerator and checked to be certain no one had taken the food he'd worked so hard to steal. The sandwich slices and bread were still there. It was a good thing Elizabeth hadn't checked the refrigerator or she'd have noticed that someone had been putting fresh supplies inside. Then she would have known where he was hiding.

Now he had to get busy. If Elizabeth was going to take scuba supplies from the garage, then he was going to have to find his own tanks and equipment, and that wasn't going to be as easy as stealing ham slices and bread.

ELIZABETH TESTED the tanks and nodded to Michael. Everything was set. Without another word, they slipped the boat out of its berth and moved very slowly toward open water.

Somehow the moon had conspired with them. The night was pitch black. Much more dangerous in some regards, and so much safer in others. It was the kind of night that Elizabeth hated. It was as if the entire world was closed off from the universe. As if a dark hand had wiped across the sky, blotting out the light for some evil purpose.

Michael had taken the wheel, so she settled into the passenger seat as he made his way south, away from the shore and toward the island. His lean body was barely an outline as he stood at the wheel, watching for any other ship foolish enough to run at night without some kind of light. That was another of the many luxuries they couldn't afford—light.

The wind was bitter cold. Elizabeth knew it was because she was afraid, and worried for her brother, and for Michael. She had so much to lose this night. So very much. What if Michael was injured or killed? Would she ever be able to forgive herself for bringing him into this?

Michael notched up the speed as they left the coastline behind and headed for open water. Elizabeth couldn't see the spray cast up by the boat. It was too dark even for that.

When they were parallel with the western coastline of the island, Elizabeth touched his leg. The wet suit was odd-feeling, and she missed the touch of his skin. She was surprised at how important such a little thing could be. Michael brought the boat to a slower speed, gradually notching down until he cut the engine and let her drift.

From the waterproof case on the floor of the boat, Elizabeth retrieved the binoculars. She scanned the horizon, but the dark night kept all of its secrets. Nothing showed.

"Infrared?" Michael whispered.

She nodded, then remembered he might not be able to see her, even as close as they were. She handed the binoculars to him.

He looked for at least forty-five seconds, long seconds to Elizabeth, before she heard him draw in his breath. "There she is. A big pleasure boat, very nice."

"What's she doing?" Elizabeth asked under her breath. Sound carried so easily on the water.

"She's just sitting. Bobbing along, like we are. I don't see any activity at all from here."

Elizabeth's heartbeat accelerated. It was time now. They were going to slip into the water and swim over to the boat. With any luck, they'd be able to surface and listen to the conversations of the deckhands. That might tell them a lot, especially if another ship were to also come along. A ship with a cargo to unload or load.

"How is the boat riding?" she asked suddenly.

"Very low." Michael knew what she was getting at. Did the boat look loaded or empty?

"She may already be loaded." Elizabeth felt panic. "Maybe we should hurry."

"No." Michael was adamant. This entire business was filled with risk, and he wasn't going to compound the odds against them by getting into a hurry. He wanted to watch the boat and make certain it was as safe as possible.

Elizabeth slipped into the heavy tanks, making as little noise as she could. When it was time, she didn't want to waste another second. She calculated the minutes it would take to swim to the other vessel. Maybe fifteen minutes. The plan was for them to surface just at the hull and cling to the side of the boat. The men aboard, unless they were sleeping, would talk. They'd do their best to figure out how many men were aboard and what the cargo was.

Michael kept the glasses trained on the ship. It was awfully quiet. Almost too quiet. The feeling of doom prickled along his neck once again. Was it possible someone knew they were coming and the ship was a setup? It didn't *seem* possible, but then, none of the things that had happened in the past few days could really have happened. Could they?

He slipped a glance at Elizabeth. She was waiting, almost beside herself with eagerness to begin. She was such a beautiful woman, in every way. She couldn't conceive of the danger they faced. In her life, in her world, people weren't capable of horrible cruelty, because she wasn't capable of it herself. But he knew better. And it was his responsibility to take care of her.

"Elizabeth, I want you to stay right with me. Even if you think I'm going in the wrong direction, you stay with me. Promise?"

She nodded, then softly said yes. She knew he spoke out of love and concern. She didn't bother to mention that she had more training and hours under the water than he could ever dream of, but it didn't matter. She'd stay beside him.

"Let's go." Waiting wouldn't solve anything. Michael hefted his tanks, adjusted his equipment and together they eased over the side and into the water.

They stayed close to the surface. They needed to be only deep enough so that a guard on the boat wouldn't see their approach. Looking behind him, Michael saw the flash of Elizabeth's dark-suited body and the reassuring rise of the air bubble. It would be very easy to lose each other in the water. Even though they were only twenty feet below the surface, the darkness of the night gave no visibility.

They cut through the black waters, drawing closer and closer to the boat. Michael found the anchor line and waited there for Elizabeth to look at him. He gave her a signal saying he was going up to check the name of the ship. They'd discussed the plan at great length, and she understood. She was to wait at the line.

Michael circled the boat and then worked his way to the surface. He eased in as close to the hull as he could, breaking the surface with what sounded like a roar to him. He lifted his mask and listened. There was the soft lull of conversation toward the bow. He couldn't make out the words distinctly, and then he realized the language was Spanish. Easing along the hull, he found the name. *Liberty Lady.* She was a beautiful ship, and he had a pang of regret for the people who had owned her. They were undoubtedly floating somewhere in the gulf, very dead.

He listened to the conversation, trying to adjust the language to the dialect he heard often in California. The Spanish of Miami had a different flavor, different pronunciation. It was subtle, but enough to throw up a roadblock for someone who wasn't fluent. Given a few moments, though, he'd adjust to it.

The word "Uzis" was clear enough. Mirage, Diablo and *veinte-cuatro.* The twenty-fourth—of November. Thanksgiving. He might not be able to understand everything, but he caught the drift of that. Delivery date for the cargo was only three days away.

His logical mind balked. Three days? Did the boat intend to sit off the island for three days? That didn't make any sense.

His first warning was the soft rattle of wood against wood. Not even waiting to draw on his mask, he slid beneath the water. Only a few feet from where he'd been clinging to the side of the ship, he saw the outline of a much smaller boat. A skiff that someone was rowing. His heart began to beat rapidly. Some lucky hand of fate had touched them—they'd made it just in time for the delivery. He had to get Elizabeth. If they shifted to the opposite side of the boat, they might be able to hear something crucial, and the crew would probably be so busy they wouldn't think of looking on the port side.

He surfaced on the port side of the boat only long enough to adjust his mask. Moving very carefully, he followed the anchor line back to the place where Elizabeth was waiting.

In the dark it was difficult to tell, but it seemed he was going much deeper than where he'd left her. Foreboding that had been a mere warning earlier slammed into him, almost as physical as a blow. He forced himself to remain calm. Panic would accomplish nothing except using up all of his air. Elizabeth was there. She couldn't just vanish into the water. She'd moved or shifted or gone back to the boat for some good reason or...

Or someone else had been lurking in the water, waiting to snatch her.

Michael followed the anchor line to the bottom. Elizabeth was nowhere around it. In the deep water, he lifted the flashlight at his waist. The beam wouldn't go far, but he blinked it, moving his body in a complete circle. If she was in the water, maybe she'd see the light and come to it. They'd agreed on the prearranged signal, and she carried her own light. He looked for an answering blink. Nothing.

Moving back up the line, he circled the boat, hoping against hope that she'd decided to go up on her own. Nothing. A strange noise vibrated through the water, and as he watched, the boat's anchor began to ascend. They were leaving. And there was still no sign of Elizabeth.

Chapter Eighteen

Elizabeth stared at the man in the flickering light of the candle. As frightening as her surroundings were, the man who refused to show her his face was even more terrifying. In the poor light, she saw nothing about him that even faintly resembled Sean Campbell. Not a trace of her brother lingered in the man's stance, attitude . . . or his touch.

He'd come upon her from behind in the water and nearly choked her. He'd cut the hose on her regulator, effectively leaving her without air. Only when she'd given up all resistance to him had he allowed her to breathe from his air supply. Whenever she attempted to break free of him, he held her until she was suffocating—and effectively subdued her. Sharing his tank of air, he'd brought her to this place, an underground cave where long, well-secured crates were stacked. She didn't have to make too many guesses to figure out that the crates contained weapons, especially since some of them were stamped with the words U.S. Government.

His voice was unexpected in the thick silence of the cave. "There's no escape, Elizabeth. Not without oxygen tanks."

As terrified as she was, she tried to find something of her brother in the voice. Michael had said Sean might be terribly injured, unbalanced. But totally different? Was that possible? She didn't know.

"Sean, I can help you." She spoke gently, trying to keep the emotion out of her voice. "I want to help you."

"You have no choice. You will help. The good doctor will help, too, if he wants to see you alive again."

He turned to face her fully and Elizabeth had to bite her lip to conceal the shock. He was badly burned. "Michael would help you without threats. He's a doctor."

"So were the other two. But they didn't want to help." The man turned away. "There's enough air here, for a while. The real danger, though, is the guns. Diablo will send his men for them. November twenty-fourth, I believe. Maybe the day before. That doesn't give your friend long to set to work. If he doesn't, no one but Diablo will ever find you. And if you haven't suffocated, then he'll kill you."

Before Elizabeth could respond, the man picked up his diving gear, and hers, and waded into the water that lapped at the hole where they'd surfaced. In seconds, he disappeared.

Elizabeth reached for the candle. Fire consumed oxygen, but she didn't want to be in the dark. Especially when she had no way to relight the candle. Taking it in hand, she started to explore the cave. There had to be another way out. There had to be.

MICHAEL PACED the kitchen of the old house on Mirage Island as he tried to think of a plan. Elizabeth had vanished, as if she'd never been. There wasn't a trace of her that he could find. He knew she'd never abandon him, or the search for her brother, voluntarily. She'd been taken.

By whom? And more importantly, had they hurt her? The very thought was like a sharp needle stabbing into his brain.

Ever since her disappearance, Michael had been distraught. On the off chance that somehow she'd managed to swim to Mirage, he'd come hunting her. But she wasn't on the island.

As a last resort, Michael started toward the telephone. He had to call help. Carl Williams would be able to get the coast guard. They had helicopters. They'd be able to track the *Liberty Lady* and get Elizabeth back.

He heard the sound of a motor through the open window. Someone was speeding around the western coast of the island. As he listened, he heard the boat slow. It was moving into the little harbor.

Michael started walking, hoping against hope it might somehow be Elizabeth. At the dock he saw the lone figure and knew it wasn't the woman he loved. It was a man, also dressed in diving gear. Before he could really see, Michael knew who it was. Sean Campbell. He waited, telling himself that Sean would not hurt his sister. No matter how desperate he was, he wouldn't hurt Elizabeth. But Michael didn't believe it.

"Raybin?" the man called from the boat.

The voice was familiar, but much stronger. "Right. Where's Elizabeth?"

"She's in a place with limited oxygen and a short time to live. Will you help me?"

Michael hesitated. What should he say? The man hadn't gotten off the boat yet. He could still leave. "What is it you want?"

"My face back. You can do that."

"It'll take months of surgery. Months. This isn't some minor repair."

"Will you do it?" The man paused, his hand on the throttle. "Elizabeth is safe, but I'm not kidding. She's underwater, in a place with a lot of guns. It's just a question of whether the air runs out first or the men go back for the guns. Either way, she'll die."

"She's your sister." Michael couldn't believe it. "She's done everything to prove your innocence. Even with everyone against you, she still believed in you. What kind of monster are you?"

"A very rich one." He chuckled. "Elizabeth is such a beautiful woman, isn't she? It would be a shame."

"How do you know I won't kill you instead of helping you?"

"The way I figure it, Elizabeth has about thirty-six solid hours, give or take another twenty-four. If I'm not well enough to get her or bring oxygen to her, she's dead. You can't afford to hurt me." He motioned Michael over to the boat. "So quit stalling. Let's drive into Mobile. Your good friend Dr. Van Hugh has an excellent facility, and I understand it's badly underutilized at this time." He laughed. "Pompous fool wouldn't help me, but I guess I showed him."

Michael turned back toward the house, his head thumping with possibilities. What it all boiled down to was that he was at an impasse. He couldn't do anything without risking Elizabeth, but he couldn't allow Sean to see how weak he really was.

"Hey!"

Michael turned around.

"Get in the boat or kiss Elizabeth goodbye."

Michael wanted to pull the gun out of the waistband of his jeans and kill the man who stood before him. He'd always known that in certain circumstances any human could be provoked to violence. He was ready to kill—except it would jeopardize Elizabeth.

Climbing into the boat was one of the hardest things he'd ever done. Ten minutes later he looked back to see Mirage Island, a dark hulk against a soft black sky.

It took Michael nearly an hour to thoroughly examine his patient. The burns were cosmetically tragic, but Sean Campbell was luckier than he'd ever know. He could be repaired, over time and with a skilled surgeon. His eye might even be mostly restored.

"Quit wasting time. Give me the shot and get on with it."

"You need general anesthesia, and I need a nurse, some assistance. This is delicate and fragile surgery."

"Scrub up and quit whining." He pulled the picture from Elizabeth's annual out of his pocket. "No nurse and no general. Use a local. I went to a lot of trouble to steal this photo, so use it."

"Sean, you can't just pick up your life here and pretend nothing has happened. Sandra is . . ."

"Dead. That's right, and the girls are happier with Aleshia. I don't intend to stay here, but I can't leave looking like this. I'm a monster, a freak, something that people are afraid of."

Against all odds, Michael felt his heart twist. Sean was pitiful, a man who frightened others because he'd been in an accident. Maybe...

"I'll repair your face, but you have to let Elizabeth go first."

"You don't have any bargaining chips, doc. It's my way or none at all, so start carving."

Michael led him to the surgery. He cleaned Sean's face and studied the wounds once more.

"Just remember, Elizabeth's life is in your hands."

Michael nodded and withdrew a syringe. "This won't knock you out, but it will relax you. If you jump, I won't be able to do any work." He put the needle in the left vein and slowly released the medicine.

It took only a few moments for the drug to work. "Hey!" The clawlike hands grabbed Michael's shirt. "You said..." He was under.

Michael looked through the supplies until he found restraining straps. In less than five minutes he had his patient thoroughly rigged so that he couldn't move. "Good night, Sean." He hurried to the car and headed for the island. Elizabeth had to be there, somewhere close by.

He reviewed the decision he'd made. Any man who'd use his sister's life as a bartering chip wasn't the kind of man he'd trust to keep his word. If Elizabeth was going to have a chance, it was up to him to find her.

Mirage Island was the logical place to begin. He'd figured out that Sean had nabbed Elizabeth underwater and dragged her somewhere. He didn't have time to go far, so it had to be around the island. But the shoreline was flat, and there weren't any caves. He'd walked every inch of the place, and Elizabeth knew it by heart. If there'd been a hiding place, she would have been investigating it long before.

Spinning gravel, he turned into the side yard and dashed into the house. He went straight to the den.

The ancient mariner's map might hold an answer. All along he'd been looking at it, hanging on the wall. It had intrigued him, but he'd never understood it, and in all the times he'd meant to ask Elizabeth, he'd forgotten.

He took it down. In the bright light of the kitchen, he examined it. The outline of the island was clear and true as far as he could tell. But there were strange words and markings. He'd assumed the language was Latin, but upon closer examination, he discovered it was not. It seemed nonsensical to him.

Anxiety hit him like a hammer. He'd risked Elizabeth's life because he thought he might be able to interpret these markings. And he couldn't.

He held the map, staring at it. There had to be a way. There had to be. He thought of Guy Fallon. If anyone could help, it would be the feisty newspaper editor.

He picked up the phone. It was close to 5:00 a.m., but he knew Guy wouldn't mind. Especially not if Elizabeth's safety was hanging in the balance.

Guy answered groggily, but it took only the mention of Elizabeth's name to get his full attention. Michael explained the map and heard Guy's low whistle.

"That's a smuggler's map," Guy said. "I didn't realize there were any left, but back in the days when the house was owned by a smuggler, there were rumors about that cave. Since the island has been private property, no one's really been allowed to explore it, but it's possible."

"If there is a cave, and it's on this map, I can't manage to read it. The language isn't Latin or Spanish. I don't know what it is."

"The smugglers had their own code for the island." Guy paused. "It wasn't difficult, as I recall."

"You've heard it?" Hope almost made Michael shout.

"It's part of the history here. Elizabeth knows it . . . and Sean. And Aleshia! Call her."

"Guy, another favor. There's a man tied up at Steve Van Hugh's office in Mobile. Call the police to get him." Michael didn't wait to say goodbye. He called the hotel and waited until he heard Mrs. Campbell's voice. Somehow Michael managed to sound sane while he talked. He didn't want to tell Aleshia the truth about Elizabeth or Sean until he had to. But he was scribbling furiously as she explained that it wasn't a code, not really, but a method of counting. The letters N, S, W and E represented directions, and the number of letters in between signified the number of feet or fathoms or whatever measure they'd used.

"Whatever measure?" Michael hoped he'd heard wrong.

"I can't remember whether it was nautical or regular."

Michael stared at the map. Maybe it wouldn't be too difficult to figure out.

"Where's Elizabeth?" Aleshia asked. "I thought she was with you. She knows about the map."

"Ah, she's ... I've got to go. We'll call when we finish." He hung up before he had to lie to her. Using a ruler as a guide, he worked the map in meters and then yards. The second time around, he found himself looking at an area about a hundred yards off the coastline. It was very close to the place where the *Liberty Lady* had been anchored.

"That's it," he said, slapping the map on the table. He pulled on his wet suit, grabbed his tank and headed for the boat. He couldn't think about Elizabeth. He couldn't allow room for doubt.

It was still night, but dawn wasn't far away when he eased up on the spot where Elizabeth had disappeared. In the darkness he saw the shift of another large object. The *Liberty Lady* was back! Anchored where she'd been before and silently riding the waves. "Damn!" The boat was another complication now that he believed Elizabeth was not on board. He swept the ship with the infrared binoculars—still no movement. Very strange. They were obviously loaded, so why hadn't they left?

His question was answered when a coast guard cutter slipped up beside the boat. Several packages were trans-

ferred from the cutter to the boat before the government
ship slowly arced and went back the way it had come. The
entire incident had happened in less than five minutes.

"Great," Michael said. "Now I've got to watch out for
the coast guard. I wonder if anyone in this operation isn't
on the federal payroll."

He didn't wait for an answer. Every minute he delayed,
Elizabeth was closer to death. His air tank was half full.
Enough, he hoped, for himself and Elizabeth. It would all
depend on how long it took him to find her.

He didn't notice the shock of the water or anything else
as he made the swim to the point he believed was indicated
on the map. The water slid around him, not the beautiful
azure of the day but a dark purple, difficult to see through.
Below him lay the gently rolling floor of the ocean. Plants
and sea creatures wavered and floated in his line of vision,
but he ignored them. Elizabeth was the only creature he
cared about finding.

His calculations on the map had been ballpark at best, so
he searched the gulf up to the coastline of the island and
then back out in a spiraling pattern. With each sweep, he
moved further east. Beneath the water it was impossible to
tell exactly where he was.

It didn't seem possible that there was any type of cave.
Not on Mirage. The island was a sand spit, too flat to support a cave. He fought back the impulse to give up and
continued swimming.

He was about to turn back when he spotted the piece of
wood stuck in the sand. It was the way the wood jutted, as
if some hand had forced it into the floor of the ocean. He
swung his light around and looked closer. A tiny hope
throbbed back to life. It was the same kind of wood used to
kill Tommy. Teak. He picked it up and dropped it. What
was it doing in this particular place? Using his hands, he felt
along the bottom. Sand filtered between his fingers, leaving his hands empty.

He swam onto a ridge and swung the light along its surface. An unusual clump of weed caught his attention, and

when he touched it he knew it wasn't real. In a moment he had the dark entrance to a crevice exposed, and he knew that if Elizabeth was alive, he would soon be with her.

The crevice fed into a tunnel that seemed to run just beneath the surface. At the end, it was blocked by a steel door. Michael worked the door lever, finally opening it. When he was inside, he closed it carefully behind him. He found himself in a narrow chamber that ascended. Pointing the light up, he let his body rise.

When his head broke the surface, he saw only blackness and he heard a loud sound. A large piece of crate struck him on the shoulder, and he dodged instinctively back under the water. He surfaced again. "Elizabeth!" He didn't have time to really see her, but he knew it was Elizabeth—a fighter to the end.

"Michael!" He heard the clatter of wood, and then he felt hands drawing him to the floor of what appeared to be a cave. He crawled up on dry land and took Elizabeth into his arms. "You're safe," he said.

"Sean is completely insane," Elizabeth managed to say. Now that she was with Michael, her fear subsided and sorrow flooded through her. "He's like a different person. Totally different."

Michael didn't want to argue with her—not with a boatload of men anchored not so very far above them. As soon as dawn arrived, his boat would be visible and the crew members on the *Liberty Lady* might be more than a little curious about where he'd gone. "Let's get out of here."

"That man can't be Sean," Elizabeth said, suddenly aware that she was crying.

Michael swung the flashlight around the room. The teak crates were empty, and the others bore the stamp of U.S. government. "They're stealing our guns and repackaging them in teak. That way they don't even raise an eyebrow when they go into whatever country they're destined for."

Elizabeth followed Michael's gaze. So that's what it was all about. Guns. Sandra, Tommy, Van Hugh, two young boys and who knew how many other people were dead over guns. If she had her way, she'd blow up the entire stash.

"This place is man-made. It's like an underwater bubble," Michael said, swinging the light around with wonder. "It must date back to the smugglers. They must have stored booze or something here, hiding it out until they could safely bring it into the country. There must be some pipe to the surface for air."

"How did you find me?"

"The map, that old antique thing on the wall. I also had a little help from Guy and Aleshia. Now let's go."

He didn't wait for an argument but took her hands and stepped into the water. They'd have to share his air, and it would be tricky, but he knew they could do it.

Out in the gulf once again, they saw that the water was beginning to brighten. Day was dawning. Michael urged Elizabeth to swim faster. They had to get to their boat, and fast.

They broke the surface at the stern of the boat. Michael clambered aboard, then helped Elizabeth. It wasn't until he turned around that he saw the man sitting in the captain's seat.

"Dr. Raybin," the man said, his voice lightly accented. "I've heard so much about you and your lovely friend, Elizabeth Campbell." He stood. "My friends, and my enemies, I fear, call me Diablo."

Michael put his arm around Elizabeth. There was nothing they could say or do except stare at the immaculately attired man. His dark hair gleamed, and the cut of his suit, even while he sat, was flawless.

"I'm afraid that you two have been too...intrusive. It's all very well to love one's family, Ms. Campbell, but sometimes it's better to mind your own business. Too bad you couldn't do that."

"My brother is—"

"Be silent, woman. My mind is on a crook." Diablo grinned, and in the pink light of dawn his teeth were beautiful. "A double-crosser." All humor disappeared. "He has my money, and he's going to give it back. His burns are minor compared to the fun I'm going to have with him. Now where is he? I know you've been helping him."

"He kidnapped Elizabeth," Michael said. "We have no reason to help him. I don't know where he is."

"Lying to Diablo is not a good practice." He pulled a knife from the left pocket of his jacket and whipped it open with a snap. "My men are on the ship over there, watching everything that happens. You, Dr. Raybin, are a plastic surgeon. Perhaps you could repair the damage I intend to do to Ms. Campbell's face. Perhaps not. How skilled are you?"

Michael's arm tightened around Elizabeth. "You're going to kill us, anyway. We don't have anything to tell you."

The sound of a motor in the distance made Michael look up. Elizabeth, too, picked out the direction and soon spotted a cutter headed their way. A big cutter. Possibly coast guard. She turned to Michael. His answer was a shake of his head.

"So, you know about our friend, Agent McMillan. He has been extremely useful to us." Diablo smiled. "He has contacts in many of your government's agencies."

Elizabeth felt all hope of rescue die when she saw the tall, thin outline of the ATF agent aboard the coast-guard cutter as it pulled up. She felt Michael's arm tighten, a gesture of support.

"McMillan's been selling weapons to this gentleman," he said. "I'm sure for some peace-keeping measure."

Diablo laughed. "You are very amusing, for a doctor. And very skilled. I know some of the actresses you've...helped. They're going to miss you."

The coast-guard cutter pulled up beside the small boat Elizabeth and Michael had rented. Agent McMillan looked at them, then at Diablo, who stood at the bow of the boat. "Get rid of them and let's finish the deal. All of the weapons have been delivered. If you'll step aboard—"

"No deal until the traitor is mine." The first sliver of sun moved over the horizon, and a shaft of light caught Diablo's dark eyes and made them almost glow.

"Forget him. He'll do enough time so that you'll never have to worry about him again," McMillan said.

"It's against my code to forget a betrayal. If word gets out that he is alive, there are others who might get the idea that they can betray Diablo. That is not a message I intend to send."

"Look—" McMillan's voice was angry "—you've got enough guns to sell to the rebels down in that jungle to make fifty million dollars. Your man is at Van Hugh's office. The authorities will take care of him."

"I want him." Diablo's voice was just as angry but far colder.

Michael felt Elizabeth begin to shift her weight. He had no idea what she was planning, but he knew she was going to do something. He put his arm on her to restrain her, but she shook it off.

"Make the deal now, or I'll take my guns somewhere else. Perhaps the enemies of your family would like them." McMillan glared at Diablo.

Elizabeth braced her feet. With one sideways lunge, she pushed Michael backward, throwing her body after him. Together they tumbled over the side of the boat and into the water.

Gunfire sounded all around her as the water closed over her, and she couldn't be certain if the bullets hit or not. The shock of the water almost took her breath, but she felt Michael's arms around her and he gave her the mouthpiece from his tanks. Together they sank deeper into the water.

Checking the gauge, Michael knew they didn't have enough air to stay down for long. He judged the distance to the island to be ten minutes. There wasn't enough air, but they could dump the tanks and swim for it. Diablo and McMillan would be searching for them, but that was their only chance.

Above them, the water churned as both boats cranked up. The rental boat sped away, and for a moment Elizabeth thought the cutter would pursue it. Instead she saw the cutter turn back, slowly circling the area where they'd gone overboard. In another moment a diver dropped into the water.

Elizabeth clung to Michael. They didn't stand a chance of swimming for it, not sharing air between them. She tried to push Michael away from her so that he, at least, could escape, but he wouldn't leave her.

The diver came forward slowly. The first thing Elizabeth noticed was that he was unarmed. He made several hand signals, then motioned them up.

Michael's fingers squeezed into her arms, and they started for the surface. Only seconds after they surfaced, the diver bobbed up. He removed his mask, and to Elizabeth's extreme relief, she saw Carl Williams, the police chief.

"Get in the boat," Williams said. "Hurry!"

Michael held Elizabeth back. "McMillan," he tersely reminded her.

Carl leaned down, giving Elizabeth his hand. "It's okay," he reassured them. "It looks bad. In fact, I was ready to kick his butt all over the coast. But he's not a bad guy."

Elizabeth looked over at the agent. He was standing on the deck, signaling them in.

"He's been trying to trap Diablo," Williams continued. "Someone on the ATF payroll has been arranging gun sales to Diablo. McMillan has been after him, and he had to look like he was on the take, too."

"And Sean?" Elizabeth was still treading water, with Michael behind her.

"We don't have time, Elizabeth. Diablo will be on his way to Van Hugh's clinic. Revenge is what's driving him, and if we're ever going to catch him, it's going to be now."

"Sean is at the clinic." Michael started climbing aboard. "He's a sitting duck. He's tied up in there, unable to even defend himself."

"Let's go." Williams hefted Elizabeth over the side. "I thought we had Diablo for sure. Our men have already gotten on board the *Liberty Lady.* We've disarmed the crew, and we could have taken him from your boat, but it was too risky with the two of you standing right beside him."

As soon as Michael and Elizabeth were on board, the powerful engines of the cutter kicked in. In the distance, the small rental boat piloted by Diablo was making for shore.

VAN HUGH'S OFFICE was empty and forlorn-looking as Elizabeth and Michael, in a car with Williams and Mc-Millan, drove up. There was no sign of Diablo, and police roadblocks hurriedly thrown up at the radioed request of the ATF agent had yielded not so much as a glimpse of him.

"He's tough," McMillan said, "and ruthless. We've got him nailed, and we've picked up the men who were working with him. It's difficult to admit, but one of my agents was involved. That's how he's been able to dodge our dragnet. We've got him this time, though."

"Then you know my brother is innocent," Elizabeth said, leaning up to the grill on the back of the front seat of the patrol car.

"Elizabeth—" Carl spoke softly, but McMillan interrupted.

"Let's get in there and see what's happened."

When Michael and Elizabeth started forward, McMillan balked. "Raybin, we might need another man. Ms. Campbell, you stay in the car."

"I'm going." Elizabeth's eyes glared green.

McMillan got out and motioned Michael to do the same. Before Elizabeth could get out of the patrol car, the doors were closed. She was locked in the back.

"Michael!" she whispered furiously. "Michael!"

"You're safer here, Elizabeth." Michael knew the risk he was running. If anything happened to Sean, he would be as guilty as the two officers. Without time for regret, he surreptitiously opened the door. "Stay back until we're inside," he whispered. "Stay safe."

Elizabeth sank back into the seat, biding her time. Michael had indeed stopped playing God.

Inside the office, Michael took the officers to the surgery where he'd left Sean tied. He could only hope that Diablo hadn't gotten there first. Sean would be a helpless victim, tied and unable to even run. The thought weighed heavily on him.

Motioning Michael back, McMillan pushed open the door. The injured man was lying on the table, just as he'd been left. It took a moment to see the slow chest movement. He was alive. Williams and McMillan moved around Michael, each sliding along a wall, peering behind equipment and into the dimly lighted room.

Michael went to the table. Sean was coming to. The anesthesia he'd administered had been a healthy dose, but it was wearing off.

"Sean—" Michael shook his shoulder "—wake up. We have to get you out of here."

The crack of a gun exploding twice made Michael flinch. Across the room, he saw McMillan crumple to the floor. Williams threw himself behind a cabinet but not before a bullet found his leg. He gave a groan of pain.

"So, we meet again." Diablo edged forward into the room. He'd obviously hidden outside and waited for the agents to openly lead him to his victim. With his gun trained on Michael, he walked forward. "Wake him up," he ordered, his dark eyes taking in the burned man's features without a shred of pity.

"Listen, he's still groggy. There's nothing I can do."

Diablo's gun whipped out, striking Michael in the jaw. Michael felt the blow all the way to his eye sockets, but he didn't fall down. The butt of the gun had opened a cut along his jawline, and blood began to drop on the clean sheets that covered Sean.

"Wake him up. He's going with me."

"No." Michael met Diablo's gaze. "I don't care what he did, I won't send him off with you. Kill us all now."

"You're such a fool." Diablo was angry, but it was an anger that froze rather than burned. He was not a man who allowed rampant emotion to govern him. He was controlled. "This man is not Sean Campbell. Campbell is dead. Long dead. This man is one of my employees. A very bad employee. He thought he could trick me by stealing Sean Campbell's face and life, and he almost succeeded.''

Diablo's eyes widened suddenly. A look of disbelief touched his face, then disappeared beneath his tight control.

"Drop the gun, Diablo." Elizabeth stepped out from behind the smuggler and gave Michael a crooked smile. "I did wait—until I saw Diablo follow you inside."

Michael couldn't believe it was Elizabeth. The slim outline of her body was almost hidden by the smuggler, but he could see she was pressing something into Diablo's back. A gun? No, it was a surgical probe! A completely useless weapon.

The smuggler lunged sideways, but Michael was too quick. He brought his fist down on the back of the smuggler's neck, smashing him into the floor. Diablo's gun skittered across the tile.

"I've got it." Williams picked up the gun and hobbled over. Blood soaked his pant leg. He leaned down and put the weapon on Diablo's temple. "What about McMillan?" he asked, nodding toward the agent who was on the floor, blood seeping from a wound in his torso.

Michael drew Elizabeth away from Diablo before he went to the agent and worked to stanch the flow of blood. "It's a chest wound. Elizabeth, call an ambulance." He spoke with urgency but complete control.

"He said it wasn't Sean." Elizabeth was still staring at the man on the table. "Sean . . ." She eased forward. "Sean?"

On the floor, Diablo had pulled himself to a sitting position. He rubbed the back of his neck and eyed Williams. His gaze strayed to Elizabeth. "Your brother was killed in the beginning. We needed the boat in a hurry, and Larry said it would be perfect."

"Larry?" Elizabeth spoke like a zombie.

"Steele. The man you've worked so hard to protect. He's the murderer of your brother. And your sister-in-law. And the two doctors." Diablo spat out the facts. "He is a very bad man."

"And so are you," Williams said. He nudged Elizabeth toward the door. "Call an ambulance and the mobile P.D. Hurry, Elizabeth. There's no time to waste."

THE SUN DROPPED on the western coast of Mirage Island as Michael and Elizabeth sat huddled together in the sand. An empty champagne bottle rested beside Michael, along with two empty glasses. Elizabeth watched the sunset with a terrible sadness. Michael was going back to California the next day. He'd stayed a week longer than he should have, long enough to help her adjust to the fact that her brother was dead. Long enough to make sure that McMillan would heal properly. Long enough to break her heart.

"You know, I can't help but wonder why Larry Steele wanted Sean's face." Michael pulled Elizabeth back against his chest and held her against the wind that grew chillier by the minute.

"Steele had double-crossed Diablo, and I'm certain Larry Steele thought that if he pretended to be Sean, he might be able to get Diablo off his case. That's what he was planning, and that's why he made it appear that Sean's body was his. Diablo had no quarrel with Sean Campbell. Larry, as Sean, could have returned to Gulf Shores, bided his time and then cut out with the money when he felt it was safe."

"But he could have looked like anyone. Why Sean Campbell?"

"Guy's theory is that it would be easier to start over somewhere if he had a social security number, an identity, all of that. Besides, Sean was due to inherit considerable money. Larry Steele was a greedy man."

Michael tightened his arms around Elizabeth's slim form. She still couldn't say the word murderer. She couldn't label Steele for what he was, a callous killer. But he was behind bars, where he'd stay for a long, long time, along with his close friend, Diablo. Even Carmalita, Igor and the other man were cooling their heels in jail while their roles were being investigated.

"The guns were going to a rebel faction in Panama." Elizabeth couldn't remember if she'd told Michael that tidbit or not. She was having trouble remembering a lot of things. It took all of her concentration not to let him see that her heart had broken wide open.

"I'm going to miss this place," Michael said. "I'm going to miss you."

"Come back in the spring." Elizabeth swallowed. She wanted so much to tell him to come back forever. But since the night when she'd discovered Sean was dead, there had been a hesitancy between them. Their lovemaking was tender and wonderful, but neither talked about the future. They both knew that with the arrest of Steele and Diablo, their reasons for staying together were over. All the reasons except that they were in love.

"I was thinking more along the lines of coming back at Christmas."

Elizabeth turned slightly in his arms and looked at him. Christmas was less than a month away. "Really?" She could hear the excitement in her own voice.

"Well, that's the proper time for formal gift giving, and besides . . ." His eyes were teasing.

"Besides what?"

"That's when I close the deal to purchase Mirage Island."

Elizabeth turned to face him completely. "You bought the island?"

"In deed, no pun intended." He pushed her hair out of her eyes. The wind was blowing stronger and colder, and the light was fading away.

"So you'll visit often?"

"No."

Her hopes dropped.

"I'm moving here. I'll live on the island and open a practice in Fairhope, at the hospital there. It'll be a small practice, and I'll have plenty of time to see some of the children from these parts who can't afford surgery. Tommy would approve, and it's something I've always wanted to do."

"Michael . . ." She didn't know what to say.

"There's only one clause to this." He paused. "You'll have to agree to marry me. I want to spend a lot of time with you, without the pressures of murderers and gun smugglers and people trying their best to kill us."

"Marry?" Elizabeth felt her heart stop.

"Not right away if that's too much pressure. I know you've been through a lot. But at least consider my proposal."

"Yes." She kissed his nose and his chin and his lips.

"Yes, you'll consider my offer?" He couldn't believe the rush of emotion her answer had given him.

"I love you, Michael." Elizabeth touched his warm cheek with the tips of her fingers. "I know my heart, and my answer is yes. I don't need any more time."

"And I love you." He forgot about the cold and the wind as he kissed her.

The night drifted down upon them, and they were together with the sound of the surf.

SPRING fancy '94

They're sexy, single... and about to get snagged!

Passion is in full bloom as love catches the fancy of three brash bachelors. You won't want to miss these stories by three of Silhouette's hottest authors:

CAIT LONDON
DIXIE BROWNING
PEPPER ADAMS

Spring fever is in the air this March— and there's no avoiding it!

Only from

Silhouette®

where passion lives.

Three new stories celebrating
motherhood and love

Birds, Bees and Babies '94

NORA ROBERTS
ANN MAJOR
DALLAS SCHULZE

A collection of three stories, all by
award-winning authors, selected
especially to reflect the love all
families share. Silhouette's fifth annual
romantic tribute to mothers is sure
to touch your heart.

Available in May,
BIRDS, BEES AND BABIES 1994 is a
perfect gift for yourself or a loved one
to celebrate the joy of motherhood.

**Available at your favorite
retail outlet.**

Only from

—where passion lives.

INDULGE A LITTLE 6947 SWEEPSTAKES
NO PURCHASE NECESSARY

HERE'S HOW THE SWEEPSTAKES WORKS:
The Harlequin Reader Service shipments for January, February and March 1994 will contain, respectively, coupons for entry into three prize drawings: a trip for two to San Francisco, an Alaskan cruise for two and a trip for two to Hawaii. To be eligible for any drawing using an Entry Coupon, simply complete and mail according to directions.

There is no obligation to continue as a Reader Service subscriber to enter and be eligible for any prize drawing. You may also enter any drawing by hand printing your name and address on a 3" x 5" card and the destination of the prize you wish that entry to be considered for (i.e., San Francisco trip, Alaskan cruise or Hawaiian trip). Send your 3" x 5" entries to: Indulge a Little 6947 Sweepstakes, c/o Prize Destination you wish that entry to be considered for, P.O. Box 1315, Buffalo, NY 14269-1315, U.S.A. or Indulge a Little 6947 Sweepstakes, P.O. Box 610, Fort Erie, Ontario L2A 5X3, Canada.

To be eligible for the San Francisco trip, entries must be received by 4/30/94; for the Alaskan cruise, 5/31/94; and the Hawaiian trip, 6/30/94. No responsibility is assumed for lost, late or misdirected mail. Sweepstakes open to residents of the U.S. (except Puerto Rico) and Canada, 18 years of age or older. All applicable laws and regulations apply. Sweepstakes void wherever prohibited.

For a copy of the Official Rules, send a self-addressed, stamped envelope (WA residents need not affix return postage) to: Indulge a Little 6947 Rules, P.O. Box 4631, Blair, NE 68009, U.S.A.

INDR93

INDULGE A LITTLE 6947 SWEEPSTAKES
NO PURCHASE NECESSARY

HERE'S HOW THE SWEEPSTAKES WORKS:
The Harlequin Reader Service shipments for January, February and March 1994 will contain, respectively, coupons for entry into three prize drawings: a trip for two to San Francisco, an Alaskan cruise for two and a trip for two to Hawaii. To be eligible for any drawing using an Entry Coupon, simply complete and mail according to directions.

There is no obligation to continue as a Reader Service subscriber to enter and be eligible for any prize drawing. You may also enter any drawing by hand printing your name and address on a 3" x 5" card and the destination of the prize you wish that entry to be considered for (i.e., San Francisco trip, Alaskan cruise or Hawaiian trip). Send your 3" x 5" entries to: Indulge a Little 6947 Sweepstakes, c/o Prize Destination you wish that entry to be considered for, P.O. Box 1315, Buffalo, NY 14269-1315, U.S.A. or Indulge a Little 6947 Sweepstakes, P.O. Box 610, Fort Erie, Ontario L2A 5X3, Canada.

To be eligible for the San Francisco trip, entries must be received by 4/30/94; for the Alaskan cruise, 5/31/94; and the Hawaiian trip, 6/30/94. No responsibility is assumed for lost, late or misdirected mail. Sweepstakes open to residents of the U.S. (except Puerto Rico) and Canada, 18 years of age or older. All applicable laws and regulations apply. Sweepstakes void wherever prohibited.

For a copy of the Official Rules, send a self-addressed, stamped envelope (WA residents need not affix return postage) to: Indulge a Little 6947 Rules, P.O. Box 4631, Blair, NE 68009, U.S.A.

INDR93

INDULGE A LITTLE
SWEEPSTAKES

OFFICIAL ENTRY COUPON

This entry must be received by: APRIL 30, 1994
This month's winner will be notified by: MAY 15, 1994
Trip must be taken between: JUNE 30, 1994-JUNE 30, 1995

YES, I want to win the San Francisco vacation for two. I understand that the prize includes round-trip airfare, first-class hotel, rental car and pocket money as revealed on the "wallet" scratch-off card.

Name_____

Address _____ Apt. _____

City_____

State/Prov._____ Zip/Postal Code_____

Daytime phone number_____
                        (Area Code)

Account #_____

Return entries with invoice in envelope provided. Each book in this shipment has two entry coupons—and the more coupons you enter, the better your chances of winning!
© 1993 HARLEQUIN ENTERPRISES LTD.   MONTH1

INDULGE A LITTLE
SWEEPSTAKES

OFFICIAL ENTRY COUPON

This entry must be received by: APRIL 30, 1994
This month's winner will be notified by: MAY 15, 1994
Trip must be taken between: JUNE 30, 1994-JUNE 30, 1995

YES, I want to win the San Francisco vacation for two. I understand that the prize includes round-trip airfare, first-class hotel, rental car and pocket money as revealed on the "wallet" scratch-off card.

Name_____

Address _____ Apt. _____

City_____

State/Prov._____ Zip/Postal Code_____

Daytime phone number_____
                        (Area Code)

Account #_____

Return entries with invoice in envelope provided. Each book in this shipment has two entry coupons—and the more coupons you enter, the better your chances of winning!
© 1993 HARLEQUIN ENTERPRISES LTD.   MONTH1